BENITO'S GAMBIT

BENITO'S GAMBIT

by Ronald R. Koegler

Tremonto Press
Santa Barbara, CA

Benito's Gambit
by Ronald R. Koegler

Published by
Tremonto Press
Santa Barbara, CA
www.chasingthestargazer.com

Publisher's Cataloging-In-Publication Data
(Prepared by The Donohue Group, Inc.)

Koegler, Ronald R..
    Benito's gambit : [a novel] / by Ronald R. Koegler.

    p. ; cm.

    Sequel to the novel, Chasing the stargazer.
    ISBN: 978-0-9882549-0-9

    1. Psychiatrists--Fiction. 2. Political candidates--United States--Fiction. 3. Mafia--United States--Fiction. 4. Assassination--United States--Fiction. 5. Man-woman relationships--Fiction. 6. Psychological fiction. I. Title.

PS3561.O317 B46 2013
813/.54   2012948246

Editor: Gail M. Kearns, www.topressandbeyond.com
Cover and Interior Design: Robert Aulicino, www.aulicinodesign.com

Book production coordinated by To Press & Beyond

Printed in the United States of America

Dedicated to the memory of my mother, Bessie Koegler—
"the best hotel lady in Atlantic City."

INTRODUCTION

Readers of my 2011 book, *Chasing the Stargazer: With Help from Luigi Pirandello, Nucky Johnson, and Thomas Wolfe*, asked what had happened to my characters, particularly psychiatrist Don Carter—did his wife Delia divorce him when he accepted Benito's money and was gone to Sicily for months? Did the stargazer continue to harass him?

Pirandello, the Sicilian playwright and author, who plays a recurrent role in my novels, explores a similar lack of resolution in his play, *Six Characters in Search of an Author*. In my book, as in Pirandello's play, the characters are left without full resolution, waiting for . . .? But, of course, a person's life is never resolved. It plays on and on.

People do seem to change under the influence of outside events, such as divorce, marriage, money, poverty, illness, and aging. As Pirandello states, "Each of us is lots and lots of people."

Delia Carter declares, describing part of her husband's mysterious character change in *Benito's Gambit*, "He wasn't the husband I had married . . . You know, he has a frightening memory and he used to annoy his friends by his quotations. And he just stopped-boom-like that! After he returned from Italy, the quotes were gone, as if by magic."

It's time to introduce my characters.

My flawed hero is *Donald Carter*, M.D., a psychiatrist, who had returned to Atlantic City in June of 1985 searching for the "stargazer," a man he had arrested forty years earlier under the Boardwalk, while working as a lifeguard. A "stargazer" is a guy who tries to look up women's dresses through the boards over-head while he "pleasures himself," as one of my delinquent minors in the psychiatric clinic used as a euphemism for mastur-bating. Don never intended to arrest him, felt guilty about the arrest, and wanted to make amends, or at least find out what happened to him.

Benito Desimone, the uncle of Donald Carter's wife, is a leader in the Philadelphia Mafia. Doctors have given him two years to live before he dies from prostate cancer. Benito is proud that he's "never been arrested," and is a multi-millionaire as a result of criminal gain and use of Swiss banks. He has no children and makes Don "an offer that he can't refuse," establishing Don as his heir. Benito has settled his problems with the IRS and has moved back to Sicily.

Don gives up his forensic psychiatry practice and flies to Sicily to become acquainted with Benito's family and his finances, and to perfect his Italian language skills.

Delia Carter, Donald Carter's wife and Benito Desimone's niece, was originally devoted to her uncle, refusing to believe his ties to the Mafia, but she and Benito become estranged when she mistakenly believes that he's involved in her father's murder. She begins to drift away from her husband when he accepts Benito's financial offer against her wishes. He travels to Benito in Sicily, staying over three months, also against her wishes. She and Don are the parents of *Linda*, age twenty-four, and *Robert* age twen-ty-two.

The *stargazer* (Jimmy Calver), a.k.a. Pablo Cuevas, is first seen under the Boardwalk doing his thing in my first novel, *Chasing the Stargazer*. He develops a personal vendetta against Donald Carter, who insults him during his arrest, and this anger becomes more pronounced over time. The stargazer vows revenge and orchestrates an attack on Don near Atlantic City and another attack in the mountains of North Carolina.

Don is captured by the stargazer in North Carolina, escaping at the last minute by killing one man and injuring the stargazer, sending the stargazer on his way back to Venezuela with damaged vocal cords, to resume his previous career as a very successful drug dealer for the Santini crime family. The stargazer's voyeurism is tolerated by his uncle, *Giuseppe Santini*, head of the Cleveland Mafia, because he is the source of a tremendous amount of income through his skill in the cocaine trade. *Bill Santini* appears as Giuseppe's more normal nephew. He respects the manner in which Don dealt with his cousin, the stargazer.

Molly Dorman first appears in 1945 as a fifteen-year-old "gofer" for the lifeguards, but on her seventeenth birthday, as she is about to leave for Las Vegas, the virginal Molly seduces Don in her mother's apartment, with the connivance of her mother's twin sister, Miriam. Don rationalizes his cooperation in deflowering Molly because she had just turned seventeen. However, because of Miriam's lies, Don loses track of Molly.

Earlier, Don had rescued Molly's mother *Hannah Dorman* from an attack under the Steel Pier in Atlantic City, and is rewarded by Hannah's fiancé *Sam Kravitz* (in *Chasing the Stargazer*). Sam and Hannah leave in a hurry to get married in Las Vegas. The murdered body of hit man *Dan DeSilva*, who killed Hannah's husband, is found by lifeguard Don Carter a few days later, floating in the ocean off Michigan Avenue beach. Don suspects that Sam Kravitz murdered him.

Sam Kravitz, at Molly's urging, uses his influence with Giuseppe Santini to protect Don from Santini's psychopathic nephew (the stargazer), but it was only effective west of the Mississippi River. Molly had married *Arthur Stoller*. He and his father-in-law, Sam Kravitz, run two casinos in Las Vegas.

Tim Reilly was Don's first lifeguard partner on the Atlantic City Beach Patrol and had been responsible for getting the two of them involved with the stargazer. He is two years older than Don, more experienced, and much more adventurous than Don. Tim now works in construction.

Paul Marshall is a young homosexual rescued by Don and his lifeguard partner, who later becomes a close friend to Don. He and his partner later develop AIDS, and his partner dies from the disease. *Jack Marshall*, Ph.D., a professor at Stanford University, is Paul's father. He promises to help get Don into Stanford.

Laura Agazzi has Don's heart aflutter until Benito brings him to his senses with help from one of Pirandello's plays. *George Agazzi*, Laura's husband, may or may not be a crooked union leader. As *Chasing the Stargazer* nears its conclusion, Laura is on the run with a large sum of money.

Rosie Carter is Don's mother and owner of the *Carter Hotel*. *Fred Carter* is Don's father. He works as a night watchman at the bank on the corner. *Ray Carter* is Don's older brother and works nights at the hotel desk. *Karl* is Don's elderly cousin who lives at the hotel, works as a handyman around the hotel, and gets drunk every Saturday night. In a later chapter, Karl dies.

José Ramirez is a government agent, who was only a telephone voice in the *Stargazer* novel, but plays a prominent role in this sequel. Don and Benito cooperate with José to notify him when cocaine shipments are made from Colombia. In return, Benito receives a very favorable treatment from the Internal Revenue Service.

Frank Damico, good-hearted proprietor of the *Triumph* poolroom, makes a return appearance by popular request.

Tim plays a role in *Benito's Gambit*. Lifeguards *Captain Tom* and *Pat* are mentioned. Other colorful lifeguard characters get a respite in this book, but may appear in subsequent sequels.

Oh, and Miriam gives Don Carter a special present in *Benito's Gambit*.

CHAPTER ONE

Parma, Sicily
September 3, 1985

Don had tripped on the uneven terrain before the initial shot rang out. He found himself sprawled on his back on the ground, looking up at a blue Sicilian sky. Don heard more shots, and then silence. Before the shooting started, the people of the village of Parma were welcoming Don, curious to know more about Benito's successor. Suddenly, most had flung themselves down, frightened.

He rose up to a crouch and, after a few minutes, saw several villagers slowly getting up, looking around. A few were already cautiously gathering around Benito, who had been standing behind Don, but now was on the ground. A Sicilian policeman was on the telephone, talking in a loud voice, ordering the roads closed, and asking for help with the search for the gunman.

The villagers made way for Don, as he anxiously went over to Benito. He found him lying flat, bleeding from his shoulder. Benito looked up, saying, "Nothing serious. The bullet just grazed my shoulder. He won't get far. There are only two roads out, and both will be blocked."

Benito struggled to his feet, with Don helping him, but Don

caught him, as he temporarily lost his balance when he paused to get his breath. The bullet wound on his shoulder seemed to have stopped bleeding.

"I think he was aiming at me," Don said. "If I hadn't tripped, he would have shot me."

Benito shook his head. "One might think so, but I do not believe he was trying to hit anyone. It does not make sense. Very amateurish shooting."

"I'm not sure about that," Don said.

"Think about what you are saying," cautioned Benito. "In Sicily, in a small village like this, with only one road in and one out, it does not make sense to shoot someone, except in an angry argument. On the other hand, an explosive device placed in a car will give a person time to get away."

Putting his arm around Don's shoulders, Benito said, "That is why they killed Michael Corleone's new bride in *The Godfather* by placing an explosive in Michael's car, which was meant for Michael, of course. This gave the person who placed the explosive time to make his escape."

Don was not convinced, saying, "Those were real bullets, and if I hadn't tripped, he would have hit me."

Benito said, "We will see when the police make their arrest. There was no smoke from the firing. It must have been fired at a great distance. The shooter must not have had accuracy in mind."

Benito apparently thought Don needed some education regarding the Sicilian Mafia, for he said, "It doesn't sound like the work of the Corleonesi. They would not have missed.

"Corleone is an actual town not too far from here, in Palermo Province, with somewhat more than eleven thousand inhabitants, best known for producing real and fictional Mafia leaders. The Corleonesi are the bloodiest and the most violent clan in Sicily. One thousand people were killed in the First Mafia

War from 1961 to 1964, primarily Mafia members or civic officials. Hundreds just 'disappeared.'"

Momentarily interested, Don asked, "Did things settle down after the war?"

Benito shook his head. "The Second Mafia War started in 1979 and is even bloodier. It is still going on, but at a slower pace because the Corleonesi have killed most of their enemies. It is not over, and I may leave. So, I might have to die in America," Benito said thoughtfully.

Don was concerned about Benito's sudden unsteadiness, and asked anxiously, as Benito wavered, "Are you sure you're all right?"

Benito replied, "I was just a little dizzy. I am okay. Walk me over to the infirmary, but slowly. If we are lucky, there will be a nurse on duty. I will try to find out how much I should worry. Besides, there is something we need to talk about."

The path to the infirmary was uphill, and the sun was hot, but Benito had no more dizzy spells.

As they walked, he said, "I am worried about the situation in Colombia. Didn't you tell José Ramirez, our government contact man, that it was to be every *other* cocaine shipment?"

Don shrugged. "That's what I told him, but he started intercepting every shipment. Now, suddenly shipments have stopped. There hasn't been news of any shipment at all for almost a week, and I was going to ask if you had heard from Carlos."

Pausing in his walk to catch his breath, Benito said, "Our informant, Carlos, was supposedly itching to take over from Santini's nephew, as you know, but the last time I talked to him, he said something about cocaine shipments that keep 'getting intercepted' by some other organization. Then he clammed up, and his voice seemed to fade. I lost contact. He does not answer the phone, and I have not heard from Carlos in over a week."

Benito was silent for a moment, and resumed walking. "Do

not do anything until I straighten this out. No traveling back to the States. I suspect Carlos is dead or has a better offer."

Benito said, "On another subject, my spies report your stargazer is like a madman since you grabbed him by the throat in North Carolina. His voice is hoarse, and all he talked about is getting even with you. I will find out. In his agitated condition, he cannot be much use to the Santini family."

They arrived at the medical clinic, a nondescript, single story building built of stone, with two rooms, and a curtain serving as a partition in one of the rooms. A sterilizer was evident in one corner. Shelves held bandages and basic medical supplies. Don could see a cot made up in the second room.

The nurse was not there, but her assistant was, and she quickly and efficiently bandaged Benito's shoulder. As she finished, she asked, "When did you have your last tetanus shot," apparently having recognized the sound of gunfire in the distance.

Benito replied, "About a year ago, when I was living in Philadelphia. It seems so long ago. I needed stitches in my hand."

The nurse's assistant was young, slightly plump, talkative, and an attractive girl of medium height, who chatted comfortably with Benito. He introduced her as his *cugina*, Ersilia. Don said he had remembered her from when he met Benito's large family, and remembered her name, also, which got a big smile from Ersilia.

Don had noticed that the word "cousin" was used loosely in the village and included anyone with a familial relationship, although the family usually knew the specific kinship.

They said good-bye to Ersilia and left the clinic. Benito said that a doctor came for a few hours once a week, but that doctors were available more frequently in larger villages closer to Palermo. "Those who can afford it go to private doctors and clinics," he added.

"There are about nine hundred people living in Parma. We are only sixty-one miles from Palermo, but it might as well be one hundred miles. It can take several hours to drive to Palermo, depending on road conditions. Sometimes, the road is impassible in the rainy season. In the fall, we sometimes get several inches of rain, not much, but damaging, since the roads are not paved.

"That is why I say whoever did the shooting cannot get far, and must be from the immediate area—someone who is desperate for money. Maybe your stargazer wanted to make us worry. The police will have the shooter in jail by the time we get back."

"Get back?" Don asked.

"Yes, I want you to take a trip to Zurich to visit my bank. I'll go with you, of course. The economy is rising, but the bank balance is not rising," Benito explained. "I had already scheduled an appointment on Friday with Heinrich Kessler, a vice president, in order to introduce you, but I suspect something is going on with the money. We will first see Heinz Schultz, who is supposed to be managing my account.

"I'll make the airline reservations for Thursday, and we will go to the appointments the next day. My sister or my aunt will be answering the phone, and either one will call me in Zurich, or wherever I am."

He continued, "I believe that you will be safe in Italy and Sicily and will not be in any real danger of being killed until you go back to the States, but I am not sure. Just keep traveling around until I find out what is happening in Colombia."

Zurich, Three Days Later

Don supported Benito down the stone steps from the bank, at the same time saying, "He's lying." The air had become cooler as the short Swiss summer approached its end, and Benito didn't reply at first, breathing heavily when they paused at the last step.

Benito said, "I suspected that there was a problem in the bank accounts, but I could not be sure. What makes you sure that he is lying?"

Don said, "I have a natural ability of detecting lying. It's an annoying skill. People lie much of the time, and I find it distracting. But I thought to resurrect this skill, because I instinctively felt it would be useful, as useful as practicing my Italian."

Don said, "I called Professor Silvan Tomkins, who's a renowned affect psychologist. I think I told you that his mother and my mother were first cousins, and his father was my dentist in Atlantic City. He told me that Professor Paul Ekman at the University of California in Berkley, a former student of his, was studying lying, and I should talk to him. I pressed Silvan, who loves to talk, and told him about my natural ability of detecting lying, and he told me it was all in the micro-expressions in the face, and, to a lesser extent in the micro-movements of the body. And he told me that he had studied faces for many, many years and had no difficulty distinguishing when people were lying. In fact, Silvan said, when he was tested against game show contestants who deliberately lied, he was one hundred percent accurate."

"Am I to understand that you and Silvan Tompkins were born with this ability, to decide if someone was lying?" Benito asked, the tone of his voice indicating some skepticism.

Don replied, "I'm saying just that. More importantly, Silvan told me that there were a few other individuals with my natural ability, including some in law enforcement, and that Ekman had collected more of these individuals and was studying them. He suggested that I call Ekman."

Don paused, and said, "I found out what I wanted to know— that there were other persons with this ability. I didn't want to get distracted from my Italian studies, and I felt that I was doing all right on my own, studying people and their faces. It's like riding a bicycle. The skill comes back fairly quickly. But unlike riding a bicycle, the vast majority of people are never adept at detecting lying, although Ekman feels that they can possibly be taught with a lot of effort and practice."

Benito asked, "Is that how you detected Schultz?"

Don replied, "This man, Heinz Schultz, is a practiced liar and ordinarily difficult to detect, as are all sociopaths and practiced liars, but he was nervous, probably because he sensed impending disaster when we arrived. You could almost smell the lying. 'There ain't nothin' more powerful than the odor of mendacity,' as 'Big Daddy' said in *Cat on a Hot Tin Roof.*"

He started to explain the reference, but Benito nodded and said, "I saw the movie."

Don realized that he had practically stopped the constant quoting that he had been doing for many years—the quoting that seemed to occur spontaneously—and was virtually unstoppable, as though his eidetic memory was out of conscious control. This had frustrated his wife and annoyed his friends.

Don continued, saying, "He may be 'churning' your accounts, that is, making unnecessary purchases to increase his own income. But, more likely, and this is a very lucrative practice, he's being paid by other individuals to make large purchases or sales of stocks in order to affect their value. He's either a losing gambler, a drug addict in deep financial straits, or has a very expensive girlfriend."

"So, which do you think it is?" Benito asked.

Don replied, "I'm betting on gambling. He needed a large account to play with, one that wasn't closely supervised, and he needed more and more money to cover his gambling losses. The addictive gambler refuses to believe that he can't beat the house."

"We are going to the boss now," Benito said. "I had made an appointment with him at eleven o'clock to introduce you, but now we have a problem with Mr. Schultz. We are taking the long way because I do not want to alarm Schultz."

Don said, "A lot of people lose money in the market, but banks are supposed to be cautious with a client's money. About thirty-five percent of your funds are tied up in the stock market, on advice from Schultz. That's way too much. The bank has a responsibility to supervise their employees closely, and they screwed up."

They paused on their climb to allow Benito to catch his breath.

"How long have you been working with Schultz?" Don asked.

They had been wending their way slowly up the hill to another entrance to the bank.

Benito responded, "Almost ten years."

Both were silent in the elevator and neither spoke as they entered the reception area. A gray-haired, primly dressed secretary looked inquiringly at them, and Benito said, "I have an appointment with Herr Kessler at eleven o'clock," speaking in English.

The secretary spoke in German to announce them, but Herr Kessler greeted them in English. His English was flawless.

After introducing Don as Dr. Carter, his niece's husband and his heir, Benito explained, "We feel my account has been mismanaged. Herr Schultz has been responsible for the account for almost ten years, and I have not been paying proper attention. Dr. Carter feels that Herr Schultz has been lying to us."

Herr Kessler said, "Those are serious charges, Mr. Desimone. Do you have any proof?"

Don took over. "I have an ability to detect lying, and Herr Schultz is clearly lying. In addition, the account has been manipulated. If you look at the account, it will be clear to an expert like yourself that the account has been mismanaged. I expect that Herr Schultz has a gambling problem, for the amount of money lost can't be explained easily, and is most likely, in my experience, a gambling issue."

Don went on, repeating himself, "A close look at the account by a skilled observer will show that something is wrong. Of course, gambling can be a disease, and the gambler keeps thinking he'll have a big win to cover his losses, but he's out of touch with reality and that's why he ignores the house cut."

Kessler said nothing, but got up from his desk and left the room, returning several minutes later with a folder, studied it carefully for a long time, and he turned back to Don and Benito.

Kessler said, "I have to admit that there are some strange things going on in your account, Mr. Desimone. Herr Schultz has been with us over fifteen years and is a trusted employee. In fact, as you have surmised, he's been given little direct supervision because of his dependability and apparent integrity, as well as his skill. I'm going to find out what's been going on."

Kessler excused himself and left the room, while the secretary served them coffee. Finally, Kessler came back with a frightened Schultz in tow, and announced, "Herr Schultz has something to say to you."

Schultz had a defeated expression on his face. It was clear that Kessler had been grilling him.

Schultz hesitated, and spoke. He said, "I want to apologize for mishandling your accounts. I needed the money to pay for my gambling losses in Monaco, and I was just waiting for my big win to pay you back, which I fully intended to do."

He spoke in a flat monotone, with no expression visible on his face.

Kessler spoke to Schultz, telling him to wait in the outside office.

When he had left, Kessler turned to Don and said, "Well, you were right. Rest assured, Mr. Desimone, that we will 'right' your account for the money that you lost as a result of Herr Schultz's behavior. And Dr. Carter, if you ever want a job working for the Swiss bank, come to see me. I agree, it is usually gambling when such huge sums are involved."

Don said, "It probably started with modest amounts, and grew and grew until he had owed very large sums, possibly hundreds of thousands of dollars. The professionals were playing with him, of course, paying his debts, and suddenly demanding payment. They offered him a way out if he would manipulate the market by making large purchases or sales of stocks, and that's where Benito's account was used. I would imagine that had to be a stock with a limited number of shares available?"

Don looked at Kessler with a questioning expression, and Kessler nodded.

Don thought about lifeguard Doug Murphy, who was always searching for the "big win."

"He was bound to be caught, eventually," Don said. "The amounts became extraordinarily large and even a non-expert like myself could pick it up because of the large amounts invested in common stocks and frequent transactions. And the estate has actually lost money in spite of a rising stock market."

As they got up to leave, Don said, "I think you would agree, Herr Kessler, that a typical estate for a client of Mr. Desimone's age would be invested primarily in bonds, treasury notes, and similar safe vehicles."

Kessler agreed, with a forced smile. They shook hands with Kessler, and Benito said, "We'll let you handle it. I don't think this is a police matter, but it's up to you."

Kessler nodded in agreement, and Don and Benito left after Don received a copy of all the transactions for the previous ten years.

When they had left the building, Benito said, "I'll have my lawyer write them a letter to document this meeting."

They had called a taxi for Benito at the bank, and it was waiting to take them back to the hotel. They ate, and Don announced that he was going to inquire about a gym with weights and a heavy bag for his workout. Benito surprised him by saying that he wanted to go along.

"There is something that I want to talk to you about," he said. "But at supper, after we have returned to the hotel."

Don wasn't sure what Benito had planned for him, what this was leading up to, but he knew that Benito was not finished with what he would say, and would eventually get to the point. He did wonder why Benito was being so mysterious, but his thoughts returned to his workout and whether the gym had a heavy bag.

The clerk at the desk told him that boxing gyms were a fad at the moment in Zurich, and most of the gyms had heavy bags. After changing into his workout sweats, he was directed to the closest gym. He found it to be spacious and remarkably clean, as he expected, this being Switzerland.

Don went into his usual routine of three three-minute rounds at the heavy bag, the first one easy, and getting gradually more demanding. He was sweating profusely, as he attacked the bag the third time.

A small group of men, possibly prospective gym customers, had gradually assembled by the time he had finished, and several applauded. One man in white duck pants, apparently the instructor, said in English, "See, you can look like this man if you just keep working at it!"

Don laughed and continued to the weight room. He went into his routine, starting low and gradually working himself up to two hundred and fifty pounds in the bench press, and finishing off with a series of exercises, all involving weights. He followed with sit-ups and crunches, and moved to the treadmill for a half-hour run. Don noticed that Benito was watching him.

Don showered, dressed, and they took the taxi back to the hotel. Don asked, "Well, what do you think? Ready to start boxing?"

Benito shook his head and said, as they entered the elevator, "I was quite a street fighter in my younger days. You had to be in order to survive in Philadelphia." They went up to their room and rested until suppertime.

In Italy Don had become accustomed to eating the main meal in the early afternoon, and a light supper in the evening, and he followed the same schedule in Zurich. He felt quite relaxed, as he usually felt after a good workout, and not all hungry. Benito began speaking, as they sat down to eat.

"I was watching you carefully during your workout. You are friendly and personable, but your workout was always primary in your mind. You told me you had been working out with weights and aerobics since the age of fifteen. This demonstrates perseverance and the ability to stick to a goal. In addition, you have a great memory. You have all the attributes of a good political candidate."

"Yes," Don replied. "But . . ."

Benito interrupted. "You are probably wondering what all of this is leading up to. The newspapers report that Senator Boyd of California is ill with the same disease I have, prostate cancer. But his disease is more advanced, and he has not appeared in the Senate for several weeks. I personally think he will be dead within three or four months. There is probably already a field of candidates waiting for him to die or resign."

Both paused to order from the menu, and Benito continued, "The Democratic voters outnumber the Republicans by a significant margin in California, so the only Republicans who can win are those with moderate social views, like your current senator, Pete Wilson."

Don started to protest, but Benito cut him off.

Benito said, "You have a good personality and a fantastic memory. You are intelligent and know when to speak out and when to be quiet. You are a social moderate, and you believe in a tight budget. In fact, the only thing you lack is name recognition, and we are going to supply that. Or rather, we are going to find the best campaign manager in the business, pay him a good salary, and develop your public image. I believe that with an aggressive campaign and plenty of money behind you, you will be able to win the Republican nomination. You are a registered Republican, are you not?"

It was all beginning to sound ridiculous to Don. "You mean you can take a guy who has never run for office before and elect him to the United States Senate? There is something bizarre about all this."

Don had another thought. "I'm not a real Republican," Don protested. "Somebody told me you get to vote twice if you registered for the opposite party, always able to vote for the more moderate Republican candidate, so I registered as a Republican. Delia is constantly after me to change my registration, and she would really get angry when I would refuse to change. I think she was embarrassed when the Republican campaign literature would arrive, afraid her friends would see it."

"Well, it may get you divorced," Benito said. "But it might get you elected to the Senate. That is a fair trade. Which would you rather have?"

While Don was thinking about this question, startled by Benito's remark, Benito continued talking. "We are fortunate that there is a particularly weak field of candidates trying to become United States Senator, possibly because it is an unexpected vacancy. Just Matthews on the Republican side and Oates on the Democratic side.

"Yes, you are perfect. You are in favor of allowing a woman to choose what she wants to do with her own body, in favor of separation of church and state, a strong supporter of Social

Security, careful of foreign entanglements, and in favor of a balanced budget. Perfect!" declared Benito.

"What if I don't want to run?" asked Don.

"Nonsense," exclaimed Benito. "I know you will accept a challenge. And what are you going to do with your life after you speak perfect Italian?"

Don had been wondering the same thing.

Benito continued, "There are a number of things to get ready for a campaign. First, we need a good campaign manager to transform an unknown challenger into a good candidate. Second, we need money, lots of money, which I have. Third, we need a government agency, preferably the CIA, to say that we have been working with them."

"Why do we need a government agency to say we have been working with them?" Don asked.

"Because of my criminal background. Hopefully, they will admit that we were working for the CIA."

"But how can you be sure of what the CIA is up to in Venezuela or Colombia?" Don asked.

"Because I found out that the CIA has been using us to intercept cocaine shipments, not to confiscate the shipments, as they claimed, but to use the cocaine in some scheme of their own," Benito claimed. "I am absolutely certain of that, but I am not sure what they are up to."

Benito, with a wry smile, said, "You remember when they persuaded the IRS to settle my income tax problem so favorably, not paying attention to possible foreign accounts? I did not fully recognize it at the time, but that was in return for revealing the connection of Giuseppe Santini's nephew to the cocaine trade in Colombia, so they could use our contacts to intercept the shipments and do something else with the cocaine. I should have been suspicious. On the other hand, it may all turn to our political advantage, in addition to the obvious financial benefits to my estate. How is that to our political advantage?"

Answering his own question, Benito said, "I believe that our friend José is actually CIA."

"Are you certain?" Don asked.

Benito stated firmly, "I am quite certain.

"One thing in our favor is that everything is 'classified' in the CIA, more than in any other agency of the federal government. The problem is getting them to admit that we were working for them, but I think that that would be tied up with the difficulty in getting in touch with Carlos, our informant. Something is going on in South America that the government does not want anyone to know about."

Benito suddenly changed the subject, saying, "I have been associated with Philadelphia gangs most of my life, but I have never been arrested. Did you know that, Don?"

Don answered, "No, I didn't know that."

Benito said, "It was tough, coming over at age eleven, fighting on the streets and at school, working to help support the family. I was the oldest child. My father died when I was sixteen, and my mother, brother, and two sisters moved back to Sicily. One sister, Talia, later returned to America, and my younger brother, Carlo, also returned."

Don noticed he always referred to them as "gangs" or "criminal gangs" rather that the Mafia.

"Too bad," Don said. "This would have made a great book, along with the CIA business."

Ignoring Don's comment, Benito said, "Just remember one thing I learned was to bargain. It is the same in the Senate as it is on the street. You have something I want? Bargain. Never forget that. The CIA wants our silence. All they have to do is to be vague about the time I was an agent—an unknowing agent, to be sure."

Benito continued, "Some gangsters would do well in politics. Look at Nucky Johnson in Atlantic City. I read that he was Secretary of the Atlantic County Republican Executive Committee, County Treasurer, and at the same time collected from gambling, prostitution, booze—you name it. He was the crime boss of Atlantic City."

"There must be some smart people in the CIA," Don said, changing the subject.

"There are lots of smart people in the CIA, but they get involved by their superiors in some dumb operations, sometimes. I will find out what they are doing with the cocaine. I believe the CIA would be willing to trade our knowledge of their operation for our silence, and act as though I had been working for them for years. Of course, you understand that the CIA makes such arrangements all the time, bargaining for silence or cooperation, just like criminal gangs.

"In short, we will say, 'You have been naughty, but we won't tell if you give us a lollypop,'" Benito said.

Don found his remark mildly humorous, but he was still wrestling with the problem about his running for the Senate.

"I have been involved in some borderline operations," Benito continued. "But I have been lucky and never arrested. The CIA is a nut on secrecy, and it is in the nature of the organization to be secretive. Probably they would not have revealed how long I worked for them, but this is added insurance."

Benito added, "Now that you are going to be a United States Senator, I am going to avoid any mention of my criminal background, so that, if you are ever questioned, you can honestly say that 'he never said anything about that.' Oh, someone will write a book about my crime career eventually, if you, Don, become important and famous, but people are forgiving about their heroes. Remember, Ronald Reagan was only a so-so movie actor, and he became Governor of California, and then President of the United States. But for the time being, never ask any questions about my colorful life."

Benito became thoughtful and mused, "Too bad because

there were some unbelievable stories to tell."

Don said, "Nice speech, Benito. You would make a great campaign manager."

But Benito said, "I cannot be your campaign manager for obvious reasons, in addition to my poor health. So, I am going to get the next best thing, Joe Abrams. Only he does not know it yet. Well, Don, are you ready to commit to being a candidate?"

Don replied, "I'm more ready than I was, but I still have my doubts. I'll give it a try."

Benito concluded, "So, we are all set! Over the next few months, I will make all the arrangements. And I will find out what the CIA is up to in South and Central America, somehow. Thank you, Don . . . It means a lot to me."

Don realized what he meant—going from an eleven-year-old helping to supporting his family, working the mean streets of Philadelphia, to enabling his unbelieving nephew to become inaugurated as a United States Senator. It seemed impossible at first, but Don was beginning, just beginning to believe it was possible.

They rented a car in Zurich and began traveling slowly through Switzerland and down into Italy, stopping frequently as Benito talked about the history of Italy and his experiences as a youth growing up in Sicily. It was almost as though he realized this might be his last trip through Italy, and he wanted to savor the experience.

Benito directed him to Vicenza, the city of Palladio. He noticed Benito becoming more animated as they entered this city. They visited the Olympic Theater (*Teatro Olimpico*), Palladio's masterpiece and final work, which particularly fascinated Benito, and was not completed until five years after Palladio's death.

Constructed so as to give the illusion of an outdoor Roman

amphitheater, Don could see how it was ideal for the performance of classical plays. It was still being used for this purpose. And he was beginning to understand now why Benito had purchased one of Palladio's villas in near Vicenza, in a run-down condition, for Don's son, Robert, to restore.

When they visited that villa, however, the one that had been selected for restoration, Don looked it over and said, "I don't believe that this can be restored. It's too deteriorated."

Benito replied, "You are thinking of one of your American houses. My agents assure me that it can be restored and is worth restoring. It lacks only someone to spend a great deal of money on the restoration. It is a classic by Palladio. All of his villas are worth restoring."

Don asked, "Tell me, what attracts you to the work of Palladio? He seems to have stayed with the classical building principles, and I find a sameness to his villas and other works."

Benito argued, "No. There are certain design differences to all of those works. It's all in the classical mode, but there are definite differences. Palladio published four volumes of architectural studies and perfected 'Palladian style,' with certain rules to be followed based on construction styles used in ancient Rome."

He continued, "Thomas Jefferson was so intrigued by the work of Palladio that he built Monticello based on Palladian principles, and he built the University of Virginia in a similar manner. Palladio's works on architecture are reflected in many southern plantations. I considered, very briefly, building a Palladian-style home in Philadelphia, but it was too ostentatious for a man of my reputation, and I settled on the home that you admired when you visited, constructed of stone from my native Sicily. It was a wise choice for me."

Don laughed. "A Palladian-style house in Philly—that would be a real attention grabber and quite a tourist attraction."

Benito agreed, "I wanted to be an architect when I was growing up, believe it or not, but of course this was impossible for an Italian immigrant boy who left regular school after the sixth grade, so I learned all I could, and especially practiced my English. I became obsessed, in fact, with the English language, so I became very useful among the Italian community, as I told you when I spoke to you at my house in Philadelphia."

Under a different life, Don thought, Benito would have been a senator or a successful businessman, or even a professor of English or Italian Literature, rather than running a Mafia gang.

At this moment, they were sitting in the rented car, ready to leave Vicenza. A light rain was falling.

Benito spoke, "The pain in my bones has increased somewhat, so I was thinking of going back to Sicily and seeing Dr. Romani in Palermo. I wanted to see Vicenza one last time, so I was happy and my pain did not seem as bad, but now it has returned. I have enough medication for several days if I double up. The pain comes and goes, but I cannot take a chance, and I do not want to stop at some emergency hospital. They look at you as though you are some kind of addict."

Don suggested, "Why not drive to Venice, which is about an hour away, and turn the car in? We can take the train to Rome, a journey of five hours. We will stay overnight in Rome, and consider taking the train to Palermo, whenever you feel up to it. I understand they load the trains onto boats to cross the Strait of Messina, and put the trains on the track again for the rest of the trip to Palermo. Rome to Palermo takes ten to thirteen hours, according to the guidebooks."

Don added, "Dr. Romani can phone in a prescription."

Benito agreed. "I have not been on those trains to Palermo for many, many years. Yes, that is a good idea. We can always fly from Rome to Palermo if things get bad. Dr. Romani will just have me increase the dose, anyway. And you will get to see the Strait of Messina and the bridge that never gets built."

Benito explained, "It is only a few miles to travel across the Strait of Messina. A long time ago, the Romans proposed a bridge of boats and barrels, but it was never built. Over the years, the bridge was almost started many times, and has now become very expensive. I doubt if it will ever be built."

On the train to Rome, Benito dozed intermittently and Don took turns watching the scenery or re-reading *The Leopard* by Giuseppe di Lampedusa for the third or fourth time, but for the first time in Italian. It was slow going at first, but he was in no hurry, and the words finally began to flow.

Don looked over and noticed that Benito was awake, so he asked, "Did you ever meet di Lampedusa?"

Benito replied, "Yes, once. I sometimes saw him reading in the back room of the *Café Mazzara* in Palermo. Occasionally, he wrote, but he was not sociable. Twice I spent considerable time in Sicily visiting my family, and it was on the first occasion, when it was, let us say, 'inconvenient' to return to the United States, that I spoke with him."

Don suddenly remembered that Benito was in Sicily to see his "sick mother" when Don and Delia were getting married. But his mother was in good health when he and Delia visited Sicily a few years later, so Benito was definitely on the run— probably afraid for his life.

Benito continued, "Giuseppe Tomasi de Lampedusa would walk from coffee house to coffee house, stopping to talk to booksellers sometimes, and settled down in *Café Mazzara* to read or write. I stopped him on the street, on one occasion, and I said, 'I heard you were writing a book.' He appeared startled, and said, 'Yes. But publishers are hard to find,' and continued walking. He was a shy man, pale complexioned, and soft. At least he was when I saw him in 1955 or 1956. He died in 1957, I believe, and his book was finally published a year later."

Don said, "It's unsettling to think of dying and believing you were a failure, and finally getting your book published after your death, and to have it become an overnight sensation."

Benito said, "Being dead, that was of no concern to him. He was a smoker and died from lung cancer. Most pictures of di Lampedusa show him with a cigarette in his mouth.

"My wife Gasparina was allergic to tobacco smoke. Finally, she became fed up and told me that I had to 'sleep elsewhere' if I kept smoking, so I managed to stop over thirty years ago. It's a filthy habit, although I did not think so when I was smoking. My wife wouldn't let Charley Marturano in the house when he smoked, even when he cooked for us, so he also stopped smoking," Benito said fondly.

When they arrived in Rome, Benito was feeling much better, so they stayed an extra day. Don had been in Rome and had "seen" the usual tourist attractions, but they came alive with Benito. They took taxis often, because of Benito's lack of stamina, in their journey around Rome. The two of them managed to step back in time for the moment, and Don felt a closeness with Benito that surprised him.

Don found it fascinating that Benito, although not a religious person, had an encyclopedic knowledge of the *Vatican Museums* and the *Sistine Chapel*, particularly Michelangelo's *Last Judgment* on the altar wall. After lecturing Don about Michelangelo, Benito had dinner with Don at Myosotis, a lovely family restaurant with an excellent wine cellar. It was a perfect evening.

Benito slept late the next day. Don left a note for Benito and ventured out in the bustle and noise of Rome, walking around, and taking it all in. He returned before noon and found Benito getting dressed.

Benito said, "Don, I really enjoyed seeing Rome again with you, through your eyes. Thank you."

They ate dinner at the hotel, and walked a short distance as a light rain fell. Benito was still somewhat fatigued from their strenuous evening. After a light supper, they boarded the 20:30 train to Palermo.

It was after midnight before they finally went to bed. Don slept fairly well, waking a few times when the train stopped. He awoke early. Benito was still asleep.

Don shaved and dressed while Benito was gradually waking up, possibly sleepy from the effect of the narcotics he had taken for pain. There were a few early risers in the dining car, and he chose a seat by himself. Later, Benito joined him.

The waiter brought *Caffe latte* with rolls, butter, and jam— *prima colazione*. They had a typical Italian light breakfast. The *colazione* was followed by *Fette biscottate*, hard cookie-like bread, which they ate with butter and jam. Don nibbled on *biscotti*.

When the train arrived at the Strait of Messina, Don went onto the ferry deck. The train cars were loaded one at a time onto the ferry. Benito joined him, and they watched together, later, as the ferry left the dock and began plowing through the waters of the Strait. These waters were calm, but Benito assured Don that whirlpools formed in the Strait, in certain areas, and could menace passage through the waters.

Benito said, "Scylla and Charybdis are two immense rocks between Italy and Sicily. A sea monster lived there that alternately swallowed the waters and threw them up, causing the whirlpools. Homer in the *Odyssey* and Virgil in the *Aeneid* describe this 'sea monster.'"

Benito was obviously enjoying himself, as he continued, "This gives rise to the saying, 'Between Scylla and Charybdis' to describe a bad situation with no obvious solution."

He turned serious. "That describes the situation of my balls, 'Between Scylla and Charybdis.' If I have anti-hormone injections, there are side effects. If I have them removed, they are gone forever. Either solution will ease the bone pain, hopefully."

There was long silence.

Don asked, "Are you wondering what I would do in the same circumstances?"

Benito said, "Yes."

Don said, "Well, all things being equal, if I were interested in having sex, I would postpone any decision until the pain became intolerable and was not relieved by medication. If I were not having sex currently, but had hopes, I would wait, depending on the pain. I would have injections first to see the effects and side effects. If I were sure I never would have sex again, I would consider removal of my testicles."

Don added, "As far as I know, the decision doesn't change life expectancies."

Benito said, "Thank you. Time to get back on the train."

The train was hooked back together on the tracks, and they started on the three-hour journey to Palermo. They arrived at the scheduled time, much to Benito's surprise, and took a taxi to Dr. Romani's office, hoping that Dr. Romani would have an earlier appointment available.

The secretary was surprised to see them, saying, "The train is almost always late, but you're in luck because a patient cancelled, and Dr. Romani wants you to join him for lunch."

As they entered the restaurant, Romani saw them, stood up, and embraced Benito. Obviously, they had a close relationship and enjoyed each other's company. Benito and Don had spoken Italian almost entirely during the journey, and Benito introduced Don in Italian. Romani was almost alone in the restaurant, and he explained that it was early for Italians to eat *pranzo*, or lunch, but he was expecting two friends to join them later.

They sampled a local red wine while discussing Benito's medical problems, and Romani's friends arrived, an attorney and a local businessman. Don ordered a bottle of "Tancredi" from the Donnafugata Winery. The wine was excellent and led to a discussion of the meaning of Tancredi's famous statement in *The Leopard*, "Things must change in order for things to stay the same."

They had a spirited dispute over the meaning of di Lampedusa's words, as the restaurant became crowded. The attorney was elected the winner of the argument for pointing out that little had changed in the world over the years except in technical areas, and the nations still fought over the same territorial disagreements, but with more dangerous weapons.

He said, clinching the argument with a conspiratorial whisper, "And the Mafia only changed from knives to AK-47's!"

The conversation was fast, loud at times, and Don had to ask occasionally for a translation. Two hours passed very quickly, and they were all good friends by the end of the dinner. Don thought about the hurried lunches he had had in America.

The friends left, and Dr. Romani gave Benito a prescription for a larger number of pain pills, as well as the reassurance that the surgery to remove his testicles would be performed under mild sedation, if he chose surgery, and most people were not hospitalized.

"It's a simple office procedure," Dr. Romani assured Benito.

Benito replied, "Yes, but it is 'good-bye, *coglioni!*'"

Dr. Romani said, "It's true that removal of the testicles doesn't alter progress of the disease, just reduces the pain. It's not like a mastectomy for women, which gives hope for a cure, and women are willing to accept disfigurement for this hope of survival. For that reason, I recommend that you hold off and only consider this surgery if the pills don't work well anymore, or the pills interfere with your balance or make you too sleepy, or otherwise cause uncomfortable side effects. And I already discussed with you the side effects from anti-androgen injections."

"Well, enough discussion about my balls," Benito declared. "It is time to allow Dr. Romani to get back to his practice."

Early in the morning, they left for Partinico, about nineteen miles from Palermo, with Don driving. In the jail at Partinico, waiting for them, was the shooter.

Benito said, "It is the nearest jail, and the police are expecting us. The population of Partinico is about thirty thousand. You will be happy to hear that there is a gym in Partinico with a heavy bag. As a matter of fact, they have occasional boxing matches in town. It's one way to escape from the poverty of Sicily, becoming a successful fighter. Few succeed."

They arrived at about ten in the morning in Partinico, and Benito directed him to the police station, where the policeman on duty said they could get nothing out of their prisoner to explain his actions. Don interviewed him alone. He was short, maybe forty years old, with his skin darkened by fieldwork, and he was obviously frightened and suspicious.

Don offered him a cigarette, which Don had procured from one of the officers, and the man accepted it. He asked his name, and the man replied, "Guido Venanzi."

Don explained that they knew that someone paid him to shoot in the direction of the crowd, but that he accidentally hit someone. This man he had hit was a very important man in the community and was very angry, but would excuse Guido's action if only he would tell who put him up to this, since he was angry only at the person responsible, not at Guido. In fact, if Guido told him the whole story, he might ask the police to let him off with a fine or a short time in jail.

Guido considered the offer. He said that many people knew he was having financial problems and had been ill and unable to work, and was only just recently feeling a little better. One day he received an unsigned note asking if he wanted to make a lot of money to play a joke on someone.

"Of course, I said, 'okay.'"

After a long pause, Don asked, "What happened?"

He started talking more rapidly now. "A new gun appeared, from nowhere. At my door. There were bullets already in the gun, and a note saying to go to Palma and scare the American visitor. I never saw that kind of gun before, but he sent a lot of money. It was enough to end all my money problems!"

The effect was predictable. Guido was unaware that the gun would carry that far. "And it shot so many bullets!" he continued.

Don said, "Guido, just tell your story to Mr. Desimone, and I'm sure that he'll understand."

He called Benito from the other room, and Guido repeated his story. Guido asked Benito about the money he had received, saying most of it had already been spent to pay his debts. The police had confiscated the automatic rifle.

Benito went back and advised the officer, "I will not press charges, and I will take Guido back home. The police can keep the rifle to cover their costs."

They signed a few papers and Guido was released, while the officer kept his eye on the gun. He did not mention the money that Guido had received. In fact, if Guido could get cleaned up, he would like to take Guido to lunch after he took Dr. Carter to his boxing workout.

The police officer, who gave his name as Arturo Nelli, said, "The only shower at the jail has not worked for a month, but there is a boxing gym nearby with a shower."

Benito and Don left with Guido, stopping to get him some clothes, which he put on after showering at the gym. Guido appeared mystified at his good fortune and followed along hesitantly, as if he expected to have to do something in return.

Don had his usual workout with the heavy bag, but was only able to scrounge up two hundred pounds of oddly assorted weights, so he did more repetitions. He also worked on the light bag, trying to get his rhythm back. Afterward, Don showered, and they had lunch at a common restaurant frequented by local workmen, not wanting to have Guido feel ill at ease. It seemed to work, because Guido seemed to relax.

He said he and his wife and three children lived on a small farm about an hour from Parma. "But I haven't been able to work much lately because of pain in my side," he said, pointing to his left side. The local Mafia boss kept after him for the *pizzo* that he was supposed to pay every month for "protection."

Guido suddenly started grimacing, saying, "It hurts," pointing to his side. "The pain has started again." He was unable to eat his lunch, which the waiter had just set on the table. Guido hadn't visited a doctor because he was worried he might have to go to the hospital. He added, "And I was afraid of dying at the hospital."

Don told Guido that he was a doctor, and felt his abdomen, eliciting a sharp cry when he pressed on Guido's left side.

"It's probably appendicitis," Don said, and looked at Benito questionably, while telling Guido not to eat anything.

Benito said, "Well, on to Palermo and Dr. Romani. It is less than an hour back to Palermo. Dr. Romani has surgery in the morning today, and will be getting back from dinner about now."

Dr. Romani was in his office, about to see a patient, but he examined Guido immediately and confirmed that he did have classic symptoms of a soon-to-burst appendix. He sent him to the hospital and had him on the operating table within the hour.

They saw Dr. Romani after the surgery, and he said, "Just in time. It's nice to get them before they burst. Otherwise, it's quite a mess." Romani's secretary called Guido's wife, telling her that her husband was resting comfortably after surgery and would call her in a few hours. The secretary said that Guido's wife had burst into tears at the news.

They went to see Guido, who said the pain was gone, and

Benito told him that he and Dr. Romani had arranged for a car to take him back to his farm whenever he was released from the hospital, and the money he had received for the "joke" was his to keep, but it would be better if neither he nor his wife told anyone about it.

In spite of the late hour and the light rain falling, Benito wanted to return to Parma. Don drove more slowly because of the rain, while Benito talked about the conditions of much of the population in Sicily, eking out a living on small farms, always on the verge of poverty.

Benito said, "And if they, through some miracle, manage to build a successful business or farm, there is always the Mafia demanding a share of the profit, the *pizzo*. The Mafia is heavily involved in hospital and medical matters, influencing the contracts for unnecessary hospital construction and purchases of useless equipment. Front men for the Mafia run supermarkets, electronic stores, and medical clinics—bribery and kickbacks are a way of life for the Mafia!"

Don said, "I remember your telling me that Sicily was a wonderful land when the Greeks arrived seven hundred and fifty years before the birth of Christ. It was covered by forests, and Plato wanted to establish his Republic on Sicily. The trees have been cut down many years ago. You said the soil is mostly clay, worn down, not really good for growing anything."

They arrived in Parma in the early evening, just before dark. It had cooled down slightly and had stopped raining. Benito said, "Palermo, the capital of this province, typically has less rainfall annually than any other city in Italy."

Benito's house was one story, built of stone, on a slight knoll at a distance from the village, and deliberately modest so as not to draw attention. Nevertheless, it may have been the best house in the village. It had three bedrooms and as many baths, in addition to a large kitchen, a study, a comfortable living room, and a patio in the rear.

Benito's sister, Angelica, and aging aunt, Concetta, were preparing a light supper and greeted them warmly. They talked about some of the events of the day. In the very small village of Parma, there were no secrets, and Angelica and Concetta, of course, knew about Guido's family and his financial problems, and both had heard about the shootings.

Neither Don nor Benito mentioned the money that Guido had received. Benito did explain about the "joke" that Guido thought he was playing, and said that he was not pressing charges against Guido. He told how Don had correctly diagnosed appendicitis, and how Guido was now recovering in the Palermo hospital.

Don had met Angelica and Concetta, both widows, when he first arrived in Parma late in August, and he had been examined carefully by them and the many cousins, who gave their final approval when he used a few Sicilian phrases in his speech.

Benito said, "I can tell that your language instructor came from the Palermo area, for the dialect is quite different in other parts of Sicily. A Sicilian can understand the variations, but you would not be able to understand. The Sicilian language is not taught in the schools, and younger generations tend not to speak Sicilian. It is a family language, spoken in the home, mostly."

He and Benito went out and sat on chairs on the patio. There was thunder and occasional flashes of lightning, but no rain. The weather was warm and humid, and there was a slight breeze outside that mitigated the temperature somewhat.

"I would like you to come to our Pirandello discussion groups, which are held four times a year, either in Palermo, Rome, or Milan," Benito said. "Lawyers, doctors, professors, shopkeepers—they all argue and talk about Pirandello, and they eat and talk some more. They get up in the morning and talk again until noon, all about Pirandello. The next meeting is in late September in Milan. I will check on the date."

"Great! I would like to go," Don replied.

The two of them sat quietly for several minutes, and Don said, "There's one thing that bothers me, Benito."

"Just one thing?" Benito joked.

"Let us say we are successful in convincing the CIA to say we were secret operatives for an unknown number of months or years."

"Yes," Benito answered.

"Won't Giuseppe Santini get pissed?"

Benito sighed. "Of course he will, if he is still alive at that time, as he has a serious heart problem. He owes you a favor for not killing his stargazing nephew when you had the chance in North Carolina, but he may ignore that. Put yourself into his head. He might be earning more money than ever, which is all he really cares about."

Benito continued, "He will be puzzled. All the wise guys will be puzzled. What were we doing for the CIA? Is there any crackdown on the Mafia as a result of our CIA involvement? They will get nervous and be careful for a while, and life will go on."

Benito laughed, and said, "Another motivation to become a United States Senator. The Mafia would never kill a senator. Very bad publicity.

"But, at the moment, I am more concerned about the Corleone family than Santini," Benito said. "They are truly vicious. And they read the newspapers."

Benito became thoughtful. "Seventy percent of Sicilian businessmen throughout Sicily pay protection to the Mafia every week, and a larger percentage in Palermo. And where is the Mafia most thick? In Palermo, of course. The restaurant we ate in and had such a good time? They pay a substantial sum to the

Mafia for 'protection.' Protection from what? Protection from the Mafia, of course. Protection from firebombing, being beaten, cars destroyed, or being robbed."

Benito continued, "There are twenty-eight different Mafia clans in Palermo. Each with its own territory, but the boundaries are obscure, which lead to disagreements and shootings. Every province has its resident clans. Even the poorer farmers are assessed. They are not sure what to do with me because I am sick and presumably dying, but they want to know how much money I have, and they snoop around. Of course, they know of my Mafia connections."

"You can always return to the United States," Don suggested.

"Perhaps. I am still a United States citizen. Most of the retirees that you will be responsible for are planning on retiring to Fort Lauderdale, of all places, and not returning to Sicily to live. Only one widow in my group of retirees is still in Sicily. Others decided it was too dangerous and returned to the United States, to Florida.

"Oh, hell," Benito said with a laugh. "Those who live by the Mafia die by the Mafia. I will go down to see Paolo, the local clan leader, tomorrow and arrange for protection!"

"Protection?" asked Don.

"Yes, protection. For example, to make sure my phone messages are not being listened to by anyone, neither the Mafia, nor the U. S. Government, and especially not the Italian police. Or Giuseppe Santini, for that matter, trying to find out if he is in danger from the CIA."

Don asked, "But what about the local Mafia listening in?"

Benito answered, "In the first place, Paolo does not speak English. But he does know how to check the line for bugs. Also, he has no interest in and does not understand American politics. And, strange to say, our local man considers himself a 'man of honor' and would not listen in on the line. The Italian police are very involved in listening to phone conversations, and the judges allow them to do that without a warrant. It keeps crime a little bit in check, but people are nervous when they talk on the telephone. I have known Paolo for a long time, and he respects me. His clan has a poor area to monitor, and I have given him money from time to time. But it is better if he can say to his friends that he is protecting me. That will give him status and a regular income, and everybody will be happy. It will keep the bosses off my back for a while."

He added, "And as they say in America, we have a win-won situation."

Don appeared puzzled, but brightened up.

"Yes, a true win-won, and maybe even a win-win!" Don said.

CHAPTER TWO

Atlantic City
August 30, 1946

"DROP YOUR PANTS!"

"Wait a minute. The clap! That's impossible!" Don exclaimed.

Dr. Francis was a handsome man, about forty years old, erect, rather huskily built, and looked more like a boxer than a doctor. He said, "You have all the symptoms—a discharge, pain in your penis and scrotum. And you have a frequent urge to urinate.

"And come over here," he said, bringing Don over to where he had a microscope set up.

"Look," he said. "See those little specks under the microscope? They're bacteria, *Neisseria gonorrhoeae*, and your smear is full of them, after I did a Gram stain of the discharge from your penis."

Don looked into the microscope, but he wasn't sure what he was seeing.

"But the good news is that you'll be cured with two shots of penicillin," he said.

Dr. Francis continued talking as he went to the cabinet and removed a vial. He said, indicating the vial, "This is penicillin, a miracle drug, and I'm going to give you one injection today and another in two weeks. Now, drop your pants."

Don hesitated, but complied.

"Ow!"

"Sorry. I have to use a large needle because I'm giving penicillin."

Dr. Francis removed the needle from the syringe and said, "You're lucky. Until a few months ago, you would have gotten sulfanilamide pills, and the bugs were becoming resistant, so it wasn't working anymore. And before 1940, they were treating gonorrhea with Protargol. It's a silver preparation that they would shove down your penis, made by the Bayer Corporation, but it's only about seventy-five percent effective."

He looked at Don's chart and added, "But of course, you would have been about thirteen at the time they were using Protargol, so you probably wouldn't have needed it."

Don, however, wasn't listening to Dr. Francis's effort at humor. He was still trying to deal with the fact that he really had the "clap."

Dr. Francis washed his hands, and turned to Don, who was fumbling with his fly. "I see by your history that you were in the service. Are you going to go to college?"

Don answered, "Oh, I was accepted by Penn State before going into the Navy, to become an engineer, like my brother, but after I was discharged from the Navy, I got a letter saying that only applicants from Pennsylvania would be accepted. So, I'm going to go to Philadelphia College of Pharmacy and Science, and to Stanford next year. I know one of the professors there. I changed my mind about becoming an engineer, and decided to go to med school."

Dr. Francis said, "Great. Look me up when you graduate medical school. And if you do go to Stanford, try Floyd Pages's gym in Palo Alto. You look like a weightlifter. I was there at Stanford for five days at a seminar last year and worked out at Floyd Pages's."

Dr. Francis said, "No sex for two weeks. I'll test you again and give you another shot. And stick to older women in the future."

"She is an older woman."

"Well, in that case, she probably doesn't know she has gonorrhea. In women it's often difficult to tell, and it becomes chronic, with virtually no symptoms. So, don't be surprised if she blames you."

Don hesitated, recovered his nerve, and stammered, "Can you get gonorrhea in your mouth?"

Dr. Francis successfully managed to keep a straight face, and said, "Yes, you can. Don't worry, penicillin will cure that, too, but gonorrhea of the mouth usually doesn't cause symptoms."

"Oh, no," Don said hurriedly. "I didn't mean I did anything. She wanted me to go down on her, but I refused."

Dr. Francis said, "A wise decision in view of the gonorrhea. Wait 'til you're married for that sort of adventurous activity."

Don thanked Dr. Francis and turned to leave the doctor's office.

"Wait a minute," Dr. Francis said. "You'll be having some discomfort for up to a week. I'll give you some aspirin to take— up to four a day. Call my office if you continue to have pain after one week, or if the pain gets worse."

He handed Don a package, saying, "And don't worry. You'll do fine," clapping on his back to reassure him.

Don turned to leave, but Dr. Francis called back again, and said, "It's too late now, but next time, wear a rubber. You should know better."

Don replied, "There wasn't much time to think, and I only had one rubber, so I figured she was older and knew what she was doing. Besides, as I told you, I couldn't think that quickly.

She wanted it again, and I made it okay. I thought we were through, but she wanted it again. The third time, I barely made it, you know, trouble getting it up. I needed a lot of help.

"And she said she couldn't have children, now that I think about it," Don said.

Dr. Francis looked at Don's chart thoughtfully, and said, "You're nineteen years old, Don, and you work as a lifeguard, according to your chart."

He looked up and asked, "Weren't you tired the next day, at work?"

Don thought a minute, and replied, "No, well . . . maybe a little."

"Did you see her again?"

"Oh, yes. I saw her the next night, and again the next night. She was gone for two nights, and again the next night. Then, I felt this burning, and I made an appointment with you," Don said.

He added, "I thought I would get better at it, but I was never able to make it the fourth time."

"They say men are at their sexual peak between fifteen and nineteen, so it must be true," Dr. Francis said. "You don't plan on seeing her again, do you?"

Don said, "You must be kidding. I'm going to call her on the phone and tell her what you said, that she gave it to me, and never go near her again!"

"That's good," Dr. Francis said. "She seems to have a condition known as nymphomania. Sexually she never feels satisfied. You may never meet up with another like her. It's not very common."

He thanked Dr. Francis, shook hands, and went into the waiting room. He paid the receptionist at the desk in cash, and was assured by the elderly women in the office that no receipt would be sent to his home.

Upon leaving Dr. Francis's office, Don first looked around to make sure no one he knew had seen him. He had selected Dr. Francis because he was far away from his home, and had scouted out his office to make sure it was well hidden. And Dr. Francis was a "urologist," which he had looked up and found was the right doctor for his "burning" problem.

Don figured out that it could only be Miriam who had given him the gonorrhea. In his mind, he went back over all that had happened since Molly Dorman, Miriam's niece, had moved to Las Vegas with her mother Hannah and new stepfather Sam Kravitz. It was a sudden move, the day after her seventeenth birthday.

He had held off dating Molly because he thought she was "too young," but Tim, his lifeguard partner, kept pushing him to date Molly, so he had celebrated Molly's seventeenth birthday with Molly in her mother's apartment, on the night before she was leaving for Las Vegas. Miriam, her mother's twin sister, was supposed to be supervising, but later, he realized that Miriam and Molly had conspired together for Molly to lose her virginity on her birthday.

In looking back on the experience, Don realized that he had been manipulated, but in a very pleasant way. When they were in bed together, before they had sex, Don said he was uncomfortable about what was happening.

Molly had said, "But it's my birthday!"

And, when he had laughed about being her "birthday present," Molly had become upset, and Don realized, finally, how much this meant to her.

Molly promised to write, but Miriam had called to tell him that Molly said she didn't intend to write to Don, because she had found a new boyfriend who was "very cute."

Don thought about Molly's soon-to-be stepfather, Sam Kravitz, who had left for Las Vegas suddenly with Molly's mother just before Don and Tim had found Dan DeSilva's body floating in the water at Michigan Avenue beach. He had suspected that Sam had killed DeSilva, and married Hannah Dorman, Molly's mother.

Don thought about Hannah's twin sister, Miriam. She had invited Don up to her apartment, and five minutes later, they were having sex, and the next night, and the next. They had sex over and over each night, until he was unable to get it up. They skipped the following two nights because she had to go "out of town," and they had another session.

He shook his head. Weren't identical twins supposed to be alike in personality, like the Marshall twins he had gone to school with? Hannah, Miriam's twin sister, had a lot of class, but Miriam had very little class. Besides, she was very demanding. She did have a nice body, though. Miriam was urging him to go down on her, and he hadn't agreed yet. Thank God for that!

He went to a payphone and called her number. Miriam picked up the phone on the first ring. She recognized his voice.

"Don. I'm expecting you. It's six thirty. You're late."

Don replied, "Well, I'm coming from the doctor's office."

Miriam said, sounding puzzled, "Oh? Are you ill?"

"He's treating me for gonorrhea."

Silence.

A string of curse words came out of her mouth, "I don't have it. I hope you haven't given it to me. Of all the goddamned luck!"

"Calm down," Don said. "Dr. Francis says you gave it to me."

Miriam hung up the phone with a crash.

Well, Don thought, that was that. Don felt relieved to be done with Miriam, who just wanted sex all the time. He got into the jitney to go home, almost glad that he had the clap.

His mother was happy to see him. He knew she was worried

about his late return the last few nights, but she didn't ask any questions. And she had been curious about his coming home early and changing out of his lifeguard uniform to go to the appointment with Dr. Francis. Of course, he hadn't told her where he was going. He had changed clothes because the red lifeguard uniform was too conspicuous.

It was Friday night on a Labor Day weekend and it hadn't rained. They had only seven vacancies in the seventy-room Carter Hotel. It was turning out to be the best weekend of the year for the side avenue hotels. They might have a little business with the Miss America Pageant the following week, but the season was over after this week. The Carter Hotel would start closing the top two floors, which were unheated, placing cardboard over the stairwells.

The lifeguard force would be cut back, and stations would be closing. Only the older guards and the captains would continue working, and the beach would soon close down completely.

Don sat down for dinner. He ate pork, mashed potatoes with gravy, sauerkraut, baked beans, and apple pie. His mother mostly cooked German style, probably because his father's German mother had cooked for the family before Don was born, and his father liked that style of cooking. Hell, he liked it, too.

Don had heard the story many times of how the family name had been changed to "Carter" from "Schroeder" at immigration, and that "Carter" was a man who repaired carts, which was his grandfather's trade. And how his grandfather kept the name because of discrimination against persons with German names.

Fred, his father, had looked at his pocket watch, and had gotten up from the table as Don sat down. His father always was interested in what had happened at his lifeguard job that day, but Fred had to go in early to his job as night watchman at the Boardwalk National Bank because someone was ill.

But he had time to ask, "Any rescues today?"

Don said, "Only one, Pop."

Actually, it had occurred as he was leaving to keep his appointment with Dr. Francis, and Pat and Tim had made the rescue, but it was a true statement.

He clapped Don on the back as he left, saying, "Be careful, son," as he always did, reached for the brown paper lunch bag, and left. Don and his mother continued eating. His mother had bought the seventy-room hotel for $6,000 in 1940, renamed it the "Carter Hotel," and converted the large dining room into rooms for the family, hidden from the guests.

After he finished, Don told his mother that he was going to the poolroom and would be back early to relieve her at the desk, and walked over to Frank Damico's Triumph Pool Room on Mississippi Avenue.

The small sign underneath Triumph said "Billiards," but there were no billiard tables to be seen. Frank welcomed him warmly, and he watched the pool tables for Frank when Frank went in the back to set up the crap game. Only the regular players were permitted in the back room. Don had only seen it when it was empty.

Frank's only son, Frank Damico Jr., a straight-A student and a great athlete, had been killed fighting with the Marines on Okinawa, and Frank was depressed a long time after his son's death. Now he was especially helpful to young men in college who has been in the service.

It was early, and only two of the nine tables were active until Don started playing in a game of two-five with an older player. In two to five, the money-balls were two, five, ten, and fifteen and total score (double if you won everything). The two of them were evenly matched, and he ended up winning a small amount of money. When they played eight-ball, he lost his marginal winnings.

Don suggested straight pool, his favorite game, with a payoff of two dollars to the first player to reach seventy-five points. Don easily won, and had one run of fourteen balls and another of twelve. Frank had come out of the back room and was observing while Don played. A small group had formed, watching the play.

The group applauded. Frank clapped him on the back when the game ended, and exclaimed, "Too good," which was Frank's highest compliment. Even young Jaime Fox, who made a living hustling in poolrooms, congratulated him.

Jaime, half-kidding, said, "I'll spot you twenty points in a game of one hundred points, straight pool." He said, "Make it twenty-five points, for five dollars," as though he was doing Don a favor.

Don laughed. He was having none of that. He knew he was not in the same league as the full-time players, who played for hours every day.

"Quit hustling me, Jaime," he said, putting his arm around Jaime's shoulders.

He looked at the time and decided to go back to the hotel, so Don notified Frank that he was leaving and walked the several blocks to the Carter Hotel. When he arrived, his mother was giving directions to the Steel Pier to a couple at the desk, and she looked up at him and smiled. After she finished, Don took over the front desk.

There was little to do at this time of night. The final train had arrived some time earlier. The Carter Hotel was on the same street as the train station, and when the trains unloaded, the exiting passengers streamed down the street to their favorite hotels.

He just needed to answer questions and requests for lost keys and for extra towels, and why there wasn't enough hot water for showers. But it seemed as though there were an unusual number of sexual glances from young ladies this evening, or was he just imagining it?

Suddenly, in the midst of a daydream, he felt arms around his neck, and a big kiss from Janet Kremens on his cheek.

"Hello, Don," she said. "Sis and I have a big date tonight with Charley and what's-his-name," she giggled. "Tell me, did we really have sex that night?"

It was a standing joke between them. She had passed out on the bed when he helped her up the hotel stairs, at his mother's suggestion, afraid that she would collapse in the lobby. He insisted that they had sex, and her sister went along with the joke. Janet was a very heavy drinker, and she had blackouts. It hadn't stopped her drinking, however.

Don said, "Oh, it was wonderful. You were very passionate."

She giggled again, and left to join her sister on the porch. She was about twenty-three and her sister was twenty-four, or maybe it was the other way around. Anyway, Don was saving money for college, and he couldn't afford them, and he was not old enough to drink legally.

His mother's friend, Nellie, arrived, and Rosie and Nellie went across the street to the River Shannon Café. Before leaving, she had reminded him that his brother, Ray, would be back to the hotel at midnight to take over, and that Karl, his elderly cousin, was on his regular weekend drunk. Don's mother would return about midnight. Of course, his mother would mostly be at the River Shannon Café, where she could keep an eye out for problems at the hotel.

He went out on the sidewalk and took in the street scene, the River Shannon and its friendly noise and swinging doors, and the little store underneath the hotel next to the River Shannon staying open until midnight, trying to sell postcards and bottles of cold pop. Did the little store stay open all year? Well, he would find out soon enough. College started the following week, and he would be commuting to Philadelphia by train from

Atlantic City three or four days a week.

He turned and looked toward the beach. At the corner, four bars were open. Ripley's "Believe It or Not" newspaper column had supposedly claimed that this was unique, having a working bar on each of four corners. Don had never found the actual column, but he was now looking at the corner with the four bars.

There was the Norwood Bar on the corner closest to the Carter Hotel, McGettigan's and McGuire's Tavern across Pacific Avenue under the Ariel Hotel, Grob's Café under the Osborn Hotel across Arkansas, and diagonally across the intersection was Dunlap's Tavern. All four bars were a half block from the Carter Hotel.

There were two more bars in the next block, just before the Boardwalk—the Killarney Café and the Nevada Café. The Killarney was known for its big crowds and Irish shows, and the Nevada was just a hangout, usually with Irish customers, despite the name. Police officer Bobby Muldoon could often be located in the Nevada, having a few beers, while he was supposed to be walking his beat.

When his mother and Nellie returned around midnight, he was feeling tired, but he had only urinated twice. The discomfort in his groin continued, and he took two aspirin before he went up to bed. During the night, he urinated twice, and he thought the discharge had decreased.

He and Tim were working the ten thirty to six thirty shift on Saturday, so he could sleep late, and he felt reasonably rested when he woke up. Captain Tom and Pat would cover their beach at Michigan Avenue until Don and Tim came in at ten thirty.

The discomfort was almost gone, and he thought, hopefully, that the penicillin was working. His mother was up and made his breakfast of scrambled eggs, bacon, and toast, handed him his lunch, and he left for the beach.

"Well, how did it go at the doctor's?" Tim asked, looking

him over when he arrived. He decided Don didn't look well. Of course, Tim blamed it on Miriam. Tim had taken a dislike for Miriam when he first spotted her talking to Don, and even when Don explained that they were discussing Molly, Tim didn't buy it.

Tim agreed that she had a nice figure "for an older woman," and he had made facetious remarks about all the sex he was getting from Miriam. "Your eyeballs are sinking into your head," he would say. But Tim turned out to be right about Miriam being "trouble."

Don shook his head, indicating that he wasn't going to talk when Pat could overhear. Pat had his own drinking buddies, and wasn't prone to spreading gossip, but a chance remark from Pat would result in the whole beach knowing about Don having gonorrhea—or so Don feared. Of course, Pat, with his huge cock and his gin drinking, must have had more than a few doses of the clap over the years.

The ocean was packed with bathers because of the Labor Day weekend, and the Labor Day crowd was enjoying the last chance to enjoy the warm ocean and the beach. But the ocean was rough that morning, and he knew they would have a busy day. Don started to say something to Tim, but he noticed a bather headed for trouble.

"I might tell you after we grab that white hat," Don said, as he stood up to watch.

Tim and Pat stood quickly and saw a woman in the white bathing cap, who obviously couldn't swim, was in an offset, and was headed out to sea—only she didn't know it. To get ready, Tim jumped down from the stand and put another roller under the front of the lifeboat.

Don said, "Let's go!" and leaped off the stand.

Don and Pat rushed to the lifeboat where Tim was waiting. Don grabbed the thole pins on one side of the lifeboat, with Tim on the other, pulling the three hundred pound boat off the rollers and into the ocean, with whistles blowing as Pat pushed them off.

The white hat was just beginning to realize that she was no longer able to touch bottom and started dog paddling desperately. Some of the bathers scattered as the lifeboat approached, but the crowd was so thick that most were unable to get out of the way in time, or didn't know what the blowing whistle meant.

Somehow the boat got through, leaving a trail of bathers hit or nearly hit by the oars, and Don and Tim discovered that there was a second victim, a man who apparently had tried to help the white hat, but ended up getting himself in trouble.

Both the white hat and her rescuer were drifting, caught in the same offset. The white hat was swallowing water and gasping for breath, while the man was swimming impotently against the current.

As Don in the bow watched the pounding surf, Tim shipped his oars and threw out the donut with the line attached. It was a good throw, right to the gasping bather, and Tim started drawing her toward the boat, as Don attempted to row farther out to sea to escape the breaking waves.

Don had just barely managed to get over the top of one wave, when they were thoroughly drenched and collected water in the bottom of the lifeboat. After Tim hoisted the elderly woman on board, Don managed to row farther out, relieved of the drag and the pull caused by the woman hanging on the side of the boat.

The young would-be rescuer could swim a few strokes and had not panicked, so he was able to grab onto the other side of the boat, Tim quickly hoisted him on board. The two passengers were seated in the stern, and Tim bounced his oars into the thole pins and resumed rowing.

They rowed out on an angle to get back to Michigan Avenue,

and rowed in stern-first, aiming for the lifeguard stand. A breaking wave caught up with them, and they rode it partway into the beach.

The usual crowd gathered, as Pat and Captain Tom helped the passengers out of the lifeboat, with the woman surrounded by anxious and grateful friends and relatives, while the embarrassed young man got kidded by his friends.

Captain Tom said, "Nice job," as Don and Tim rolled the boat on its side to empty the water out. The captain said he expected that the sea would calm down later.

Later, he and Tim were on layout for an hour at two o'clock, sitting in their lifeboat in what had become a perfectly calm ocean. After swearing Tim to secrecy—"including Darlene," Tim's fiancée, and a loose cannon, very impulsive, and talkative—he told Tim about seeing Dr. Francis.

Don told him about the gonorrhea diagnosis and Miriam's reaction when he told her about his gonorrhea. "She went bonkers, cursed me out, and yelled that I better not have given it to her. And when I told her that the doctor told me she had given it to me, she slammed the receiver down. Bang! My ear still hurts."

Tim grinned. He gently rowed the lifeboat a little farther out to sea, where there were only occasional swimmers, and Tim said, "I could tell that there was something odd about Miriam. I think she's a 'nympho,'—wants sex all the time."

"That's what Dr. Francis said, that she was a nymphomaniac."

"How many times did you bang her? I mean, how many times a night?" Tim asked.

Don thought, and said, "No more than three, and once only two. She was after me for number four, but I couldn't get it up. It stayed limp. I was totally exhausted, and she was pissed off when I couldn't make it. To tell you the truth, I'm almost glad I got the clap—almost, that is."

"Yeah, you looked like you were really dragging. My brother, Mike, had the clap about three years ago," Tim said. "He took sulfa, but he had a damn hard time getting rid of it."

"Well, I got a shot of penicillin today, and I get another in two weeks, but no sex during those two weeks. She wanted me to go muff diving, but I sure am glad I didn't do it!"

Tim laughed and turned around to check the bathers.

He said, turning back, "Life's a crapshoot. You win some, you lose some. Take Darlene and me. She watches me like a hawk, maybe worrying that I won't go through with the marriage. But I will, and she'll relax and stop worrying, and stop checking on me. It's all just because some other guy walked out on her. I've got her all figured out."

Yeah, right, Don thought. It's funny. Tim is older and more experienced because he had older brothers close to him in age. He's able to give good advice to me, but he's getting into a marriage that's probably not going to work. But what do I know? I know that Tim is right about one thing—life really is a crapshoot. You get sick, killed in an accident, or crippled. Who knows what's over the hill?

A year ago, I was headed for the United States Navy for radar training, Don thought.

The war in Europe and the Pacific were both over, the atom bombs had been dropped in August, and still I was sent into the Navy in September of 1945. And that time, I was taking a test on radar in the Navy and put the answers on the wrong line, and had to erase them all. They thought I had been cheating because of all the erasures. When I protested, that asshole Bosun's Mate threatened to put me in the brig—scared the hell out of me!

They had the nerve to offer a promotion if we signed up for the regular navy, as we were about to be discharged. Oh, well. At least I'll get the GI Bill for a couple of years.

He looked around and realized that he was expecting to see

Molly at her usual place on the sand, looking up to where he was sitting, and asking whether the lifeguards needed anything from the store?

Is it possible to fall in love with someone so quickly? There was something about Molly that made me want to be around her. Maybe that's love.

Well, Molly is gone forever, and I've accepted that fact. Damn!

CHAPTER THREE

January 4, 1986

THE TAKEOFF FROM LONDON WAS SMOOTH, and shortly afterward, Don fell asleep. It seemed he was only asleep for a short while, but when he awoke, they were serving dinner. He glanced around. An attractive woman in the seat behind him was looking at him, so he smiled at her and she quickly looked down. There were empty seats in first class. He did not have a seatmate.

Noticing the stewardess approaching, he glanced at the menu, checking off the menu items, and ordering a glass of wine before the stewardess could ask. She was pleasant and friendly, a mature woman who he assumed had been working for United Airlines for many years. He was gradually becoming accustomed to the luxury of first class.

As he ate, his mind wandered. He worried that he had not been working out regularly, and he had mentioned this to Benito before he left. Don remembered their conversation, and he went over it, bit by bit. Benito had not been apologetic about the lack of workout opportunities.

"I am more worried about making sure that you stay alive," Benito said. "I just told you that Giuseppe's nephew, your 'stargazer,' is very dead, which should be very good news, but even in death, he is causing problems."

"I just assumed it was another fake death. He's 'died' so many times," Don declared. "He pops up again."

Benito said, "He does 'die' frequently, but this time it is true. I heard from someone who saw the body. But my contact also said that, before he was killed, he heard your stargazer over the phone talking about 'taking care of someone in LA.' He may have arranged an assassination, a 'hit,' before he died. In such cases, the money is usually exchanged before the hit takes place and without any direct contact with the guy ordering the hit. The hit man will not know who ordered the hit, so if he is caught, he cannot possibly reveal who it was."

Benito paused, deep in thought, and said, "I am sure if the hit is on, it will take place in the United States, and in Los Angeles. That is why I scheduled the plane reservations at the last minute, to give you time to get there and hire a bodyguard in Los Angeles. And I will be checking around."

Benito continued, "Guido, the shooter in Sicily, was instructed to miss. By whom? By an anonymous third party who received cash in the mail, someone familiar with rural Sicily. Guido was not knowledgeable about modern weapons and almost hit you, and did shoot me in the shoulder. The real shooter will not miss."

"I still don't know why it happened," Don said, puzzled.

"Probably to scare you, when he could not arrange for a hit in Europe, lacking contacts. You'll have plenty of time in Los Angeles and Vegas to work out," he said, changing the subject. "And we cannot have something happening to the next United States Senator from California."

Don remembered feeling uneasy, and shook his head.

"I don't know about that," Don said. "I registered as a Republican, but I sometimes voted for the more liberal Democratic candidate. As I think back, I guess my first rebellion against Delia was registering as a Republican, and refusing to change my registration."

Benito said, "And, as I mentioned, you may have to change wives. Delia will be against it on general principals. Why have you not told her? Because you know what her answer will be, something about not consulting her."

Don was startled momentarily at Benito's statement. This was the second time he had suggested that possibility of "changing wives." Of course, Benito was right. He remembered looking directly at Benito when he said this, and Benito didn't look happy. Don was beginning to realize how much his candidacy meant to Benito, and, of course, Delia wasn't helping by her behavior and her coldness toward her uncle.

Don replied, "Well, we should know shortly. I'll be seeing Delia in a few days."

Benito said, "Let us get down to business. Repeat your schedule for Washington and Las Vegas."

Don said, "There's no danger of my forgetting any of this. I first go to Washington and make sure that José Ramirez will verify that we were working for the government. If necessary, I'll allude to Central America, cocaine, and the CIA involvement in the funny stuff that's going on in Nicaragua. I'll determine whether José Ramirez is CIA, which we're pretty sure that he is, and try to find out what's going on in South America, which I doubt we can determine, this being the CIA, which prides itself on secrecy. I'll use my own judgment about revealing to José the problem regarding the hit man."

Don continued, "I'll go to Vegas and tell Sam Kravitz and Arthur Stoller that we can't accept any gangster money in the campaign. I'll also thank Sam Kravitz, in private, for protecting me over the years from Santini's crazy nephew, and tell him that said nephew is deceased. I'll personally thank Molly Stoller for her concern and for keeping me from being beat up or killed."

"That was her name," Benito exclaimed. "Molly. I could not remember her name. We talked with her on the telephone from

Asheville last June. She is still in love with you, protecting you all those years."

He thought about Molly and wondered what she would look like after almost forty years, and whether she would stir up old memories.

Don finally continued, "From there, I'll come to LA and see that Delia is on board with being a senator's wife. I can tell you now that she isn't presently on board, especially not as a Republican senator's wife. But I hope she'll see the light."

He was not sure about Delia. She could be very stubborn. Perhaps Delia has made up her mind, Don thought, one way or the other, about our marriage, and about her once-favorite uncle Benito. Thinking back over our life together, I've always given in when she was adamant about something, because, frankly, it was no big deal to me. But running for the Senate is a big deal.

He added, to Benito, "By the way, I call Delia regularly, and she said that her mother talked to her and told her you had tried to talk her father, your brother Carlo, out of distributing drugs, and you weren't involved with his murder. But I had to pry it out of Delia, and it didn't seem it made any difference to her."

Benito said, "You are to referring my brother's murder in Florida, when he wanted to be a big-shot, and make a lot of money by dealing drugs without proper protection. Yes, I tried to warn him, but he would not listen. During those years, I expected, at any moment, to hear the telephone ring and hear a voice saying that something bad had happened to Carlo. So, when the call finally came, I almost felt relief, as though a heavy weight had been lifted from my back."

Benito shook his head sadly. "And yes, I now believe that Santini's nephew, your stargazer, was responsible for Carlo's death," he declared.

Benito continued, "It all fits—Maria Lucia, my brother's wife, even remembers people joking about this American, who was the boss of the Cubans and the Colombians, joking over the American's behavior with women, just like your stargazer would go under the Boardwalk in Atlantic City and masturbate, while looking up women's dresses on the Boardwalk above."

Benito paused, and said, "This American and his group were arguing with Carlo over money, so my brother became angry and decided to deal with Meyer Lansky instead. Carlo always was hot-headed, like Sonny Corleone in *The Godfather*, who also ended up dead. Sure, Lansky had the connections, but he could not offer protection. Mind you, Lansky was good with a gun, and in his younger days was a suspect in several murders, but by the time my brother dealt with him, Lansky let others do the shootings. My brother was stubborn, anxious to prove he was a big man, and bigger than his older brother. I never dealt in drugs, but I bankrolled Carlo because he kept after me."

The stewardess interrupted his thoughts, asking if he wanted coffee, which he turned down, and it took a few minutes to get back on track.

Benito had been talking about drug traffic, and he said, "The drug trade is a murderous business. Only Luciano escaped, and he died of a heart attack in 1962, while waiting for a film producer at the Naples Airport. He was considering authorizing a film about his career."

"That would have been a very interesting film," Don said.

Benito continued, "I was in Italy at the time, and his death was headlined in newspapers all over Italy and Sicily. Luciano had been active in sending cheap heroin and cocaine into the United States, and this caused the drug business to expand explosively. The dealers met with Luciano at the Grand Hotel in Palermo, by the way, sixty miles from Parma."

Benito said, "But, getting back to the business at hand, José Ramirez lead us to believe that he was FBI, on loan to Drug Enforcement, presumably because of language skills, but I doubt that—he is really CIA. There is something funny going on because a lot of the cocaine is going to Nicaragua instead of the United States. You should stay out of it. Leave it to me. When I talked to Giuseppe Santini by phone about his nephew, he said his nephew was dead, and they were planning to bring the body back to the United States to Cleveland for burial. And yes, I would be interested if there were an open casket, but I did not ask."

Benito continued, "Incidentally, Giuseppe remembered you and said that his other nephew, Bill Santini, spoke highly of you. He said to tell you he appreciates you not killing Jimmy, and if he can ever do you a favor, just ask."

"Wow!" Don exclaimed. "He can do me a favor by staying away."

They both laughed.

"There was nothing said about any drug interceptions," said Benito, returning to business. "In dealing with the CIA, you should make it clear that all you are asking is that José, or whatever his real name is, will verify that you are a 'good guy,' and he should protect you when the questions come up. Otherwise, the CIA will make José hard to find when you go looking for him."

Benito went on, saying, "For some reason, this is a very important project for the CIA, and when that happens they will not stop at anything, even murder. They undoubtedly scared the hell out of Giuseppe. He may be a power in Cleveland, but he is no match for the CIA. I just have to find out why the CIA is supporting the Contras in Nicaragua. That is the key!"

Benito nodded that he was finished with this subject, and Don went on. "I'll go to meet Joe Abrams, my campaign manager. I've only spoken to him on the phone, and he's quite enthusiastic. I think it's because you're paying a lot of money."

Benito replied, "No. He's the best. It's his business to size up potential candidates. I had the attorney call ahead. You must have made a good impression on the phone. I called him after you called, and he was quite positive. It is his regular fee, by the way."

Benito went on, "As to the money, so many good candidates have been hampered by lack of funds. He just likes to win, and you are a good candidate. With your perfect memory, you will not have to use a teleprompter and you are good at thinking on your feet."

Pausing for a moment, he said, "Speaking of money, when I die, you will be trustee for the rest of the money in my will, money for pensions and annuities for former employees, money for my nieces, my sisters, for Delia's mother, and some gifts to charities. And you will start paying United States taxes. I told the tax attorneys it was important that we not get into problems over taxes, no fancy maneuvers to make money for the lawyers, and I believe that they understood. They will more fully understand when . . . when . . . ."

Suddenly, the sound of a disturbance came from the coach section. There were loud voices and the sounds of scuffling, followed by screams, with the noises getting louder, and a male voice urging everyone to "remain in your seats, everything is under control."

It didn't sound to Don as though everything was under control.

Ignoring the command to remain in his seat, Don hurried down the aisle, pushing passengers aside. He found a tall white male, about age twenty-five or thirty, trying to open the emergency door, yelling and throwing off passengers as they attempted to stop him. A woman, trapped in her seat, was screaming.

"Stand aside," Don commanded in his loudest and most authoritative voice, and the tableau in the aisle halted momentarily, long enough for Don to feint with his right fist, and hit the young man in the gut with a left hook. When the man doubled over, Don hit him with a right hook to the jaw, and he collapsed over the seat.

Don felt a sudden, sharp pain in his right hand. The man smelled of alcohol.

His seatmate, the screamer, wailed, "You've killed him!" She also smelled of alcohol.

"No, ma'am, I just put him to sleep for a few minutes, long enough to put these cuffs on him," he replied, as he watched the stewardesses quickly attach plastic cuffs.

Don asked a stewardess to get him some ice for his hand, while the passengers were congratulating him. At the same time, the woman was still complaining in a loud voice, threatening to sue.

Don went over to her and said, "I'm Dr. Carter."

She gave her name as "Sally."

"Are you both Americans?"

She nodded.

Don said, "You know the British will throw the two of you in jail for being drunk and disorderly. You're both drunk, and if I can't persuade the pilot to keep flying past the halfway point, he's going to turn this plane around and fly right back to England, so keep quiet!"

She mumbled something about "getting an attorney," and shut up.

A big, burly guy with a short haircut and a modest potbelly came down the aisle rapidly, flashed a sheriff badge, and identified himself as "Sergeant Mike Kelly." He towered over Don, who was six feet tall, and said he was a Los Angeles County Sheriff. He apologized for being in the "can" while all the action was taking place.

"Diarrhea, that English food," he said in a low voice. In a normal voice, he exclaimed, "That was some right hook you hit him with!"

He added, "I'll take care of him now. He's still out. Probably won't remember much, except his jaw hurting."

Mike explained, "I was in London on police business, but the British judge changed his mind and wouldn't release my suspect, so headquarters said to come back to LA. I'm retiring, anyhow, next week."

The United Airlines pilot appeared, looked over the situation, asked questions, and wrote down information on a form. He thanked Don and held a consultation with Mike Kelly. They decided to move the drunk to the First Class section where there were empty seats.

The drunk had regained consciousness, and Mike and Don guided him to his seat. He kept asking, "Wha' happen'?"

Don found himself sitting just behind his assigned seat, alongside the attractive brunette woman whom he had noticed earlier. If someone had been sitting in the widow seat, they had been moved.

The now almost-sober and very frightened male passenger was in the window seat in front of them, with Mike Kelly guarding him. His drinking companion, Sally, remained in coach.

The brunette introduced herself as Roberta Edwards. He noted that she was about forty, and attractively groomed and dressed. He guessed she was on a business trip.

She was curious, and questioned him, asking, "I noticed several passengers clapping as you came down the aisle, so you must have been the one responsible for subduing that passenger, the one causing the commotion? And was that the man who caused the noise, the man you were guiding down the aisle?"

Don nodded, "Yes" to both questions.

She handed him her card. It read, "Roberta Edwards, Public Relations." And she added, "I'll write it up, sort of as a gift for what you've done for the passengers. I don't know what would have happened if he opened the door."

Don said, "He couldn't open the door. The air pressure at high altitudes keeps exit doors closed. Also, exit doors are 'plug-type,' meaning they're designed to resist opening under pressure. But he was physically dangerous and out of control. I was afraid that someone would be seriously injured, and the pilot would have to turn back."

He had a hunch, and asked, "You're in public relations in LA. Do you know Joe Abrams?"

She nodded, and said, "Why do you ask?"

"Because I have an appointment with him when I get back from Vegas."

"I like him. He's good. Usually works for Republicans. I worked with him once. Are you thinking of running for office?" she asked, jokingly.

Don replied, "United States Senate, to fill the soon-to-be vacant seat of Senator Boyd, retiring because of poor health. He'll be replaced by a registered Republican, me, on a platform of fiscal conservativism and social openness, geared toward independent voters and reasonable Republicans."

Don paused, and asked, "Want a job?"

"Whoa, there. I wanted to spend more time with my husband and my daughter, who's about to graduate high school. But are you serious?"

He said, "I'll check with Joe Abrams, but he won't be hiring until after our meeting next Tuesday. How did you two get along?"

Don noticed Mike Kelly standing in the aisle, moving from one foot to the other.

"I have to go to the bathroom," he explained. "Will you watch this guy for a while? He's no problem."

"Sure," Don said and moved to Mike's seat on the aisle, taking the ice with him.

He introduced himself and asked the man's name, which he

gave as Ryan Withers. They sat silently together for several minutes. Finally, Ryan looked at him, and looked at the small container of ice, which had been wrapped in a linen napkin by one of the hostesses.

He asked, "What's that?"

"It's ice. For my hand. I injured it."

He said nothing for a few minutes, and asked, "How did you hurt your hand?"

Maybe he was remembering, Don thought, so Don asked, "Do you remember getting drunk, going crazy, trying to open the escape door, fighting, getting hit?"

Ryan shook his head, "A little. It's coming back a little. And my jaw hurts."

"Do you remember getting hit on the jaw by a fist, while you were drunk and out of control?"

"Sort of. It's pretty hazy."

Don said, "Well, I'm guessing you're not going to fully remember. Do you have a history of blacking out?"

"Yes, I've had blackouts. I don't always remember what I've done."

Don continued, "Well, judging from your behavior today, you're going to kill someone if you keep drinking. Have you ever been in rehab?"

"Twice. My parents sent me."

"Airplane security is a big deal nowadays, so the police will question you and probably jail you. They will look up your record and find out if you've done time."

Hearing no response, Don asked, "Well, have you ever been arrested?"

"Two DUI's," he said, hesitantly.

"The judge may throw the book at you, maybe three to six months in jail, if you're lucky, possibly prison if you're not so lucky. If they have an AA program in jail or prison, sign up and get a sponsor. Turn your life around and learn how to protect yourself from a right hook."

Don had a sudden thought.

"Were you an athlete in high school, by any chance?"

"Yeah. I was on the track team. Ran a very fast two-twenty, and was on the relay team. But the coach kicked me off for drinking. I screwed up, big time."

Ryan became tearful.

"Save the tears for the judge, Ryan."

Don said, "My buddy, Kurt, and I worked out a program at Warm Springs Rehab Center called Psychotherapeutic Recreation, for alcoholics and drug addicts. Replace a negative addiction with a positive addiction. Replace alcohol with running and working out. I mean, *really* working out, every day! I'll have someone check on you in jail, and, if you work out in jail, I'll give you a copy of my book called, *From Skid Row to the Olympics*. It describes our Warm Springs program."

"In jail? How can I work out in jail?"

"Push ups. Sit ups. All sorts of exercises. Leg raises. Running in place. Jumping jacks. Use your ingenuity. And running around the exercise yard, if it's allowed. Okay, got to go. Mike is waiting. There will be a big crowd at the airport. I may see you again at the medical check for your jaw and my hand. And good luck," he said.

"Thanks, I guess," Ryan said.

He turned to greet Mike Kelly, and remembered something and turned around. "And get rid of your girlfriend. You two are poison together!"

"I can't," Ryan said. "She's my wife."

Don said, "So? If she stays sober while you're in jail or prison, keep her, but if she drinks, get rid of her, because she's part of the problem. It will be good for her and good for you."

After greeting Roberta, Don returned to his seat. Roberta

had been writing in her notebook, and Don filled her in on his conversation with Ryan. "Dr. Carter's fifteen-minute cure for alcoholism! It will be a miracle if he stays sober, and with an alcoholic wife, a double miracle."

"Well, at least you tried," Roberta said.

"On another subject, how did you get along with Abrams?"

"Fine," Roberta said. "I was brought in as a temporary replacement, but he wanted me to stay on. I had promised someone else I would work for them, but I managed to get another PR person for Joe, and I think he was happy with her."

Don declared, "Okay. I'll call Joe from Dulles and get back to you, and confirm the offer. I have a meeting in Washington, and on to Denver to catch the plane to Vegas, and a short meeting, and finally back to LA. No PR about the airport fight until we decide on the timing."

Roberta nodded in agreement.

"And now, I need a bodyguard," Don said, and got up to talk to Mike Kelly.

Mike was quietly guarding his prisoner when Don spoke to him about a job as bodyguard, but they were interrupted when his prisoner had a sudden urge to go to the bathroom.

It was a while before Mike returned, explaining that the prisoner "had the runs." Mike said he had done off-duty work guarding celebrities in the past, and mentioned a salary, which Don quickly agreed to.

The rest of the flight went smoothly. The police and FBI were waiting inside the gate and checked all the passengers, and interviewed the stewardesses, Don, Mike, and the pilot and co-pilot at length. They were told to be available for a hearing later in the week. Mike Kelly said he would be at the Los Angeles Airport to meet Don and start his guarding duties on Monday, when Don returned to LA.

He called José Ramirez, and said he'd be late. José said that would be fine, as he had come in on Saturday to move his office and it would take him two hours to finish.

He got hold of Joe Abrams at home in Los Angeles and told Joe about the fracas on the plane and his role in it, and his arranging for an interview with Roberta Edwards. He would be seeing Joe on Tuesday morning and Roberta later in the day. He called Delia and left a message, saying that he loved her and would be home on Monday, and had some exciting news.

Just wait 'til she hears what it is, running for senator as a Republican, Don thought.

Don grabbed a taxi and went to see José, or whatever his real name was.

He went through a screening and pat down and was seen almost immediately. José was still in the process of moving, judging by the boxes piled up. There was a nameplate on the desk, partly askew, saying "José Ramirez."

They shook hands, and José explained, "Came in on Saturday to clean out my desk. I'm moving. I was on loan to Drug Enforcement."

This was the first time he had seen José in the flesh. He was a heavyset, muscular, tan-skinned, personable man, about five feet, ten inches with a trace of a scar across his right eyebrow.

"Hey, you look happy, so I guess I should congratulate you. Are you returning back to your position at Langley?" Don asked.

José looked at him sharply and said, "A promotion. Back to training some of the new recruits, temporarily, and on to a new job."

But he didn't answer Don's question about Langley, the CIA headquarters. By not answering Don's question, he seemed to be confirming that he was CIA.

"I guess you know about the death of our drug trafficker, Santini's nephew," Don said. "So, the reports will stop."

José didn't seem perturbed, indicating that he had already heard, and continued filling boxes. He reached over and recaptured an errant box, returning it to its rightful place.

It appeared that he was following CIA protocol, saying, in effect, "We're the guys who ask the questions, not you. Your job is to answer questions." Don was amused by the game. He figured something noncommittal would follow, and a question would be asked.

Finally, José said, "That's the way it is with those guys. But it was very valuable while it lasted. What are you up to these days?"

"That's why I'm here."

Pausing for dramatic effect, he said, "I'm preparing to run as candidate for the Senate to replace Boyd in California, who's retiring because of illness. But I want to check with you. It's sure to come up about my wife's uncle, Benito, and his criminal past."

José stopped filling boxes. "Well, I'll be darned," he said. "I'll have to check with the higher ups, but I like it."

"I just want to know if you'll be able to say that we were 'working for the department,' or something equally mysterious."

José said, "Sort of turning it to your own advantage. I like it. The supervisors know about your help, but I'll remind them. But seriously, it's good for the department, having someone sympathetic in the Senate. Running as a Republican or Democrat?" José asked.

"Republican," Don answered. "I probably could not get past the primary as a Democrat in California. I'm going after Hispanics, independents, and the centrist Republicans."

José said, "Well, it's a long shot, but you're smart, and they will overlook you because California is a Democratic state and they will think it's all over when their Democratic candidate wins the primary."

"Did you get a bulletin about the fracas on the United Airlines plane this morning?" Don asked.

"Yeah," José said. "The guy hit him with a right hook, and he was bye-bye!"

"Well, that guy was me," Don said. "And I'm going to win this election."

José looked at him with new respect, and said, "I do believe you will. U.S. Senator. I'll be damned."

Don said, "One other question, José. You authorized a temporary gun permit, which I have. I had to dispose of my gun after my confrontation with Giuseppe's nephew in North Carolina. At your request, I didn't kill him, but had to use a choke hold to subdue him, and he suffered apparent permanent damage to his throat. This made him crazier than ever, determined to get even with me, and his obsession about me possibly led to his death."

José hesitated, and said, "I really didn't realize that you were responsible for his throat injury, but we knew about his obsession with you. We did request that he not be killed in North Carolina, and his uncle also asked that he not be killed. I was busy with other matters at the time, and we slipped up.

"Are you expecting trouble?" José asked.

"There's a strong possibility that Giuseppe's crazy nephew hired a hit man before he was killed," Don said. "You know how that operates—money up front, arranged though a third party, the hit man doesn't know who hired him, and the guy ordering the hit sure doesn't want any publicity."

José suddenly became interested, and asked, "Could you tell the source of your information."

Don replied, "I don't know. Benito probably knows, but he won't tell you. At the moment, he's dying in Sicily. You see, if I want to stay alive, I cannot depend on the CIA because they often have other responsibilities. In this case, there's a need for secrecy, and ongoing covert operations in South and Central America may prevent action to save individual citizens."

"Point taken. I may alert Los Angeles, however. We have some responsibilities toward elected officials, even potential elected officials," José said.

"And your gun permit is permanent, effective immediately," José declared.

They shook hands and the visit was over. Mission accomplished. José is CIA, and whether the CIA would confirm that Don and Benito were working for them was up in the air. That is, until Benito finds out what is really going on in Central America. Don was betting on Benito finding out. Anyone able to lead a Mafia organization for twenty-five years without being arrested is able to outwit the CIA.

Don was on his way to Las Vegas for part two of the assignment, after a night in the hotel. He was early to bed and up at 4:00 a.m. to catch the first flight to Denver and Vegas—and Molly.

CHAPTER FOUR

January 5, 1986

HE BEGAN THINKING ABOUT MOLLY—what did she look like after forty years, how was her marriage going, and was she still attracted to him? Don had gotten up at 4:00 a.m. in Washington, and had only slept intermittently on the flight into Denver, but now he felt alert as the plane headed to Las Vegas.

He remembered talking to Max, Hannah, and Molly last June from the Grove Park Inn in Asheville, the first time they had spoken in forty years, and he especially remembered Molly's voice, and how it sounded—eager, youthful, and fresh.

Remembering Molly's voice brought back memories of lifeguard days, Tim and Pat, a very young Molly, and having sex with Molly—it all came rushing back.

He was thinking about those memories, as he exited from the plane and searched for her, wondering whether he would recognize her after all those years. Suddenly, she magically appeared and fell into his arms. It seemed so natural, as though time had stood still. They kissed, tentatively.

She said, "Oh, what the hell," and kissed him harder, and they held each other.

"It's been a long time," he said, stepping back, but holding her hand, recognizing she was still attractive to him.

"You never answered my letters," Molly said.

He said, "I didn't know your address, and Miriam told me that you told her that you were not going to write to me. She also said you had found a new boyfriend who was 'very cute.' I remember her exact words—'very cute.' Over the years, I began to realize that it didn't make sense, about your letters, but by that time, I was married and busy becoming a psychiatrist. As I was flying in today, it hit me—Miriam had lied. She had kept those letters or destroyed them. And there was no 'cute' boyfriend."

As they started walking out of the airport, Molly said, "I trusted Miriam. She did some strange things later on, things that upset my mother a lot. I should have realized that Miriam was holding the letters, and probably destroying them. I never see her. I think she's living with some guy in Phoenix."

She asked, "How long did it take for Miriam to seduce you after she lied about receiving the letters?"

About five minutes, he thought, but he didn't answer Molly's question. They were walking along, and he was pushing his single bag.

He was no longer holding her hand, and Don finally said, "The way you asked the question—'how long did it take for Miriam to seduce you'—shows that you know her problem. The answer to your question is 'five minutes,' by the way. She gave me a case of the 'clap'—gonorrhea. So, I called her, and she cursed me out, claiming that I gave it to her, and hung up on me, with a bang! That's the last time I talked to her, August 30, 1946."

Don paused, and said, "Dr. Francis, who treated me for my gonorrhea in 1946, listened to my description of the sexual experiences with your aunt and said she was a nymphomaniac. I had thought I was inadequate, so I found these comments from Dr. Francis quite reassuring."

Don continued, "And, I would be willing to bet that the 'strange things' that Miriam did that upset your mother were of a sexual nature. So, this guy she's living with in Phoenix better have satyriasis. I think that's the word for a man with an uncontrollable sex drive."

Molly was laughing as they arrived at her car, a Jaguar Salon. She turned and said, "I shouldn't laugh. It's very sad, really. She had a pelvic infection that wouldn't clear up, probably the 'clap' that you received, gonorrhea, and it made her sterile. It's just as well. She shouldn't have children. She's so different psychologically from my mother, and they were supposed to be identical twins. They looked the same when they were young, but they looked less and less alike as they got older."

Neither spoke for several minutes, as Molly was driving away from the airport, and Don had an opportunity to observe Molly closely. She seemed to sense that he was looking at her, turning her head very slightly, but kept her eyes on the road ahead.

She asked, "Do you like what you see?"

"Yes, very much," he said. "I was concerned that I would not recognize you, but I shouldn't have worried."

He remembered thinking that her mother, Hannah, was the most gorgeous woman he had ever seen, but he had not looked very closely at any women when he was a nineteen-year-old lifeguard with surging hormone levels.

Molly was attractive in a different way than her mother, with higher cheekbones and a straighter nose, more slender, taller, and she had a certain way that she carried herself. Of course, he had not had sex in three months, which might have had a lot to do with the attraction.

"Do you have a 4.2 liter engine in your Jaguar?"

Molly appeared startled. "Why, is it important?"

Don said, "No. I was just changing the subject from your attractiveness, which I found disconcerting, to the subject of your Jaguar. The Jaguar came with either a 2.8-liter or 4.2-liter engine. I'm sure that yours has a 4.2. It's a show car for the Strip."

Molly replied, "My husband says it's important in Vegas that you have a presence. Thus, the Jaguar. But I've grown to like it. In the circles we travel, everyone has a Mercedes or a BMW, and a few have Jaguars. Of course, it's in the shop a lot. It's definitely a high maintenance car."

She drove on for a few minutes, and Molly said, "Sam would've been very disappointed if I hadn't married a Jewish man. I thought I was in love with Arthur, and Arthur is Jewish, which seemed perfect at the time."

Don was a little startled by the abrupt change in topics, but he liked her directness.

He asked, "Do you still think you love Arthur, now?"

Molly answered, with some hesitation, "I gradually realized, over the years, that I wasn't in love with Arthur, but I did miss his company when he was gone. In recent years, he's been spending a lot of time traveling. Today he's leaving for Atlantic City, and he has another trip scheduled next week. Naturally, with all the traveling Arthur did, our sex life became almost nonexistent."

"I'm not sure if Delia loves me," Don said. "She's very cool in her letters."

They were silent for a while, and he suddenly said, "My mother was Jewish." Don said this casually, wanting to see her reaction.

Molly was obviously startled. "I'll be darned. That means that I could have married you. You never told me you had a Jewish mother. But it all happened so quickly, back then. You kept telling Tim I was too young, and I found out my mother was getting married and we were moving to Vegas the next day, so I was desperate. As least Miriam did one good thing, arranging for us to come together."

They stopped at a light, and Don said, "One thing puzzled me. How did you find out that Giuseppe Santini's nephew was after me?"

Molly answered, "Sam found out and told me. Santini and Sam were close and had business together, but not in recent years because of stricter casino gambling regulations. I panicked and told Sam he had to do something, so he went to Santini and arranged to have you protected, at least west of the Mississippi River."

Don said, "Well, you saved me. I never knew what was going on. Santini's nephew is dead, by the way, killed in South or Central America. I don't know the circumstances, but his uncle Giuseppe confirmed his death."

"Are you sure?" Molly asked.

"I hope that it's true. And Benito is certain that he's dead," Don replied. "I'll be telling Sam about his death today, so don't say anything yet. Fortunately, I had nothing to do with the death of Giuseppe's nephew, because I was in Italy at the time, studying Italian. Did you know that he's the guy we arrested under the Boardwalk for 'stargazing' on that rainy day, when the captain was making jokes and the two elderly ladies went for the police?"

"No, I didn't know," Molly exclaimed.

"I think Giuseppe told Sam, and Tim says you called him sometimes. Didn't Sam or Tim tell you?" Don asked.

"No, Tim never said a thing, and I sort of gave up calling regularly. Sometimes, I thought about you, especially when Arthur was traveling, and I was lonely."

Don was silent, wondering about how much he could tell Molly.

His thoughts turned to his marriage, and he said, "I didn't marry until I was twenty-seven years old, and I married a Catholic girl. All I had to do was sign an ironclad contract to bring the kids up Catholic. Besides, the last thing I wanted to do at age nineteen would be to get married. I certainly wasn't ready for marriage. I had college and girls and a career in mind."

Molly didn't respond immediately, as she drove up to the attendant. She greeted him by name, and said, as the attendant drove her Jaguar away, "Boys always feel that they're not ready for marriage."

They parted until dinnertime, and he took the elevator to his room. Don was impressed with the tasteful décor in the casino, with muted colors and subdued patterns, in sharp contrast to the gaudiness of Atlantic City.

After freshening up, Don hurried down to the small private dining room where he was to meet Sam Kravitz and Molly's husband, Arthur Stoller, for a late lunch. Molly had said that Arthur was flying with some business associates to Atlantic City, where they were considering investing in a casino, and he had to leave for the airport that afternoon.

He shook hands with Sam, who was in a wheelchair, and they embraced awkwardly, hampered by the wheelchair.

Sam said, "It's been a very long time since Atlantic City."

Don shook hands with Arthur Stoller, a man about medium height, balding, talkative, and friendly. He seemed genuinely curious about the reason for their meeting, which Don had set up, but Don ate slowly and collected his thoughts. Then, he went directly to why he had asked to meet with them.

"I'm going to be a candidate for the United States Senate from the State of California. As you know, Senator Boyd is very ill and may die soon. I'll be running as a Republican. California has many more registered Democrats than Republicans, so my plan is to appeal to the independent voters and fiscally responsible Republicans. My campaign will depend primarily on private monies, and I'm asking you to be cautious about donating significant campaign funds."

Don continued, "And why don't I want you to give any large sums to my campaign? Sam already knows the answer. I can still picture you, Sam, trudging across the sand of the beach in Atlantic City in 1946, with your suit jacket on in the heat of summer. I used to wonder why Sam wore that jacket when it was so hot outside. One day, Pat, my lifeguard partner, told me why Sam never took his jacket off."

He looked directly at Sam, who grinned.

Don spoke slowly and carefully. "My wife's uncle, Benito Desimone, contacted you, Sam, last year, and I spoke to you, Hannah, and Molly one time from Asheville. Our phone conversation brought back many old memories of Atlantic City. Benito is living with extensive prostate cancer and had settled completely with the Internal Revenue Service earlier this year. He has retired to Sicily for his final days. There are no charges against him and he's never been arrested, believe it or not."

Sam interrupted, saying, "I, also, have never been arrested, believe it or not!"

Don and Arthur both laughed, and Don said, "You're both very smart, very careful, and, more importantly, very lucky!"

The three of them laughed, and Don said, "The one thing that Benito wants, before he dies, is to see me taking the oath of office in Washington as the United States Senator. I aim to provide him with that pleasure."

Don paused and said, "Las Vegas has a checkered history and, in the mind of the American public, has a reputation for gangsterism and violence. I guess that's part of the reason that people come to Vegas, although, in reality, Vegas has more or less reformed itself. But the public thinks otherwise. So, if I were to receive substantial monies from Vegas, it would not look good."

Don added, "Politicians have to be careful about accepting gifts, so I'll pay full price for my accommodations and my meals."

Arthur nodded approvingly, and he turned to Sam and asked, "What did you have under your coat, Sam?"

Sam said, with a straight face, "I was just cold."

Sam shook his head sadly, saying, "We were lucky to stay alive."

Changing the subject, Sam asked, "Who's your campaign manager?"

"Joe Abrams."

Sam nodded approvingly. "Expensive, but he works hard and gets results."

He said, "Anything we can do, just ask."

Arthur had a newspaper in his hand, and said, "Say, a guy with the same name as you knocked out some drunk who was going bananas on a United flight into Washington, knocked him out cold."

Don said, "As a matter of fact, it was me."

Arthur whistled, and said, "I wouldn't bet against you in the Senate race."

He looked at his watch, stood up, and said, "I've got to get moving if I want to make the flight. I haven't finished packing. I'll be at Resorts, Sam, as usual. Good luck with your campaign, Don."

He had a brief discussion with his father-in-law about the upcoming negotiations, and Arthur left.

Don turned to Sam and asked, "How are you doing? Physically, I mean."

Sam replied, "Pretty good, I guess. Very weak left leg for about two years, since my stroke, but now I'm out of the wheel-chair every morning for my therapy. But you're doing okay physically, according to today's newspapers."

"I try to work out at least three times a week," Don said. "I know you have a fitness center in the casino, by the way, and I would like to have a workout before dinner. But first I have to tell you what's been happening to me in recent years."

Don continued, "I went back to Atlantic City in June, searching for the guy I arrested for trying to look up women's dresses under the Boardwalk—'stargazing'—in 1946, and all hell broke loose. I didn't know he was Giuseppe Santini's nephew. I learned later that you were protecting me west of the Mississippi, and I want to thank you, but I didn't know about it for many years. Finally, I ended up fighting with Giuseppe's nephew, Jimmy Calver, in the mountains of North Carolina, and I managed to avoid killing him, at the request of Giuseppe. But the nephew sure was pissed off at what I did to his vocal chords with a choke hold."

Don paused, thinking, and said, "Jimmy Calver, probably through an intermediary, hired some poor villager who needed money desperately, to shoot near me when I was in Sicily, visiting Benito. An unknown person gave the villager a fancy gun, which the guy didn't understand, and he was told not to hit me. It was just a 'joke' on the American."

Don continued, "It was just to make me worry, I suppose. They knew he would be caught. He didn't have contacts in Italy for a hit, so he wanted to scare me. But he didn't understand the gun, and nicked Benito in the shoulder."

He went on, "Anyhow, the federal government would seem to have solved my problem, because they arranged to have Santini's nephew killed. Apparently, they wanted the Santini cocaine supply to support the Contras in Nicaragua, and Jimmy Calver may have balked. It's all connected in some mysterious way to the hostages in Iran. Only the CIA knows what the connection is. Actually, there are only a select few directing the operation."

Sam interrupted him and asked, "You mean Joe Santini's nephew was killed in Colombia? The guy who was importing all the coke for Santini, and was looking up women's dresses?"

Don answered, "The very same guy. I'm guessing that

Santini's nephew wouldn't cooperate with the government. He was too busy trying to get even with me. As I said, he was killed, and someone else took over the importation of cocaine from Colombia."

Don continued, "I'm guessing, and this is strictly a guess, that Giuseppe Santini is allowed to import some cocaine to Cleveland and Chicago, with most of it going to Nicaragua and the Contras. Santini may even be getting paid for getting the cocaine to Nicaragua, also. I really don't know. This isn't common knowledge, so keep it to yourself until you read about it in the newspapers. And, Sam, pardon me for asking, but I need to know what your connections are with Santini, or if you have any connections?"

Sam said, "I understand your need to know because of your campaign. Joe Santini did still have a small interest in one of my casinos, but I bought him out eleven years ago, mainly because I was anticipating pressure from the State Gaming Control Board and the State Gaming Commission. I sold my interest in this other casino—the Majestic—to provide cash while I was building the Crystal. I also own one other casino, the Showplace. So, I own the Crystal and the Showplace, neither connected with Santini in any way."

Sam paused, and went on, "The Crystal Casino was built four years ago. Santini has no connection and never had a connection with the Crystal. I also built a hospital for the community, a library, a golf club, and other buildings. So, I am a completely respectable community leader."

Don shook his head in admiration and said, "You have done a great job in rehabilitating your image. Congratulations!"

Don asked, "What exactly is my problem, with Santini's nephew dead?"

Answering his own question, Don said, "My problem is that there may be a hit man gunning for me somewhere, waiting to strike, probably in Los Angeles. He doesn't know that the crazy nephew has been eliminated, and there's no one to cancel the contract for the hit. Because this all occurred in Colombia with no publicity, and the hit man was undoubtedly paid in advance, with no direct contact with the nephew who ordered the hit, the gunman is still looking to kill me. I understand that this is customary practice with professional hit men, to not know who ordered the hit. And you see, I may have a problem, or may not have a problem. But I do have something to be concerned about. Don't you agree?"

Sam nodded in agreement, and said, "Hannah's husband was killed by a man who was part-time hit man, part-time gambler."

Don said, "Dan DeSilva."

Sam looked at him, startled. "How did you know that name?"

Don said, "I was the lifeguard who pulled him out of the water. He floated through the Million Dollar Pier onto Michigan Avenue beach several days later. I remember him because he had a lot of what looked like crab bites on his body, according to my partner, but it looked to me that they were from banging around under the pier. Anyhow, he was quite dead."

What Don did not mention was that Sam had probably killed him, and that he and Hannah had almost immediately arranged to move to Vegas to get married.

Don had taken a calculated risk. He knew Sam may have murdered Dan DeSilva, and Sam realized this and would keep his silence about the hit man who was after Don.

Don said, "DeSilva was killed when he made the mistake of gambling in Atlantic City. But did you ever find out who ordered the hit on Hannah's husband, and why?"

Don added, "And, I understand DeSilva was tried in court and mysteriously found not guilty. So, it's different in my case. I don't know who the gunman will be."

Sam didn't answer immediately, and said, "Yes, your situation is more traditional. I understand the guy ordering the hit on Hannah's husband didn't follow protocol, didn't discuss it with Santini, probably knowing that Santini would not approve, and he's disappeared. I think he probably told DeSilva it was approved by Santini. I truly don't know the circumstances of his disappearance and don't want to know, and the whole procedure was botched. Santini was furious. Hannah, naturally, was very upset, so she was greatly relieved when DeSilva died."

Sam noticed that Don had not been paying full attention, thinking of Molly, and said, "Are you daydreaming about the old days?"

"Sorry, Sam. I was in another world. Briefly, I hope. But you understand that this is confidential information about the hit man. You can tell Hannah about Santini's nephew being dead. I've already told Molly. And I definitely would keep quiet about the CIA business in the jungle. I suspect the project isn't going well and there surely will be a congressional investigation.

"Why am I telling you this?" Don asked. "It's because you have just enough information to open the can of worms about Santini's nephew and his fate, enough to be subpoenaed as a witness if you let something slip in casual conversation. You and I don't want to be witnesses and have to face the dilemma of either squealing or lying and committing perjury. I appreciate your protecting me over the years, so I'm passing this advice along. And Hannah should be warned, also."

Sam said, "I understand. But what about yourself?"

Don said, "Well, if the campaign is successful, you'll receive your answer in the newspapers. That's all I can tell you. The funny thing is, neither one of us knows what's really going on with the CIA and the cocaine traffic in Nicaragua and Colombia, but we don't want to be investigated or subpoenaed—you, because you have carefully built a solid reputation in the community and your old history will be in the newspapers, and I, because I'm just starting out on a political career and can't afford to have Benito's past exposed. I've hinted at the solution for my problem, but, as I said, the answer will be in the newspapers."

Don declared, "In fact, only William Casey, head of the CIA, and a few others, know what's happening. I know the plan changes frequently, which is a sign that the plans are not working."

"All right," Sam said. "I get the picture, and thanks for the warning. I'll be waiting and reading the newspapers. But we should get moving, if you want a workout before dinner."

His wheelchair was motorized, and Sam zipped along, speaking as he went, "I'll have you transferred to one of the security suites. And the fitness center is on the fifth floor. You did say you're staying just the one night?"

"Yes, I've been in Europe three months organizing Benito's finances and studying Italian, away from my wife and the kids, so I'm anxious to get home."

Don added, "I hope you have a heavy bag for my workout."

Sam nodded and said, "We'll see you at dinner, around seven. Have a good workout."

The Crystal Casino had an elaborate fitness center, with all the latest equipment, including a light punching bag, and they were in the process of dragging the heavy bag out of storage when Don arrived, dressed in sweats. The manager apologized, saying that they had put the bag away because it was rarely used. Sam Kravitz had obviously called and commanded that the heavy bag be produced.

He was called to the phone. It was Sam.

Sam said, "I thought you'd want to know that Senator Boyd died. And a reporter from the local newspaper is here, about that incident on the plane yesterday. She somehow found out you were staying at the Crystal."

Don said, "Thanks for the news. And send the reporter up. It looks like my campaign is off to an early start."

He got Joe Abrams on the phone. Joe was at home, hoping to watch the Lakers game on television, and had already heard about Boyd's death.

He said, "Dazzle the reporter with your fancy footwork and tell her that you're thinking of running for Boyd's seat, and what a great guy Boyd was.

"By the way, what did you think of Boyd?" Abrams asked.

"Great guy. Good senator. Spent too much money, however," Don replied.

Don reiterated, "You got it. That's our platform—'Great guy. Good senator. Spent too much money.'"

Abrams laughed, and was laughing as he said, "I'm going to enjoy this campaign. You've got good political judgment." And he said, "See you Tuesday at eleven."

Don left the private phone room and found the reporter waiting for him. She introduced herself as Sue Hopkins, and she was accompanied by a photographer named "Bud" Nelson. She was young and energetic, and Bud, belying his name, appeared old and tired.

Don said, "I'll have an important announcement in three or four minutes, so if you'll be patient, I'll be with you presently."

He went into his usual workout routine, warming up with his leather bag gloves, dancing around the bag, using punching movements and hooking with light blows.

The promise of an announcement seemed to perk up the interest in both the reporter and Bud, and he began shooting more pictures, as Don went into the heavy bag punching. The first punches were tentative because of his fear that he had injured his hand the day before, but when he experienced no pain, he began punching more savagely.

At the end of three minutes, he rested, and he said, "I was

sorry to hear of the death of Senator Boyd this morning. He was a good man and an excellent senator. I'm considering entering the race for the Senate to replace the late Senator Boyd in the Senate from California."

He resumed punching the heavy bag, pausing only briefly to say, "As a Republican!" emphasizing this point with a particularly heavy blow to the defenseless bag. Sylvia wrote in her notebook, and she and Bud waited for the next statement.

He paused at the end of three minutes. Don had worked up a sweat in spite of the air-conditioning.

Sue asked, "When do you expect to decide?"

"I'm meeting with my staff on Tuesday, and I'll have an official announcement later in the week."

An older man in the audience who had come to watch him punch the heavy bag said, "I'm a Republican from California. Why should I vote for you?"

"Right now my platform is to have another three-minute round with a heavy bag, but if you wait, I'll tell you how to win another Senate seat for the Republicans."

With that, Don attacked the bag again for three minutes. Breathing heavily and removing his bag gloves, he shook hands with his questioner and asked, "Why do Republicans keep losing in California in the Senate?"

Don answered his own question, "Because they get bogged down in ideology and offend the Democrats and independents and the regular Republicans. I'm a fiscal conservative and social moderate. I'll add to the Republican voter block in the Senate and keep your taxes down, balancing the budget by controlling excessive government spending. I believe in a woman's right to choose, to control her own body."

Don went on, "Some Republicans get too involved in social problems like abortion and homosexuality, and not enough involvement in immediate questions, like the budget and the national debt. You can get away with that in some states, but not in California. If you want to lose elections in California, just keep talking about abortions and homosexuals. If you want to win elections, both in the primary and in the general election, vote for me."

Don continued, "Now, I need to get on with my workout. Further details can be expected later in the week when I officially announce my candidacy for the Senate seat vacated by Senator Boyd's death."

He shook hands with the Republican from California, noting his name.

As he moved to the weight area, he had a sudden feeling of panic. He had forgotten about Delia, his wife. She would be angry to find out about it in the newspapers. But maybe Delia wouldn't get around to reading the paper early, and if he were super lucky, it would not be picked up by the Los Angeles papers. He needed to call her and tell her.

The photographer took some more pictures of him, following his workout routine with the heavy weights. Sue, the reporter, apparently was mostly interested in the plane incident and seemed to be in a hurry to leave, looking at her watch. So, he said goodbye to her and the photographer and continued his workout.

There were no "muscle-heads" present, and those working out in the weight area seemed to be impressed as he gradually increased from one hundred and fifty to two hundred and fifty pounds in the bench press. He decided to try two hundred and seventy-five, stopping at four reps, fearing injuries because of irregular workouts. Don reminded himself to be more careful in his workouts, now that he was older, both on the weight he lifted and on his heavy bag work. He had been lucky so far and had avoided serious injuries.

He completed his workout and went to the security suite on the tenth floor. It required a key to operate the special elevator.

An employee followed him to his room, helped him enter, and provided instructions on the security system.

He called Delia, told her how much he loved her, and eventually told her that he was thinking of running for the Senate in California as a Republican for the seat left vacant by the death of Senator Boyd, and he'd tell her all about it when he got home the next day. He was in a rush, he said.

Suddenly, the phone went dead, and he realized she had hung up on him. Well, the last time he had that experience was forty years earlier when he told Miriam she had given him the clap. At least Delia had hung up quietly.

Don realized he was running late for dinner. He was distracted from his marriage problems when he entered the ultra-luxurious shower in which he was assaulted by a dizzying assortment of knobs and showerheads, including one that gave off steam. He was finally able to arrange for a normal shower, shaved, and dressed for dinner, while looking at the lights of Las Vegas shining below.

He went down in the special elevator and found the restricted dining area. Sam and Hannah had just arrived, and Sam was called away on a phone call. Hannah must have been in her seventies, but she was still strikingly attractive. She greeted him with a surprisingly long hug and looked at him mischievously when they pulled apart. He remembered the sensual kiss under the Steel Pier is 1945 when she rewarded him after Don rescued her from an attack under the pier, but he remembered that she was just teasing him on that occasion.

For some reason, he thought of one of May West's quotes— "Is that a gun in your pocket, or are you just happy to see me?" But just then, Sam returned from his phone call, and a few moments later, Molly arrived.

Molly had obviously dressed for the occasion, and she looked spectacular. Her mother, Sam, and Don were temporarily speechless, but recovered quickly and complimented Molly on her appearance. Not only her appearance had changed, but she carried herself differently—more vibrant and more confident. Don suspected some competition between mother and daughter.

After they were seated, Sam asked, "Will you tell them?"

Don said, "Why not? It'll be in tomorrow's papers."

Hannah and Molly looked at Don questionably.

Don said, "I'm entering the race for Senator Boyd's seat in the United States Senate as a Republican on the platform of fiscal responsibility and social moderation."

Molly and Hannah both applauded, and Molly asked, "What's your stand on women's rights? I warn you, if you give the wrong answer, I'm going to leave right now!"

They all laughed, and Don answered by saying. "I'm pro-women's right to choose and, in general, am pretty liberal with the exception of fiscal policy. I'm after the independent vote and the vote of reasonable Republicans who want to win elections, rather than spouting ideology."

Molly said, "We'll all celebrate and drink to your success!"

Don said, "And let us not forget another toast, this time to the Crystal Casino, which puts the Atlantic City casinos to shame, spectacular without being gaudy, very tastefully done!"

They drank to the Crystal, and Sam said, "Thanks, Don. A lot of planning went into the casino, and Molly gets much of the credit for the atmosphere. Plus, we give a slightly better payoff to the customers, and the people know it. And, we give back to the community, so we have a lot of regular gamblers. We have the highest return per table in Vegas."

As they ate, Sam and Hannah expressed curiosity about what he could possibly do for three months in Italy. So, Don engaged their Italian waiter in a lengthy discussion, in Italian, about Italian politics that had the waiter laughing. The waiter said, in English, that Don "knows what he's talking about."

Don added that he and Benito had many private confidential business talks, necessary because he was Benito's heir and Benito had serious health problems. Benito had suggested he do this to establish Don's credentials as a "player" and to establish that he was financially independent.

Sam and Hannah excused themselves after dinner, and Molly went to her suite to change into "something more comfortable," while Don walked around the casino.

When she came down, Molly and Don took a brief tour before going for a drive. He noted she didn't take the Jaguar. Don thought he knew where they were going, but didn't say anything. Molly drove to the outskirts of Vegas, looking, finally stopping in a dark area behind one of the many motels.

"Here, let me get you ready," she said.

She attached a mustache and short beard to his face, saying, "Can't let the new senator get in trouble. This is guaranteed not to fall off."

She laughed. He had noticed the perfume that she was wearing.

Don drove to the motel entrance and signed for the night, paying in cash. The clerk was not curious. Obviously, Molly had prepared for this occasion well in advance and had scouted out this particular motel.

As for the mustache and beard business, it was a dramatic gesture, but quite practical, even though Molly had not known about the Senate campaign. The local newspaper would have pictures tomorrow, so it was just as well he was in some sort of disguise.

Their room was on the second floor and was spacious, almost luxurious. He took off the beard and mustache and turned off the lights. They undressed each other, and he kissed her body as each part was revealed. They held hands as they got into bed, and they pressed their naked bodies together. Neither spoke.

At first their sex was languid and unhurried, but became tumultuous, as she had multiple orgasms.

Molly finally spoke, saying, "You see, I've learned a few thing over the years."

But she held him close, seemingly startled.

After a silence, she said, "I've never had sex with anyone except Arthur since my marriage. Maybe I was waiting and hoping to see you again, but I wasn't aware of that. I don't know about Arthur. He has a lot of opportunity, always on 'business trips,' but now I'm interested in finding out. What about you?"

Don hesitated, and said, "Delia is a dedicated Democrat and I can't see her giving that up. I was just hoping that she would see that I have a liberal platform and go along with this, but it's probably a fantasy of mine. She has a big problem with my taking over and making decisions about our future. This really bothers her, and now I've done it again, deciding to run for the Senate without consulting her."

Don said, "It's funny. Delia has this thing about not being an 'Italian wife' like her mother, so she gets upset when I make a business decision. I'm sure she regards Benito as a bad influence on me. Probably I did let Benito influence me to become a senator, because he sees in me the fulfillment of his own immigrant dream. He told me that he had wanted to become an architect, but he had to give that up almost immediately when he had to work to help support his family. His parents were immigrants from Sicily, and he was the oldest son, eleven years old when his family came over, and he didn't know a word of English."

Don continued, "The nuns permitted him to go to school for a few hours in the mornings, because he had to work in the late morning and afternoons. He was fascinated with English, studied hard, and became a translator for the non-English speaking immigrant Italian and Sicilian families by age thirteen. The call for his services would come at all times of the day or night, and he would study English or read late at night. Benito is an example of what you can do if you dedicate yourself and you have reasonable talent for what you want to accomplish."

Don paused to think, and went on, "I want to campaign and become a senator, not only because of Benito, but also because I've started forming my own ideas about the country's future. I'll tell you about them later. It's a golden opportunity. I have Benito's money behind me, as Sam suspects. We'll see what happens."

He said, "I do love you, whatever happens." The words came out spontaneously, surprising him.

Molly held tight. "I'll always love you. You're my first and only love."

CHAPTER FIVE

January 6, 1986

MIKE KELLY WAS WAITING as Don's plane landed at LAX, and they discussed his bodyguard responsibilities later over lunch. Don said, "We'll have to avoid using the word 'bodyguard,' but that's mostly what you will be doing, at least at first."

The first assignment for Mike would be to watch for any person behaving suspiciously near Don's home in Pacific Palisades. Don explained the problem of the hit man who didn't know that the man who hired him was dead. Generally, Mike was to park down the street from Don's house and watch for any unusual activity.

He asked Mike if his problem with diarrhea was still a concern, but Mike laughed, and said, "It was that English food. Too much fish and chips. I'm fine."

Don was upfront about his marriage problems, indicating he likely would be getting a divorce, "Unless some miracle happens. Delia hung up on me when I told her I would be running as a Republican. She's made up her mind, and when Delia makes up her mind, that's it. I've been kidding myself about my marriage, thinking I could leave for three months and find her waiting when I returned. She turned down my invitation to join me

99

in Italy, so she was thinking of divorce for some time. And I couldn't tell her about the hit man. Now, it's time to face the music."

Mike drove Don to his home in Pacific Palisades, parking out of eyesight. In the parked car, Mike handed over a gun, a Beretta, somewhat larger than the one he had killed the man with in the North Carolina mountains, but fairly light. Mike fitted Don with a shoulder holster and placed the gun in the holster. Mike answered his questions about operating the Beretta, including the use of the safety, and said he would follow-up with Don on the firing range.

Mike said, "This is a 9mm weapon, but it's light and you'll forget you're wearing it. Have you ever shot a pistol?"

"Yes," Don replied. "Once. Also a 9mm, but smaller, and specially made to fit a groin holster, with a silencer. I was told it was effective only at close range—for people, that is."

Mike was startled briefly, and said, "Well, I won't ask about the circumstances. I'll go around the block and park down the street."

All was quiet. He waited until Mike and his car disappeared. Don went to the front door and let himself in with the key. At least his key still worked. She hadn't changed the locks, yet.

Delia must have heard Mike's car, and she was waiting in the living room. After a perfunctory kiss, Delia rose to the attack. It was interesting to Don that both Delia and Molly were very direct. And both were very passionate.

"What did you mean, you're going to run for the Senate? Without discussing it with me? And as a Republican? What kind of craziness is that?"

"I guess, all things considered, I have to run as a Republican. I've always registered Republican."

Delia said vehemently, "Well, you'll do it without me!"

It was like a poorly played stage production, and very unlike

Delia. Don looked directly at Delia, and finally asked, "Is there someone else?"

His question felt stagey, also, but it brought the desired result.

Delia briefly looked like a deer caught in the headlights, then she relaxed, and said, "I was never good at covering up or lying. Yes, there's someone else, someone who wants the things I want and will stay home with me, live with me, make decisions *together* with me. And yes, we have had sex and it was quite satisfactory."

"Satisfactory" sex? Don wondered what "satisfactory" sex felt like, but he didn't inquire. Strangely, he didn't feel any anger about his wife bedding down with someone else. At least, not at the moment. Usually, at this point in the production, the cuckolded husband asks, "Is it anyone I know?" But he was not curious. He would find out, eventually. Besides, Delia wanted him to ask.

Of course, last night's episode with Molly had a lot to do with how calm he was in the face of his wife's infidelity. He thought about Molly, starting over with Molly. How pleasant that would be, not to have to deal with all this garbage.

It occurred to him that, knowing Delia, she would not be having sex with anyone else if she had not filed for divorce, so he asked, "When did you file for divorce?"

She said, after some hesitation, "Three weeks ago. The papers are on your desk, in the study."

But Delia was not finished, of course. She probably had been rehearsing this speech for months.

She said, "I don't want to be a political wife, anxiously awaiting the results of the next elections. You've changed, Don, or maybe you were always that way underneath. I wish you all the luck in the world, but I'm not the wife you need."

Delia continued, "I had sort of made up my mind when you

accepted Benito's money without talking it over with me and went off to Sicily, again not talking it over with me. This political business, which I don't quite understand, confirmed that I had made the right decision."

Don realized that Delia was justifying the divorce in her own mind, easing any guilty feelings, so he didn't contest the logic of her statements. And she was right—what did she say? "I'm not the wife you need?" She was fucking-A right!

"Don, are you listening?"

"No, as a matter of fact. Your speech time is up. You have already filed for divorce. What's the point?"

There was a period of silence, and Don asked, in an even tone, "What about the children?"

He had sent postcards regularly from Europe to Linda and Robert, as well as occasional letters to Delia. He received return cards from Linda, as well as one card from Robert, and one letter from Delia. Delia's letter asked when he was coming home (probably to make sure she had started the divorce proceedings before he returned).

Delia was silent for a moment, and she said, "Linda is interviewing for a translator's job this morning. She lives in her own apartment now. Robert is on Christmas break from Cal. He only needs three units, plus his dissertation, to finish his master's degree in architecture. He's with his girlfriend today, somewhere. I warned both children that I needed to talk with their father, and to stay away."

Don had felt a little nervous at the beginning of their talk, but he gradually realized Delia had made her decision a long time before. She never had said, "Come home immediately or I'll divorce you." What would he have said? "I can't come home. There may be a hit man waiting to kill me?"

He said, "It will take me a little while to move out. I'll be sleeping in one of the spare bedrooms and . . . "

The doorbell rang and Don answered the door, suspecting possible trouble. It was Mike, and he said, in a low voice, "I've got someone trapped in the alley next to the house next door. The house is dark—there's a 'for sale' sign on the lawn. I don't think the guy can get out as the fence is quite high. He's armed, and his gun has a silencer. I heard something whistle past my ears."

Don shouted to Delia that he would be right back, and he hurried next door. The house was locked up tight and apparently was empty.

He whispered to Mike that the owner was "paranoid" and the neighbors had threatened legal action about the height of the fence and the barbed wire strung along the top. He motioned to Mike, and the two of them crept along the house wall, keeping to the shadows, pausing frequently. Both he and Mike had their guns drawn but were unsure of their next move.

Suddenly, while Don and Mike were trying to decide what to do, a figure rushed toward them. Don instinctively went for the man's knees and flipped him over on his back. As he hit the ground, a gun fell from his hand. Don grabbed the loose gun with the attached silencer and Mike quickly applied cuffs.

The man put up a brief resistance, but Mike's vast bulk evidently discouraged him, and the loss of the gun took all the fight out of him.

Don said, in a low voice, "He's okay. Go into the house with him. Get him on his feet."

The man struggled to his feet, and Don hurried him and Mike into his house, and through the den and into the kitchen. Don and Mike listened. The neighborhood was quiet.

He asked Mike, "Did anyone notice us?"

"No," Mike replied. "At least, I don't think so."

Don left the kitchen to find Delia, who was headed into the bedroom, and Don stopped her. "Don't call the police. Under no circumstances will you call the police. Do you understand? Everything is okay."

Delia raised a questioning eyebrow but nodded, and Don went back into the kitchen.

He took a camera with him and silently snapped five pictures of the man sitting in the kitchen chair in handcuffs. He was a short, stocky, dark-complexioned male, middle-aged, and possibly Italian. There was a bruise on his forehead, probably from being tackled.

He sat there, sniffing occasionally. There was a strong after-shave smell and a hint of body odor. He was wearing a windbreaker jacket over a long sleeved, checkered shirt.

Don pulled up the man's jacket and shirtsleeves far enough to reveal needle tracks.

Don said, "We have a problem. The man who paid you to kill me is dead, but I'm sure you don't know his name. If I can prove to you that the guy who ordered the hit is dead, you could keep the money and walk away. If you don't believe he's dead, you have not fulfilled the contract and you worry about that because you have already spent much of the money on heroin, so you can't pay someone else to take on the contract. You can't fulfill the contract yourself because we have your picture, and it's been my experience you boys are afraid to have their picture taken."

Don paused and walked around to directly face the man in the chair. "If you'll tell me where you're from, perhaps we can work something out and not go to the police," he said.

The man hesitated.

"By the way, are you a Democrat or Republican?"

The man looked startled at the question and said, "Republican," in a low voice."

It was the first word that the man had uttered, and Don said, "Wonderful. I'm going to be the Republican candidate for

Senator from the State of California. I need to concentrate on my campaign and not worry about being killed. Now tell me where you're from."

The man thought about this request, and said, "Cleveland."

Don said, "Good. I know lots of people from Cleveland. I know the Santini family. Joe is the boss and Bill is his nephew who helps Joe run things. He has another nephew who was running the cocaine operation in Colombia, and perhaps Venezuela. He ran it under the name of Pablo Cuevas and was killed in a drug raid in Colombia about a week ago. He was crazy and I pissed him off, so he ordered me killed. But he's very dead."

Don asked the man, "By any chance do you have the phone number of either Joe or Bill Santini"

The man opened up and suddenly became very talkative, possibly convinced of the logic of Don's argument, but more likely afraid that Don would call the Santini family.

He said, "Naw, I don't know the number. All I know is that some guy from South America wanted you killed. Your story makes sense. Ain't Colombia in South America?"

Don nodded, and said, "Yes, Colombia is in South America."

The man went on. "I know the Santini family, sort of, but I'm not really a member. But I respect them. Sometimes they send business my way. Oh, I do other things," he said, as though he didn't want to be pictured as a full-time hit man.

Don asked, "By the way, what's your name? And I saved you a lot of trouble from the Santini family, because if you had killed me, they would be very angry, especially Bill Santini, who's a very good friend of mine. And now you get to keep the money! How much did he pay you?"

"That's sort of private."

"Well, if you got paid a penny less than twenty or twenty-five thousand, you got taken. He wanted me killed real bad."

"Yeah. My name is Al Bonanno. You can just call me 'Apples.'

I got thirty thousand and five thousand for expenses," he said, proudly.

Mike Kelly whistled.

"But someone had to check the plane reservations for more than two months, to see when you was flying back to the States. That cost four thousand. And they wouldn't pay me the thirty thousand until you got here," Apples said.

Don said, "Bill Santini and his uncle Giuseppe Santini owe me favors, so if anyone gives you a hard time about the contract, go to them. Are you a member of the Bonanno crime family?"

Apples responded, "My mother used to say we were relatives." He asked, "Can I go now?" Don had noted that his hand had started to tremble and he was sweating. He needed to fix, badly.

Don asked, "Do you have something to help you in your car?"

Apples looked at Don gratefully and replied, "Yeah."

Don look questionably at Mike, who said, "I patted him down. He's good to go."

Mike took the cuffs off, and Don led him through the house, opened the door, and said, "Say 'hello' to Bill Santini for me." But Apples didn't respond and rushed out, presumably in the direction of his car.

Turning to Mike Kelly and locking the door, he motioned him to head back into the kitchen, and a few moments later, Don said, "I could kick myself. Here I was being cool and casual about being killed, only half believing it, and the very day I hired you, it came off."

They embraced, and he noticed how much taller and broader Mike was than he was, and how heavily muscled. He realized that Apples must have been equally impressed.

Mike said, "I don't think I ever busted a hit man. He was a weird one! A junkie hit man. But he had real ammo in his gun, and he really was going to kill you. You did a great interview, but how'd you know all those people in Cleveland?"

Don answered, "Giuseppe Santini is the boss of the Cleveland Mafia, and Jimmy Calver, his nephew ran the cocaine operation in Colombia. Bill Santini, another nephew, is second in command to Giuseppe. Jimmy is now dead. He is the one who looked up women's dresses under the Boardwalk in Atlantic City. The Santini's think they owe me a favor for not killing Jimmy Calver when I could have, but I just want them to stay away."

Don went on, "Jimmy Calver didn't know people in other states very well. He probably called someone not in the family, in Cleveland, and paid them five or ten thousand dollars to find a hit man. He couldn't call anyone in the family because they knew me. So, this other guy found this junkie hit man for him. Maybe all the hit men are junkies nowadays, but I doubt it. And the guy who set this up knew he could not use someone from the Santini family. He must have been warned by Jimmy Calver. Maybe he knew Calver was crazy or about to be killed, and he was too lazy to get someone from out of town. Calver definitely paid too much."

Don paused and after thinking about it for a moment, he continued, "Lucky for us he needed a fix. There was no way I was going any farther into that dark alley. We would have been sitting ducks."

Mike agreed, "And we couldn't have called for police back-up, only he didn't know that. He thought the police would arrive at any minute. And nice tackle, by the way. I'd pick you for my team any time."

"That's a wrestling move," Don said with a laugh.

Don became serious and said, "Okay, not a word to anyone about this incident. Not a word to your wife, children, fellow sheriff deputies, Joe Abrams, girlfriends while in the sack, or anyone. Like it never happened."

Mike said, "Understood. I'm divorced, with two grown children. No steady girlfriends. After all, he didn't commit a crime, except, maybe, carrying a loaded firearm."

Don asked, "What about the loaded firearm?"

"I'll take care of that and the silencer, too," Mike replied.

"And, I'm getting divorced, so I'll be moving. I'll talk to Joe Abrams about where he thinks I should move, maybe in a secure building, if there's such a thing. I truly think that now I can relax and plan the campaign. Come on, I'll introduce you to my soon-to-be-ex-wife."

Don started to lead Mike into the living room, intending to call Delia from the bedroom, but stopped, and said in a low voice, "The story for Delia is that he was a suspicious person in the neighborhood who was looking for someone else, so we let him go. I doubt that she'll totally believe it, but she'll go along with it."

He went to get Delia, who didn't ask questions about the story.

She said to Mike, "You looked like a bodyguard type, so I was nervous when you brought a man in handcuffs into the house."

Mike replied, "No, I'm just a problem solver, a professional problem solver."

Don said, "Our criminal turned out to be a false alarm. I'll be gone as quickly as possible, hopefully in a matter of days. After that, you can just turn on the alarm and relax."

Delia said, "Well, I guess you solved Don's problem for him, Mike. By the way, Don, one of your buddies, Paul Jeffers, called. He heard you were back in town and running for the Senate. Paul left a phone number. It's on the fridge. I told him you were having a brain fit and you'll call him after being checked out at UCLA. And I'm going out later. Remember to turn on the alarm when you leave. Mike, it's been nice meeting you," she said, offering her hand.

Delia turned in the direction of her room and was gone.

Mike shook his head, and said, "I see what you mean. She can be quite a handful."

Don remarked, "She has a sense of humor when she's not mad, as you probably noticed, when she mentioned the 'brain fit.' But now you know why I can't campaign with her. She's divorcing me, and for the first time in months, as I said, I'm really relaxed and ready to become a senator. You'll note that she never did ask what my platform was, or why I was running, or ask about her uncle Benito, who is dying, and whom she was very attached to at one time."

Mike said, "Well, I've been divorced for about seven years. There was another guy involved, and I had a short affair earlier in my marriage. But I thought things were okay. She told me she wanted a divorce. My wife has remarried, but she didn't marry the guy she was seeing before. I just think I don't understand women."

Don continued, "Freud said, despite thirty years of research into the feminine soul, he's never been able to find out, 'What does a woman want?'"

They both laughed at Don's quote, and Don said, "I know what Delia *didn't* want. She didn't want me making my own decisions, and when I started doing this, that's when the shit hit the fan! By the way, she does have a boyfriend, she tells me, and when I didn't ask who it was, she was disappointed. I predict she'll tell me tomorrow."

Don said, "I'm going to call Paul Jeffers and may go to dinner with him. You should take off. It's almost four o'clock. I'll see you at the office tomorrow. And thanks, again, for saving my life."

After Mike left, Don called Paul Jeffers. He was not sure where Paul got his money from, but he didn't seem to have financial problems and was home a lot. He had revolving girlfriends who came and went but sometimes returned. Don knew he played the stock market.

Paul was enthusiastic about having dinner together, and he said he would pick Don up. They drove down to Santa Monica to a favorite restaurant of Paul's, and all the while, Paul was questioning Don about how he was financing his run for the Senate.

Don suspected Paul could be having some kind of financial trouble, and finally Don asked bluntly, "Paul, why are you asking all the questions about how I'm financing my campaign? Are you running short of cash?"

Paul laughed, as he took the stub from the parking attendant, and he asked, "Is it that obvious?"

He didn't say anything more until they were seated, and he and Don were served appetizers and were handed the menu. Both ordered wine.

Don waited for Paul to speak, and Paul finally said, "This is embarrassing, but I heard that you had left your practice and would be in Europe for several months without Delia, maybe studying Italian or some crazy thing. Next you're back, and as a Republican, running for the Senate in the primaries, with no visible means of support. It didn't make sense because I know that Delia is a fierce Democrat.

"I hear that Joe Abrams is your campaign manager, and I know he's expensive. And I've got ninety-five thousand that I owe to the IRS. So, you see . . ." Paul said, as he spread his hand and looked at Don helplessly.

The waiter interrupted to take their orders, and Don said, "That's really tough. I guess the market zigged when you expected it to zag."

Paul nodded glumly. "I guess you're right."

Don said, "My personal situation is almost comical. I suppose I'm in the male menopause. I had money saved, and I closed my practice and took off for Europe. When I returned, I filed for the primaries and hired the best campaign manager in town, and prayed for good fund-raising. But my wife has left me for another man and thinks . . . what were her words? Oh, she said, 'You're having a brain-fit' and kicked me out of the house. Right now I'm about to move into an apartment somewhere."

Paul was sitting with a dazed expression on his face.

"There's some good news, Paul. My campaign is going well. My advice to you, Paul, is not to be discouraged, keep plugging away, and earn the money back, stall the IRS, and work your ass off!" Don almost shouted the words.

"Damn it, I will," Paul said, leaping to his feet and holding his wine glass up in the air.

Don stood up and joined Paul, clinked his wine glass to Paul's, and declaimed, "Damn it, you will!"

Men at several other tables stood and shouted, "Damn it, he will!"

There was general laughter, and several shook hands with Paul, who looked like he was enjoying himself.

One man recognized Don from the newspaper, and asked, "Say, aren't you the candidate on the plane who's going to fight for us in Washington?"

"I'm that guy," Don admitted, as the two shook hands.

"Well, I'm a Democrat, but I'm seriously thinking of voting for you."

"You should vote for me. I have similar social views. The only thing different is that I strongly favor a balanced budget," Don said.

The man looked thoughtful for a moment, and said, "By George, you're right! You have my vote. It's about time the government had to balance a budget, same as the ordinary citizens!"

Don and Paul sat down to finish their dinners, and Don sensed that Paul's feeling of euphoria might be wavering, so he said, "You should make an appointment with Larry McIntire immediately to arrange for a settlement with the IRS. Keep a positive attitude."

"It's not easy," Paul replied, shaking his head.

Don said, "I'll tell you my little secret, if you promise not to tell anyone, because my solution for maintaining my courage will seem somewhat silly. I have a future problem that could wreck my campaign when it comes up, and it certainly will come up in the general election. I believe I can solve it if I maintain my courage and use ingenuity."

"I promise," Paul said.

Don continued, "You know, when you seem to have your back against the wall, and you're worried that you might lose everything, it is important to keep your wits about you. But you can't stop worrying. At the very moment that you need to think and plan, you can't, because you're too busy worrying?"

Paul nodded, anxious to hear the secret.

Don paused, and said, "Well, *The Wizard of Oz* is one of my favorite movies—you're not going to laugh, are you?"

"No, no," Paul exclaimed, forgetting about dinner temporarily, fork held in midair.

Don fully realized he was playing with Paul, leading him on, for his own good, presumably. But it was so easy when the subject was desperate, and Don filed the information away in his mind.

Don went on with his analogy, "You know the scene where the Cowardly Lion, along with the Scarecrow and the Tin Woodman are confronting Frank Morgan, the Wizard, after he's been exposed as a fraud? The Wizard desperately and successfully placates two of them, by giving the Scarecrow a diploma for a brain, and the Tin Woodman a ticking watch for a heart?"

Paul nodded, his attention riveted on Don's words.

"He gave the Cowardly Lion a medal!" Don exclaimed. "And

he said that was for 'conspicuous bravery against wicked witch-es.' In your case, replace 'witches' with the 'IRS.' And he award-ed the Cowardly Lion the 'Triple Cross.'"

Noting that Paul continued listening with rapt attention, Don went on, "The Wizard told the formerly Cowardly Lion, 'You're now a member of the Legion of Courage!' Just regard life as a test. It has its ups and down, or, in your case, market gains and losses. Go to McIntire, arrange a settlement with monthly payments, and get on with your life. Maybe get a job. The Cowardly Lion in *The Wizard of Oz* felt courageous after he got the medal, so his attitude improved. But he was the same Lion, now with a positive attitude."

Don added, "And watch for a seemingly insurmountable problem that will arise early in the general election and how I'm going to wiggle out of it."

Paul, who seemed to have recovered his poise, said, "I'm more interested in how you're surviving your marital struggles."

"Oh, that," Don said, as he looked appraisingly at the last bit of tuna sitting at the end of his fork. "Delia just could not stand the idea of being married to a Republican. She just could not deal with it at all. And I would not give up my dream."

Don looked directly at Paul and said, "I'll be the next United States Senator from California."

CHAPTER SIX

January 7, 1986

Mike picked him up at 8:30 a.m., and they had breakfast in the Pacific Palisades before heading for Joe Abram's office in Century City. Don wanted to phone Benito and Molly, but he was not comfortable making the calls from his own home. The realities of the divorce were sinking in. He hadn't slept well the night before. He had to move—and soon.

He identified himself to Abram's secretary and called Benito a little before ten, figuring he would catch Benito in the early evening in Sicily. Benito answered the phone, and Don asked about his health, and about his prostate cancer.

Benito replied, "They took some more x-rays. They tell me it has spread, mostly to my bones, which apparently is typical for prostate cancer. But I had already doubled up on my pain pills. I think I did this while you were here. So far, it is working."

Don apologized for not having called for two days with so much happening, but Benito brushed it aside, declaring he had to learn to make decisions without him. He told Benito about what happened on the plane, and in the office of José Ramirez, the mysterious agent who would not admit that he was CIA. They talked about the publicity from the fracas on the plane, and Benito commented again about what they should do if the CIA would deny that Don and Benito had worked for them.

Benito said, "Talk about Iran-Contra. That should get their attention. That whole business is in trouble."

Don told Benito about their encounter with Apples Bonanno in full detail, including the payment of $30,000 plus $5,000. He said, "Apparently, I'm worth a lot of money—dead!"

Benito's initial comment was, "That is unbelievable! And to end up with a junkie hit man after Calver spent all that money!" He said, "You were very lucky." He agreed the hit man threat was over, but told Don to keep Mike on the payroll."

Finally, Don mentioned his pending divorce. "She was waiting for me with her prepared speech, but she said she had made up her mind months ago. She went into her speech about making decisions without talking to her, and the 'last straw' being running for the Senate. And when I said I was running as a Republican, she really lost her cool. But she had filed for divorce three weeks ago, so why this crap? I think she's upset because it didn't bother me."

After a pause, Benito finally said, "I could see that coming. American women, and I consider Delia, my niece, as 'Americanized,' want to be dominant in their relationships and become angry when men go off on their own. Their husbands are often 'pussy-licked.'"

Don was puzzled. "Pussy what?"

Finally, it dawned on him. "You mean 'pussy-whipped,' don't you?"

They both laughed.

Benito changed the subject. "The Swiss bank finally offered to reimburse my account for twenty-three million, based on how much we have lost over the years as a result of the manipulations by Schultz. My attorneys thought I should grab it, and they felt the offer was generous because the bank wanted to avoid the bad publicity of a court dispute."

Benito said, "I am not so sure. You took away with you all the Schultz material. Have you studied it?"

Don said, "I spent many hours going over the transactions of the last ten years, since Heinz Schultz began managing your account. According to my calculations, twenty-three million is less than the bare minimum amount, and not generous at all. The bank is bluffing, and they're assuming that you're also hiding money from the IRS, as so many of their clients are doing, and are therefore afraid of discovery."

"I know you have a great memory for figures," Benito said.

Don said, "Bear in mind that I had a minor in accounting at Stanford and was always interested in figures, particularly stock market figures. I would delay—let the bank sweat it out. After all, you're not in need of cash. Tell your attorneys to get a different accountant to go over the transactions, and bill them the accountant's time. Better yet, hire your own accountant. The bank is very worried about their reputation in the banking community and will offer more money. I estimate you have lost a minimum of twenty-five point three million as a result of Schultz' criminal behavior."

Benito agreed, saying, "I believe you are correct. I do not think I will do anything, for the moment. They did fire Schultz, who was responsible, but they failed to supervise him. They want to avoid publicity about their lack of supervision and did not report Schultz to the police, and he will not go to jail."

Don exclaimed, "Twenty-five point three million dollars stolen from your account and all that happens to Schultz is being fired! No prison time? You've got them by the balls. They should have reported this to the police. You did them a favor by not demanding that it be reported."

"We will wait, and see what happens. You are right," Benito decided. "I plan to hire my own accountant."

Benito went on, "I do not want some smart ass divorce attorney getting a hold of Delia, so it is just as well that we not transfer money. She will be well taken care of. After all, she is still my niece. I will gift eight million for the campaign, and you can take most of your campaign expenses out of that. I'll transfer another five hundred thousand to you for personal use, and for the house or the apartment. There will be gift taxes and our attorneys will figure that out."

Benito changed the subject. "You should have a wife appear with you, or at least become engaged to someone. What about that girl, that woman who is Sam's stepdaughter. You told me her name was Molly."

Don was startled. "Her name is Molly, and I don't see how you figured that out. Anyhow, she's married to Arthur Stoller, and we renewed our acquaintance in a surprisingly passionate manner last Saturday. At least this was surprising to me. She mentioned that Arthur takes a lot of long trips and she's going to look into that."

Benito said, "I think about how she protected you all these years. It is a very romantic story. You are her true love. You would have been killed or at least beaten up badly if it was not for her. She protected you from Giuseppe Santini's crazy nephew, the stargazer you arrested under the Boardwalk in Atlantic City in 1946, by persuading her stepfather, Sam Kravitz, to use his influence with Giuseppe. And she kept protecting you all these years."

Benito asked, "Do you find her attractive?"

"Yes. Very attractive," Don said, and he thought about Molly and the manner in which she would very slightly turn her head and glance at him.

There was silence for a moment. Finally, Benito congratulated Don on the way he handled the situation with Apples, and said he would have a private detective find out what Arthur was doing on these trips and whom he was "shacking up" with.

Don told Benito that Arthur Stoller was staying at Resorts Casino in Atlantic City. He asked Benito whether the Palladian villa near Vicenza was still available for Robert to restore, and Benito said it was, and had been waiting for Robert to start working on it.

As Benito hung up, Don realized why Benito was not upset over the divorce, even welcomed it. Benito must have given up on Delia some time ago. Don remembered that Delia had never asked about her uncle, and probably only talked to him because he had called her. Don knew that Italians were big on family and also big on grudges and proper respect. Was Delia the really strong person he imagined or was she just a pain in the ass?

He dialed Molly's private number, and she answered the phone on the first ring. "I've been waiting for your call. I couldn't concentrate on my painting. I've missed you. Arthur has extended his trip to Thursday." She added, "I think he's having an affair."

He noted her voice. It was soft, almost melodious.

Don said, "Well, I have news for you. Benito remembered you and thinks I should marry you."

There was a long pause, and Molly asked, "What are you talking about?"

He kidded, "Oh, didn't I tell you? Delia is divorcing me. I don't consult with her about major decisions, and I have the nerve to be running as a Republican candidate for the Senate, although she had already filed for divorce before I told her. She said that was the 'final straw,' which doesn't make sense, as I said. One thing more—she claims she's had sex with someone else and it was quite satisfactory. I was tempted to ask her what 'satisfactory' sex was, but I resisted that impulse."

"Wow, double wow. I think I'm going to sit down," Molly said. Her voice had risen and she was obviously excited, but her voice didn't lose its intimate quality. Don pictured her on his campaign platform, charming everyone.

She asked, "You were kidding me about Benito, about what he said, weren't you?"

"No," Don said. "He didn't remember your name immediately, but he talked to you on the telephone in June when you, Sam, and your mother called, when we were in Asheville. Benito is a good judge of character. He reminded me that you had saved my life or at least saved me from a bad beating."

Don continued, "Plus, he probably feels that Delia would be unpredictable and a liability in my campaign. He has two other nieces who won't have anything to do with him because of his Mafia connections, but Delia was always his favorite. She came to visit him frequently and was big on the family relationships, but now she never calls him, even though she knows he has inoperable prostate cancer."

"My answer is, 'Yes,'" Molly said.

Don asked, "Yes, what?"

"Stop teasing me. You know what I mean. Yes, I'll marry you!"

Don asked, "Will you marry me?"

There were giggles from the phone. She had a lovely, soft giggle. He remembered her throwing herself on the bed forty years before and giggling.

"One other thing. Benito is hiring a private detective to check up on Arthur. And if I know Benito, he's already hired an Atlantic City detective and paid him to go to work immediately!"

Molly said, "I'm falling in love with your Uncle Benito. Also, I've already talked to a divorce attorney, and I have an appointment this Thursday to go over the details, and I'm taking back my maiden name, Dorman. It's like awaking from a bad dream.

I'm angry with Sam and my mother and also with my daughter, but mostly with myself. I knew something was going on, but I didn't want to face it. Maybe we'll hear from Benito's private eye soon. Nevada has no waiting period and has no-fault divorce laws, but I admit I'm curious about his girlfriend."

"Dorman it is," Don exclaimed. "I like that name better. It reminds me of fifteen-year-old Molly Dorman, asking whether the lifeguards needed something from the store." Don added, "Unfortunately, California has a six-month and one day waiting period. The earliest Sunday for the wedding would be July 13, but I'll check with Delia about her plans."

Don thought for a moment and said, "My campaign manager, Joe Abrams, wants to start the meeting. It's in his office and I'll be seeing him in person for the first time. So, I'll tell him about my divorce, get him to help me rent a house or apartment, and move out as soon as possible. I'll surprise Joe with news of my engagement. I'm talking to the kids over dinner tonight. They have probably gotten an earful from their mother. Call you tomorrow around the same time. Okay?"

"Okay. Love you."

"Love you, too."

Don hung up the phone and went into the outer office, where Joe Abrams was waiting for him. He passed by Mike chatting with Celia, Joe Abram's secretary, who ran the office.

Joe turned out to be a dynamic, friendly person, with sleepy eyes, a stocky build, average height, and mildly overweight. He was balding and appeared about sixty years of age. He led Don into the inner office. From the window in Joe Abram's office, Don could see the Century Plaza Hotel.

Don said, "My wife wants a divorce. Obviously, she won't be campaigning with me, but I hope my children will be cooperative. My wife's last words were something like, 'I'll divorce you if you run as a Republican.' I'm kidding, sort of, but this apparently was the last straw. She's a vehement Democrat. I've registered as a Republican. It makes a good story, maybe even a headline. 'Wife divorces candidate-husband because he was running as a Republican.'"

Joe chuckled.

He said, "Well, we'll make the best of it. I'm divorced myself, and I never saw it coming. I remember meeting your wife at some political dinner last year. As I recall, she's definitely a strong Democrat."

Don nodded, and said, "I want to get out of the house as soon as possible, like, tomorrow. Can you help me find an apartment quickly? It would have to be very secure and reasonably spacious with two bedrooms, and include a small office."

Joe said, "I'll put Celia Adams, my secretary, to work on it. She'll show you a couple of places by this afternoon, and you can choose one. I'll have a moving service move you in the morning. Is that fast enough? Month-to-month lease because you're in a hurry and may change your mind about where you want to live, and partially furnished. The movers are experienced, and they will set up the bed and arrange the furniture. You just have to sign the lease and sign to have the electricity turned on."

Don nodded approval.

"Now, let's get to work," Joe said.

Joe had lunch sent up, and they worked through the lunch hour on campaign strategies. Celia took Don and Mike to look at several possible apartments in the area. With Mike's help regarding security problems, Don picked one out, and Celia arranged for Don to be moved the following day.

Mike obviously was attracted to Celia. Don looked for a marriage ring, but didn't see one. They came back to the office late and found Roberta Edwards and Joe Abrams discussing the campaign.

Roberta showed Don a video that a passenger on the plane

had taken that she had bought the rights to for the campaign. "I thought this might be useful," she said, as she projected the film. They studied it and agreed that there were some good shots.

Don said, "How about billboards, saying, 'This guy will fight for you in Washington' with no name on it, just a shot of me landing a right uppercut? Some Democrat came up to me at dinner, recognizing me from the paper, and used that slogan, 'This guy will fight for you in Washington!'"

"Great!" Roberta said enthusiastically. "But you need name recognition, so how about, 'Don Carter, Republican, will fight for you in Washington.' And the public will become aware that it's actually Don Carter throwing that punch and subduing that drunken passenger."

She paused, and added, "And I tracked down the guy you hit and he wants to know how you train. The judge put him on probation with a requirement for outpatient drug rehab, plus six months in jail. We'll arrange for newspaper and TV coverage and an interview for both of you."

"Roberta, follow up on this. You remember on the plane when I talked about 'positive addiction' to replace alcoholism when I was giving him a pep talk about working out?" Don questioned.

"Yes, he's really interested."

"Well, tell him I'll drop in at the jail if you report he's working out at the jail like I suggested. Maybe I'll bring my workout buddy, Kurt, along and put on a demonstration at the jail. But only if you report that he's developing a workout program at the jail."

Don remembered, and asked, "Is his wife sober?"

Roberta laughed and said, "She apparently is. He told her that you said to get rid of her if she doesn't maintain sobriety, and that she's 'part of the problem,' and it scared her. They're really dependent on each other."

Joe said, "Sorry to interrupt, but we've got to get moving. We'll go with the fight stuff at least through January, depending on the response. Plaster platform billboards over the state, and emphasize, also, that Don Carter will win, but ideology will lose. Balance the budget, but easy on social issues—that's if you want to win and get another Republican senator in Congress. Otherwise, same old, same old, and another loss for the Republicans in California. Understood?"

Don and Roberta nodded.

Joe continued, "We're fortunate in having a candidate with a fantastic memory who will therefore be especially effective in debating other candidates. But it's very important that you practice questions and answers and not change your answers to policy questions. So, starting tomorrow, we'll begin grilling you, preparing you for unfriendly interviewers, who will be hoping that you give them dumb answers. You probably can avoid question about the U.S. Constitution . . ."

Don interrupted, "On the contrary, I know it by heart."

"I forgot about that. So, we *emphasize* the U.S. Constitution. These interviewers usually don't know a dammed thing about it. They will be impressed, but change the subject."

Joe went on, "I've hired Tom Brady, who's an expert at working on the weaknesses and strengths of candidates. The primary election will be on March 11 and the general election on June 24, so we don't have much time to publicize a candidate with no name recognition. But the other candidates only have local recognition, and they will have their past records to haunt them, so it all evens out."

Joe continued, "I'll be interviewing candidates for different jobs with the campaign tomorrow morning, and we'll open up more office space—field manager, fund-raiser, someone to work with the media, a scheduler, volunteer coordinator, and so forth. I have people in mind who enjoy this kind of work. Celia will be my administrator, at an increase in salary, and we'll need more secretarial help. Don is moving tomorrow and meeting with his children tonight at dinner, so we'll start the meeting at noon tomorrow. The movers are arriving at eight in the morning, and if they're not done at noon, Mike or Celia will supervise the movers, and see that a phone is installed early in the morning. And, did I mention that our candidate is fluent in Spanish and Italian?"

Don interrupted, "I think I should tell you. This morning, after my wife gave me the heave-ho, I became engaged to Molly Dorman, whom I first met forty years ago. She speaks fluent Spanish, while I'm somewhat rusty."

Roberta and Joe appeared stunned.

Don looked amused, and said, "Actually it's a very romantic story. I was her true love and she waited for me over the years. Her stepfather is Sam Kravitz, owner of the Crystal Casino. I went to Vegas to ask him *not* to give to my campaign because of his mob connections. Her husband, Arthur Stoller, travels a great deal and has another girlfriend somewhere. Molly has filed for divorce."

Don said, "I might add that Benito heartily approves, and felt Delia, his niece and my current wife, would be a detriment to my campaign. He's spoken to Molly over the phone and already loves her. In conclusion, we're very much in love. I've traded a bitter, angry Italian-speaking Democrat-wife for an enthusiastic, loyal, Spanish-speaking fiancée. As much as I hate the term, it's a win-win situation."

Roberta and Joe were both laughing as he finished.

"When you put if that way, we look forward to meeting Molly and making her part of the campaign," Joe said.

Don shook hands with Joe and Roberta, and he and Mike left.

He drove with Mike to Pacific Palisades, and as they arrived at the house, Don noticed the Christmas wreath on the door. Every year the wreath would hang on this door, and Don was so preoccupied on the previous night that he hadn't noticed.

He felt himself tearing up, and memories came flooding back—his young children and Christmas. But Delia must have been waiting at the door for his arrival, for she opened it quickly and was about to speak when she noticed Mike was still present. He sent Mike to the garage to check the car and followed Delia into the living room.

She turned and said, "Well, when are you getting out?"

"My, my, aren't we in a hurry? I'm moving tomorrow to a temporary apartment and I'm having a phone installed on the same day. Is that soon enough for you?"

"That's soon enough," she admitted.

She asked, "What are you going to tell the children?"

Don answered, "I'm going to tell them exactly what you said to me. You told me that you didn't like me making decisions without discussing them with you, and that the final straw was my deciding to become a contender for the Republican Party nomination. I'm not going to mention about your having 'satisfactory' sex with someone even if they ask about possible affairs. Is that reasonable?"

"Yes," but she appeared uncertain.

Don said, "So far as the divorce financial details, this is an unusual situation because I have no professional income, and I only have the money that Benito gives me, but I believe we can settle this fairly. I'll give you half of the house, half of our savings, and half of the retirement plan. You probably will receive money in Benito's will, and I'll recommend alimony until you marry or live with someone, plus any unusual house expenditures, plus health coverage. That is, if Benito is agreeable, so I suggest you start being nicer to him. You used to be his favorite niece."

Delia was strangely quiet, so Don continued. "The children are adults now. You know I'm having dinner with them tonight. Tomorrow the movers arrive at eight in the morning and I'll be taking clothes, desks, my Kaypro computer, books, desk lamps, linens for the bed, towels, and the contents of my medicine cabinet, plus furniture from one of the bedrooms and some sets of the extra silverware, plates, cups and saucers, some kitchen knives, and pots and pans."

Turning toward the garage, Don concluded, "Okay, I guess that's it," suspecting that Delia would disclose her lover's name.

Obviously, he wasn't showing much upset about the divorce. This was a lovely divorce. No counseling to make him feel guilty about deserting her, and then 'wham!' she'd let him have it, right in the kisser (or, more likely, in the balls). He should attempt to feel sad.

This was definitely a "win-win" situation. He thought about Graham Greene's warning in *The Heart of the Matter* about the corrosive effects of pity, and he thought about Benito's observation about Molly's love, waiting for Don for forty years. He thought to himself, I almost forgot, things are happening so fast. I'm engaged to Molly, as of a few hours ago. Sounds like a movie script.

Don had gotten as far as the kitchen, on his way to the garage, when Delia called him. He turned around and Delia took a step toward him, and stopped. This was it. She could not avoid celebrating her victory in the battle of the sexes!

"You know, I decided on a divorce months ago," she declared. "I met a wonderful man while you were in Europe. Carl is warm and understanding. We're going to get married when the six-month waiting period is over, and I'll be moving in with him."

Don was rather pleased that he had guessed correctly, and said, "Congratulations."

Don thought, well, might as well get it over with, and queried, "Might I ask, Carl who?"

With suitable dramatic pause, Delia said, "Carl Bainbridge, the owner-editor of the *Times-Tribune*."

Don started choking, having momentarily forgotten about the biscuit he was chewing, and this led into a choking spasm that went on and on, finally gradually subsiding as Delia was about to call 911. He motioned to her that he was all right and wiped the tears from his eyes.

He finally got his voice back, and he was laughing in between occasional gasps for breath. "Well, you did it, Delia. You finally . . . topped me." Don was speaking very slowly to avoid another coughing fit, and laughing at the same time.

Don said, "I can't go any higher, except to the vice presidency, and then to the presidency!" He tried to control his laughter to avoid another fit.

Delia didn't see the humor in the situation, but she was concerned about a possible recurrence of the coughing spasms. Don said he was okay, opened the door into the garage, and disappeared.

His car and Mike were gone when he entered the garage, but both quickly appeared and Mike got out.

Mike said, "It's okay, but it needs a tune-up. I'll take it in some day when you're busy in the office."

Don said, "Thanks, Mike. Tomorrow, after the movers leave for the apartment, I'll be going to my regular gym in Santa Monica for a workout with Kurt, and you'll be in charge. I've got to get back on a regular workout schedule. I'll check out the apartment if I have time, afterward. Call me at the gym if there are any problems. See you in the morning around eight forty-five or so."

He went to change for dinner. There was no sign of Delia, but he noticed that the light on the phone was lit. Delia was talking to someone, maybe Carl Bainbridge, the guy who provided the "satisfactory" sex.

But wasn't Carl Bainbridge the same type of man he was, only more demonstrative at the moment, like those "second time around" couples he would see occasionally at the gym, their arms entwined as they walked or held hands? He had seen him on television and knew that Carl Bainbridge was divorced. The two of them, he and Carl, would have to have a little chat, someday.

He was still chuckling at these thoughts, as he began his drive to Santa Monica to the Vito Restaurant, but Don's thoughts changed, as he grew closer to Santa Monica. He started to wonder what Linda and Robert were thinking about their father, a man who had been absent in Europe for almost three months.

Linda was already there. They hugged and talked, and Robert appeared, along with his girlfriend, Gina Palegari. He and Robert exchanged tentative father-son hugs and Gina shook his hand. Don suspected victory was his when he heard her Italian name and Gina appeared to be more the hugging type. Robert had not mentioned bringing her, but Don was prepared and sensed an ally in Gina.

After ordering, Don said, "Gina is a very pretty name, and Palegari is a family name used for one of the characters in the Sicilian playwright Pirandello's play, *Each in His Own Way*. I'm guessing that one or both of your parents or grandparents came from Sicily?"

"My father is from Sicily, my mother from southern Italy," Gina declared.

"One of my lifeguard friends from Atlantic City declared that I was a 'natural Sicilian.' I think he meant it as a compliment," Don said.

Dinner was served, and Don slowly brought up the subject

of the divorce. "As you must have suspected, your mother and I are getting divorced. I went over this with Delia, and she agreed that this was an accurate summary of the reasons for the divorce.

"First, I've been making decisions without consulting her, important decisions, which I knew she might not agree with, and I continued doing this. This included running off to Italy to learn Italian and study about her uncle Benito's business interests.

"Second—and this was the 'final straw,' I decided to run for the U.S. Senate as a Republican. As you know, your mother is a dedicated Democrat. I never got a chance to explain my platform—I'm for a woman's right to chose, I don't think homosexuals are all going to hell, and in general, I'm liberal in my views except I'm very worried about the budget deficit. I feel Democrats spend too much money. That's the end of my little speech. My campaign has officially started.

"The primary on March 11, and the general election on June 24. That is, if we win the primary. I don't want to put either of you on the spot, so it's okay if you don't want to be involved."

Don took a breath and said, "I do have Christmas presents for you, including one for Gina, if she'll accept it. Ladies first. Linda, your present will be a trip to Italy and France for a year, all expenses paid, to travel and study. I know you enjoy working as a translator and are thinking about changing jobs, and this may be a good time."

Her appreciation was interrupted by the arrival of the waiter. Linda and Don, at Don's instigation, spoke in Italian, and the waiter joined in, taking the orders. Gina, in halting Italian, and with the waiter's encouragement, ordered her dinner. Only Robert ordered in English.

Don paused, and continued, "Robert, your great-uncle has purchased, though his foundation, a rundown Palladian villa, close to Vicenza in Italy. If you agree, he wants you to evaluate what it would take to restore it, and supervise the restoration using foundation funds. You should see some progress in about two years, and completion in, maybe, five years. It may be turned over to the government, or not, depending on government politics at the time."

Robert appeared to be both confused and stunned.

Don went on, "We visited Vicenza when I was in Italy in September, and your uncle told me it could be restored. He told me also that his ambition, as a boy, was to be an architect, but he had to leave full-time school at age eleven to help support his family. Robert, you have a project that you have to present soon to qualify for your master's degree in architecture, and I believe this would meet that requirement. You might only have to plan the project to get credit. Probably it's up to Berkeley as far as credit goes, but I'm sure you'll want to finish."

Robert had gotten his voice back and asked, "Is there a deadline? And I'll have to check with the university. A real Palladian villa? Are you serious?"

Don replied, "Yes, to answer your last two questions. You'll know soon enough whether you want to take on this project. Believe me, the money is set aside."

Don turned to Gina, saying, "Gina, you would be able to visit Robert or help him with translating on a more permanent basis. It's up to you. I don't know the dimensions of your relationship or how much you like your present job in social work. I notice your Italian is rusty, so you'll need to work on that."

Gina said, "Thank you. My father has been after me to upgrade my Italian."

Don continued, "I found it very helpful to take Italian lessons. If this works out with Berkeley, and Robert decides to go ahead with the restoration, why not both of you take Italian lessons? I'll give you my new address. Send the bill to me."

Don paused, and said, "There's one other thing. Benito Desimone, your great-uncle, had problems with the income tax people in the past. But in recent years, he settled with the IRS, has no criminal charges against him, and he's retired to Sicily to be with his extended family. He's going to eventually die of prostate cancer, probably within eighteen months, according to the doctors. To me he's a father figure and a mentor. With his encouragement, I entered politics, and he'll be happy if I become United States Senator from the State of California before he dies. I'm going to see that happens."

Don went on, "Delia was very close to him all of her life, until recently. Benito is a very erudite, self-taught man, but he's also Sicilian with strong feelings, strong family ties, and very strong loyalties. The only requirement for these gifts is that you visit him in Sicily and show him the love and respect that he deserves. This is my request, not his. I know you visited him when you were small, but not in recent years. His request was only that he gets to know you before death takes him. Your mother can visit when she wants."

He paused, and when he did so, a man rushed over from a nearby table, and he grabbed Don's hand and introduced himself as Georgio Banti, saying, "Say, aren't you the guy who knocked out that passenger on the plane?"

Don nodded, and Georgio said he subscribes to the Las Vegas newspaper and saw the article and Don's picture.

"I've been looking for someone with *'cogliones'* to take on the establishment of the Republican Party and knock some sense into their heads, and I've found him. Who's your campaign manager?"

"Joe Abrams," Don said.

Georgio exclaimed, "Good man. You're serious. I'm going to call Joe in the morning."

Linda, Robert, and Gina were talking and eating their dinners, and looking occasionally with amusement at the scene playing out with Georgio above them. Now Don sat down and started eating, while he explained to Robert, Linda, and Gina about what had happened on the airplane.

Later, he gave Robert and Linda the phone number for Benito and said Benito would fill them in and arrange for Robert to see the villa. He suggested that Linda, Robert, and Gina might consider going to Italy together for the first trip.

"One other thing." Don paused, and said, "Benito has accumulated a significant sum of money. All income taxes have been paid and there are no legal problems. I'll inherit the money upon Benito's death. The money is in Swiss banks and gradually increasing in value. After my death, I'll need someone to take responsibility as an administrator. He has about twenty men or their widows who will receive life pensions, for example. You won't have to do anything specifically. In most cases, just give your approval. And many of these people will probably be dead by the time I die."

Don continued, "I can't tell you the amount of money until Benito dies. Suffice it to say, I always fly first class or business class and you'll fly business class when you fly to Italy. It is my one luxury, by the way. It used to irritate your mother, my fantasy that I could one day fly first class. There's no urgency about this decision. It won't significantly affect your inheritance, but I would like to see someone from the family in charge of the estate after my death."

Changing the subject, Don said, "Your mother told me about Carl and I was genuinely happy for her. It's a little awkward for Delia and a little humorous, because he's the editor of the *Times-Tribune* and she's active in Democratic politics, but I have complete confidence that Carl Bainbridge will pick the best candidate for his newspaper to endorse. I must confess that I had a choking-laughing fit when she told me. Ask your mother to tell you about it. I was surprised at whom she picked, more than anything. Incidentally, I'm moving out tomorrow to an apartment in the Century City area, near my campaign manager's office. I'll give you the address."

He was glad that he brought up Carl, since they obviously knew about him, and it eased the tension. Now he hesitated, and asked, "Do you have room for one other surprise?"

They looked at him and all smiled, as though expecting a present.

Don went on, "It's sort of a long story. There was a girl I met when I was a lifeguard, when she and her mother used to bathe at my beach in Atlantic City. She would run errands for us when she was fifteen and sixteen, and she continued when we changed beaches. Our first and only date occurred when she turned seventeen, on her birthday. I was nineteen at the time. The next day, she and her mother and future stepfather moved to Las Vegas. We were going to write to each other, but because of a mix-up in addresses, we never did. Her stepfather now owns the Crystal Casino in Vegas. She married Arthur Stoller and they have one daughter, Bernie."

Don thought for a moment, and added, "I hadn't seen her in about forty years until I went to Las Vegas last year in December. I had some business with Sam Kravitz, her stepfather, and Arthur, her husband, who was leaving on a business trip. She was in the process of getting a divorce. We fell in love again, and I called her today and asked Molly Dorman to marry me, and she accepted. I haven't told your mother because it just happened and I wanted to tell you first. I'll tell her tonight, so please don't say anything until tomorrow. By the way, Molly is a lovely person who speaks fluent Spanish, and will be an asset to the campaign. It's sort of weird, old folks like us both finding romance at our age. I feel very lucky in having found two wonderful women to live with and I can't believe my good fortune."

Linda and Robert seemed to be absorbing the "surprise." Obviously, it was quite unexpected. Linda asked why the "mix up" in the addresses occurred, and Don told her part of the truth. Don said that Molly's aunt, who lived in Atlantic City and received Molly's letters, had destroyed them, and had told him that Molly had another boyfriend. Maybe she guessed that there was more to the story, but she didn't ask any more questions.

They had dessert, talked aimlessly, and said good-bye. This time, they all embraced. He knew Gina and Linda really wanted to go to Italy, and he noticed that Robert was attracted by the idea of the Palladian villa restoration.

Linda stayed behind. She embraced him again, and said, "Oh, Daddy, that was a beautiful story. If you had to be divorced, that was the best kind of divorce, with a happy ending for both of you. I'm so glad for you."

Linda wiped some tears from her eyes, and said, "I'll be able to be with you in the general elections, if you want me."

Don was delighted, and said, "That's wonderful. We sure can use you. Stay in touch. You'll have a chance to meet Molly."

They embraced briefly again, and she was gone.

Now there was one final step. Delia.

When Don arrived home, Delia was waiting. He apologized for the coughing-laughing fit, and he congratulated her on the engagement. He told Delia all that had transpired in his meeting with the children and said that Robert had not made up his mind and may want to talk about it with her.

Don said, "I was going to ask you to go with them if they all decide to go, but that may not be possible in view of your upcoming marriage. Speaking of marriage, I've signed the papers and I understand the waiting period started six months and one day after I filed them with the county clerk, which I did yesterday."

Delia replied, "Carl and I are planning on getting married on July 20. Are you, also, planning on getting married?" she asked, with mild sarcasm.

"I have something else to tell you, something I told Linda and Robert earlier, at dinner." Don hesitated. Then he told Delia about how he first met Molly, and that he was in love with her, and they planned to get married.

He noted with satisfaction that she appeared dumbfounded at his news.

Delia didn't speak, and Don said, "While you're thinking about this, there's one more item on a different subject. This concerns Paul Marshall, and the news is quite good."

He continued, "I've been talking to Paul. He is HIV positive, but doesn't have AIDS. He had been very depressed and not eating, expecting to die, wishing to die because his partner had died, so when I saw him, I thought he was in the final stage of AIDS. He looked like he had AIDS, and was quite cachectic. And the doctors, also, at first thought he was dying, but they tested him, and he doesn't have AIDS."

Don cleared his throat, and continued, "Paul is one of the lucky ones. He has a positive HIV blood test, but, so far no AIDS—they call such cases *long-term nonprogressives*. He's living with his mother Anne in Margate and goes once a month to Temple Medical School for check-ups. He's still weak, but he's starting to work out, and I gave him some advice about physical training. I told him yesterday about our divorce and he cracked a little joke, about how maybe I was changing my preference from women to men. I thought that was a good sign, regaining his sense of humor. Paul is a very bright and perspicacious attorney, and I'm hoping he'll be useful in the Senate office, but not yet. He still looks unwell. But he's getting better. You have Anne's phone number, I believe."

Delia nodded. She appeared struck dumb by Don's announcement of his upcoming nuptials, and finally said, in a low voice, "I'm so happy for Paul. I'll call Anne."

Don went on to bed in his own house for the last time.

As he lay there, he thought about Paul and the last time he felt close to Delia, on the plane returning to LA last June, when he thought that Paul had AIDS and showed her the poem in the book by Thomas Wolfe that started off, "Come back, bright boy," and Delia became tearful and reached for his hand and said, "You'll still be my bright boy, whatever happens."

Don felt a tear sliding down his cheek, remembering. *Someday I'll ask her if I were still her "bright boy." Then, again, maybe not.*

He would be glad to leave this house. The only fear most men have in the same situation is a financial fear, and a fear of lawyers, and he had neither of those problems. He slept well.

In the morning, he was up early before the movers, so he took a chance and telephoned Joe Abrams on his home phone. Joe was at home, finishing breakfast.

"I want you to know, Joe, that my soon-to-be ex-wife has disclosed the name of her blushing bridegroom. Are you ready for this, Joe?"

"Are you asking whether I'm sitting down? If you are, the answer is 'Yes.'"

"The one and only Carl Bainbridge!"

There was a moment of silence, and Joe asked, "Are you sure?"

"Sure I'm sure. Straight from the future bride herself!"

"If you're wondering whether it makes any difference in our campaign, the answer is that it doesn't. Carl is a straight shooter, and he calls them as he sees them."

Don said, "I certainly hope so. I certainly hope so." And he hung up the phone.

Mike arrived early and he let him in, and Delia left for her gym workout. Don called Molly on her direct line.

Molly said, "I received news from Benito's private eye. Arthur, my loving husband, has another sort of 'wife' he lives with when he's on those trips he takes so often. She came to the door of their suite in some sort of dressing gown at nine in the morning, after Arthur left for a business meeting. Her name is Peggy, and she's been with him steadily for almost two years."

Molly continued, "I spoke to my mother, who suspected they were having an affair, and Sam, who knew that they were having an affair. But Sam says he depends on Arthur to help run the casino, and I told him that was a bunch of baloney because Arthur is never around. The hell with the Crystal Casino! So, I told everyone I'm getting a divorce, which I already decided, and I'm going to live with you, away from the Crystal Casino. Is that okay?"

Don exclaimed, "Wonderful! I'll use you on the campaign as soon as you're ready, and maybe you'll pick out a house to move to instead of this apartment."

Then Don asked, "What about your daughter, Bernie, whom I've never met?"

Molly replied, "I seldom see her. She probably suspected or knew about Arthur's affair. I'm the only one, it seems, who didn't know about it, maybe because I didn't want to know. Bernie is now an assistant film producer and moving from New York to Hollywood with her boyfriend, so I may see more of her."

Don said, "Well, it certainly puts the pressure on good old Arthur. He probably has been telling Peggy that he can't marry her, because this would cause problems at the Crystal Casino, so Peggy had to survive on nightgowns and clothes and trips and hope. Now Peggy will want to get married. It will be interesting watching this play out. Who knows what he's told her about you."

Molly laughed, and said, "You're right. I never thought about that. Well, I don't plan on hanging around to watch. It's shifty Arthur's problem."

"Should I call Sam and ask for permission to marry his stepdaughter?" Don asked. "Will he demand to see my circumcision as proof that I'm half-Jewish? My brother had to do that once, and he was so startled that he complied. Does Sam know that Muslims are also circumcised?"

Molly found this funny, and told Don to go ahead and talk to Sam if he wanted to. "By the way, don't mention that my mother was Jewish. I want to surprise Sam," Don said.

Molly laughed, and said, "Okay."

Don said, "It sounds like the movers now. Gotta go. Love you. Bye."

Later, as Don watched his earthly possessions disappear into the moving truck, he thought about how fast things were changing. Or were they?

Maybe it's like Tancredi said, "If we want things to stay as they are, things will have to change."

CHAPTER SEVEN

January 10, 1986

DON CALLED TIM IN POMONA, NEW JERSEY, located on the mainland across from Atlantic City. He called partly because he had not contacted Tim for several months and he was feeling guilty, but mostly because he was excited about his engagement to Molly. Tim, his former lifeguard partner on the Atlantic City Beach Patrol, had known Molly since she was fifteen years old.

Tim was happy to hear from him. He had heard from friends that Don was running for the Senate, but he had been unable to follow Don's campaign because television and newspapers in the East didn't cover California politics.

Don said, "I'll send you the clippings."

Tim had divorced Darlene almost twenty years earlier, which was no surprise to anyone who knew Darlene, and had settled down with Margaret. Don told Tim of his own divorce, and Tim asked, "What happened? Did she catch you fooling around?"

"No, nothing like that," Don said.

Don asked, "Now, guess whom I'm going to marry?"

Tim immediately replied, "Molly Dorman."

Don was amazed. "How did you guess?"

Tim said, "She had to be someone we both knew, and Molly

has always been in love with you. I told you, she called me once or twice a year for a long time, to ask how you were doing."

Tim asked, "Is she still protecting you from the guy we arrested under the Boardwalk?"

Don replied, "Not any more. Our 'stargazer' is dead—killed somewhere in South or Central America, probably Colombia or Nicaragua. The family supposedly picked up the body, but I didn't hear about a funeral."

Tim surprised Don by his next statement. "I always thought you and Benito were up to something and were working with one of the federal agencies. But I never said anything. I figured you couldn't tell me."

"Thanks, Tim. I expect it will all come out in the news in a few months. So far, the campaign is very successful."

The two of them reminisced about the old days, and about Molly, and Don said he would be sending airline tickets to Tim and Margaret to attend the July 13 wedding in Las Vegas, as well as accommodations at the Crystal Casino.

But Tim said he doubted that Margaret would make the trip. "She doesn't like to fly."

Don said, "I know about Margaret's fear of flying, but these are First Class tickets. This is a completely different flying experience, believe me."

"Wow! I'll get her on the plane, somehow. Did you win the lottery?" Tim asked, jokingly.

Don replied, "No, but as Nucky Johnson would say, 'when I live well, everyone lives well!' Or, something like that."

Don asked about Laura. "What happened to her?"

"She disappeared. No one knows where she is. I thought you might know."

"Me? How should I know?"

"Well, you did have the hots for her. Her husband, George, says he's been looking for her, but he hasn't been looking too hard because 'Little Angie,' the local mob boss, is pissed off about some missing money. There's talk that 'Little Angie' planted money at George's house—George was supposed to be the fall guy—and tipped off the feds, but when the Treasury agents arrived, the money was gone—if there ever was any money."

Don was aware that Tim thought he knew something about where Laura was hiding, and Don did know, of course.

Don laughed and said, "Her body hasn't shown up anywhere, and George is still alive. Maybe Laura will surface somewhere. I hope her poetry is improving. But Laura is the ultimate survivor. Somehow she'll make out."

Don promised to "keep in touch," as he ended the call to Tim, but his thoughts were about Laura.

Joe's meeting was just starting, and he was saying, "We're making progress, running a close third, and gaining ground. For a guy who no one knew three weeks ago, that's not bad. The billboards did it. As you know, Bob Matthews was appointed to the Senate by the governor, who's a Republican, so, naturally, he appointed another Republican to serve until the election. Matthews is now a candidate for the permanent job as senator, and is an experienced campaigner who has run for the Senate before. He lost in the past because he's very conservative and wouldn't change his views, an attitude that's a killer in a heavily Democratic state like California."

They were seated around the table at 9:00 a.m. in Joe's office—Don, Roberta, Joe, John Stewart, and Maria Rodriguez. John and Mary had recently been recruited as Advisory Board members, and both were respected by Joe for their political knowledge and campaign skills. Joe had worked with them before, and Maria was active in Hispanic politics.

"We've got to keep emphasizing our platform. If you want to lose, stick to your ideology. If you want to win the election, vote for Carter," and Roberta hit the table for emphasis.

Joe said, "We'll start our phone calls this week, blanketing all Republicans with Don's message. And our contributions are coming in surprisingly well for this early in the campaign; I believe we have convinced a lot of Republicans that we might win this one. Matthews's problem is that he ran before and lost, and people figure that he's going to lose again."

Joe continued, "George Sampson, the other candidate, is short on funds and isn't well organized. He's running second, but is losing ground to Don. His platform is similar to ours, but more conservative. I think he would throw in the towel if he thought Don could beat Matthews, and he might endorse Don. He has some kind of grudge against Matthews and has run against Matthews before."

Suddenly, Molly entered the room, breathless, and apologetic. She said, "Excuse me for being late. My plane was late leaving Las Vegas."

Joe introduced himself and introduced Molly to Roberta, John, and Mary, saying, "We have spoken on the telephone and I can confirm that she's articulate and friendly. I learned from Don that she paints and has had two shows of her work, both of which received great reviews. She speaks excellent Spanish and fits right in with our plans to convince Republican voters that it's a plus to have candidates who are Spanish speakers, if we're to win in the general election."

Joe paused, and continued, "It's true that there aren't a lot of Hispanic Republican voters in the primary battles, but there are sure as hell a lot of Hispanic voters in the general elections, and most of them vote as Democrats. After they understand Don's more reasonable immigration policies, we'll be able to swing many of them our way."

Don interrupted, "Sorry, Joe, for the interruption. I want to remind the group of my immigration stance. I support a way for people who have lived here for years, with no criminal record, to apply for citizenship. It makes sense to me."

Joe said, "Thanks, Don. Getting on to other news of the day, the *Times-Tribune* announced the engagement of Carl Bainbridge and Delia Carter on the society page of the newspaper today, along with an announcement that the engaged couple plan to marry on July 20 of this year."

Joe paused, and said, "As you know, Don's soon-to-be-ex-wife is a stalwart Democrat and has been active in the Democratic Party in California. Naturally, we can't depend on the *Times-Tribune*'s support, or any other newspaper's support. The newspaper has been wrong before. That is, they supported a losing candidate."

Joe said, "The *Times-Tribune* rarely makes a selection in the elections until the general election is two weeks off, although frequently you can tell in which direction the paper is leaning. I'm reasonably sure that Carl Bainbridge won't let his marriage to a Democrat activist influence his decision regarding the candidates in the election. As a matter of fact, it would be better for him and the *Times-Tribune* if he decides that a Republican is the better candidate."

Turning serious, Joe said, "Now, let's get down to business. Don and Molly will start on a campaign swing, traveling north, and back across the state traveling southeast, on Monday, with important stops in major cities along the way, and shorter stops in smaller cities, also. The emphasis will be on convincing Republican voters to vote for a 'moderate' who's a 'fiscal conservative.' Of course, we'll point out that Pete Wilson, our present senator, is very similar to Don. That is, he's a moderate in his social views and conservative in his fiscal policy. In fact, it has been near impossible in recent years to successfully elect a Republican as senator who doesn't hold views similar to Pete Wilson and Don Carter. And, for God's sake, never use the word 'liberal' to describe our candidate. It's the kiss of death with Republican voters!"

The group around the table smiled.

"No danger of that happening," John said, laughing.

Joe said, "Don and Molly, Roberta, Mike, probably Jane as Volunteer Coordinator, extra security will all go along on the campaign bus. Kate, who's in charge of fund-raising, is off raising money as we speak. She might have to go back and forth. I'll talk to her. Use your good judgment. If it's not working in the bus, come back. Take plenty of sign-up forms and campaign donation forms."

Joe paused for a breath, and continued, "Don, you've seen or talked to a lot of prospective donors and it shows in the results. We don't want to give the impression that Don is trying to buy this election. We need to encourage donors. So far, we all are doing a good job with the fund-raising. However, up to forty percent of those who make commitments don't come through— I've seen it in other campaigns—so your fund-raising needs to watch out for this and keep after the donors."

Looking at the others, Joe went on, "Keep up with the house parties and large events. And remember, if a large event looks like it will draw poor attendance, it's better to postpone or eliminate the event. Newspapers love to show pictures of auditoriums with only a few seats occupied. Our fund-raising team is doing a great job. It takes a lot of hard work, so don't get discouraged. Molly is now officially engaged and sporting a very modest engagement ring, if you hadn't noticed." A proud Molly held up her ring to applause.

Joe continued, "A modest ring, as befits a fiancée of a Senate candidate in the midst of a close campaign."

After that, Joe got back to the tactics, saying, "We need to convince Republican voters to vote for Don even though they don't agree with him on all issues, if they want to win elections. Otherwise, lose with Matthews! We have the organization that wins elections, but it takes a lot of money to win elections nowadays, unfortunately, so that's why the fund-raising is so important. We don't want to wear our candidate out, or our staff, so we'll take the bus slowly as far as Redding, and then back to San Francisco and Sacramento, stopping to make 'state of the state' evaluations and hear citizen complaints, and so forth. I think eight days max for the trip, enough to get in the newspapers and make Don's name better known."

Joe paused, and continued, "And regular gym workouts for Don, which we'll try to schedule in the smaller towns. This has the advantage for getting questions from small-town America. This may be the only bus trip we do in the primary campaign— I certainly hope so. It's very tiring for everyone. Don and Molly, of course, will be flying to different spots afterward where our research shows they will do the most good. We'll have a group, including 'yours truly,' flying to San Francisco for the first debate on January 28, and possibly Don will give a talk the following evening in Sacramento. Tom Brady will be meeting with Don the day before, January 27th, to bring Don up to speed on possible debate topics. Don found that very helpful when the campaign was just starting."

Turning to another subject, Joe said, "If there are subtle questions about Don's religious views that come up, I'll answer for him, because it's quicker. Don's kids were brought up Catholic because his wife was Catholic. Molly belongs to a Reform Judaism Congregation, which translates to High Holy Day attendance only. I can attest to that. Don, on the other hand, goes along with the first five presidents of our country, who determined that there are dangers in organized religion, and were, therefore, strongly secular. Therefore, he'll attend different denomination churches on Sundays. I learned about the religions of our so-called 'founding fathers' from Don. I checked it out, and found it to be true, much to my surprise."

Pausing to think further, Joe continued, "By the way, Don's mother was Jewish and his father was Lutheran. Neither he nor his parents ever attended any kind of church or synagogue, to the best of his knowledge. His mother left school in the fifth grade, and his father completed the eighth grade. Both went to work immediately, his mother in a cigar factory, and his father as a machinist. They married when she was fifteen."

Joe went on, "I'm telling you this just to emphasize that your candidate comes from a working class family. He's an unknown quantity to the voters, having no previous political history. They will be curious about him and they deserve answers. You already know that he was the youngest of four children and worked as a lifeguard before and after service in World War II in the Navy, and went to Stanford under the G.I. Bill, and later Temple Medical School. Don was a research psychiatrist at UCLA for eight years."

Roberta said, "I have Don's curriculum vitae."

"Good," Joe said. "I filled Kate in on Don's history last week, and she confirms that it increases donations when they know about his background. Don isn't an elitist, and most people think that's a good thing."

Directing his conversation to Don, Joe said, "Don, you've got a busy day starting with a luncheon in Orange County at noon. Mike will drive you and Molly down there. And Maria, were you able to arrange to go along?"

Maria replied "Yes, we want to activate the Hispanic vote, making them aware that Don is with them on immigration, more than some Democrats."

Joe admonished the three of them, "Remember, there are wall-to-wall Republicans down there, very conservative. And you're due back here at three thirty for a talk in Santa Monica."

"I know," Don said, "both about the wall-to-wall Republicans and having the luncheon in Orange County. We'll be on our way shortly."

"Sorry," Joe said. "The last client I had was always forgetting appointments. From one extreme to the other—he was always forgetting, and you never forget. I much prefer you, Don."

The group discussed the campaign at length, and it was soon time for Orange County and "wall-to-wall Republicans." Molly had been quiet during the meeting, but she told the group, as she and Don were leaving, that they should make more of an effort to attract the independent and even the liberal Jewish voters.

She said, "After all, between the two of us, we have one and a half Jewish heritages. And our campaign manager is Jewish. That should count for something!"

Joe laughed, and said, "Molly's right. Interestingly, there's never been a Jewish president—plenty of senators and mayors, however. I'll schedule Don and Molly into more Jewish groups, but Jews almost always vote Democratic. And someone always will get up and ask your position on Israel, so be prepared."

Joe paused, thinking, and said, "There has been increased interest among Christian groups about Israel in recent years. They realize that the various Arab groups can't be trusted to preserve Christian holy places. Actually, the Sunnis and Shiites destroy each other's shrines, also. At the same time, many Democrats are almost pro-Arab in their attitude regarding Israel, so, as a result, Israelis are getting very nervous."

Don was standing, waiting to leave, and he interposed, saying, "The only thing standing between the West and some very hostile Arabs is Israel. Only Israel defends and protects Christian religious relics in the Holy Land! The Shiites and the Sunnis have fought wars over differing religious beliefs. And what are they arguing and fighting about? They're fighting about which is the "true" religion, of course, the same thing the Catholics and Protestants and Mormons and Jehovah's Witnesses argue about, only we don't kill one another. At least, at the moment.

"And, Jews are no different. Orthodox Jews argue with Conservative Jews and Reformed Jews. The Orthodox Rabbis don't recognize marriages performed by Conservative and Reformed Rabbis. But, so far, they only argue, rather than kill each other. So, I strongly support Israel and its remarkable and, up to now, successful struggle against some fanatical elements among the Muslim states, who would like to destroy Israel, and the whole western world. The only thing many Shiites and Sunni agree on is hostility toward the West."

Joe nodded in agreement.

Don continued on another subject, "The first thing I'm going to do after I'm elected to the Senate is to work to overhaul and beef up the security apparatus of the United States, especially the CIA. Congress was jealous of William Colby's control of the CIA under Nixon and Ford and was successful in diminishing its strength. The future is ominous for the country because there are still huge gaps in security as well as jealousy among different security agencies—including the CIA, FBI, Secret Service, and Immigration. There's competition, rather than sharing of information."

Maria asked, "Do you support a strong military?"

"I'm opposed to war unless it's necessary to protect American lives, but I do believe in a strong military. Why am I opposed to war? Because there are no winners in today's wars and war is horrendously expensive, both financially and in terms of American lives. I'm sure that an improved security will save lives and improve our ability to prevent war."

Don said, apologetically, "I'm just clearing my mind, preparing for the onslaught from wall-to-wall Republicans in Orange County. We've got to go."

Don, Molly, and Maria left, and, after a pause, John said, "Well, that will get those Orange County voters thinking, distracting them from Don's position on abortion, and maybe scaring the hell out of them. It's even got me thinking."

Joe said, "I think we've got a winner here and a real position for Republicans to support. I think President Reagan will support us and understands Don is a winner. Don is also a very quick learner. In fact, he's already ahead of us. So, let's see how we can best support him."

When Don, Molly, and Maria were leaving, they encountered Mike in the outer office, talking to Celia Adams, the attractive office supervisor, who was surrounded by secretaries typing furiously.

On the elevator, Don casually mentioned that Mike had lost weight recently, and Molly chimed in, saying Mike was looking "sharp," and asking whether he was "working out?"

"All right, you two," Mike said, as he went to get the car. "I'll tell you about it later."

It wasn't until they had settled down on the 405 freeway that Mike returned to the subject, and he brought it up himself. "It's no big secret that I've been seeing Celia, and she said something about me being so heavy. I'm six feet four and acting like I was still playing football. So, I'm working out again, which I should be doing anyhow."

He slowed down for traffic, and Mike said, "I'm on a diet, and Celia is helping me. I'm down from 255 to 240 and aiming for 215. And my diastolic blood pressure was high, running about 95, and it's come down to 90. My doctor wanted to put me on meds, but I felt I could do it this way."

"Does Celia have any children?" Don asked.

"Two. Both are married and live in the East, one in Boston, and I think the other one lives in Virginia."

Don said, "Well, the reason I'm asking is that, as a United States Senator, I have to fill fifty or so positions in Washington, so if you decide to get married, there are certainly positions on my staff for both of you. That is, if you're interested, you'll be my first hires. I haven't spoken to Joe. This is confidential, by the way. Celia is a top-notch office manager. Our office here runs like clockwork."

There was a pause, and Mike spoke. "And what would be my job?' he asked, cautiously.

Don answered, "Executive/Personal assistant. You may do some scheduling, also. Essentially, you stick to me. It's an important job. I want someone I can trust. You'll be dealing with the public, senators, congressmen, and you'll be working long hours occasionally. And it's prestigious, for whatever that's worth. Retirement and health benefits are provided."

Don added, "There's no hurry, but something to keep in mind. I've got the primary to win, first."

Mike said, "Oh, I'm pretty sure you'll win the primary, all right, but I've got a lot to think about. I might have drifted along, until Celia got tired of waiting, and now it's 'fish or cut bait' time. And I know she'd like to move closer to her kids. Thanks for the offer."

"Let me know your plans by sometime in May, or sooner," Don said.

Molly, sensing the special relationship between the two, had remained silent for some time. She finally spoke. "Mike, I hope you'll come along with us to Washington."

"Thanks, Molly."

Don said, "I'll talk to Joe about Celia. He will be in charge of setting us up in Washington, so he should be happy about Celia coming along."

They were silent as Don, in the front seat, went over in his mind what he was going to say at the luncheon, and Molly, sitting in the back seat, was watching the unfamiliar scenery of endless freeways. Molly occasionally chatted in Spanish with Maria, who was sitting with her.

They arrived a few minutes early, as the final touches were

added to the luncheon setup. Mike handed out campaign literature as Don, Molly, and Maria were introduced to the chairman, Timothy McCarthy.

There were almost one hundred Republicans at the luncheon. Lunch was uneventful, and Don's introduction by the chairman produced only minor errors about his background.

Don at first spoke in general terms about the economy in California, problems with trade, and foreign affairs for about ten minutes, and introduced his basic topic—why Republicans in California should vote for him.

He asked, in Italian, if there were any Italians present. A number of hands were raised, and he greeted them, speaking enough to show his fluency. He switched to Spanish and repeated the questions, and fewer hands were raised.

Don asked, "Do you see the discrepancy? More Italians than Hispanics in the audience. Only a few Hispanic hands were raised, and there are hundreds of thousands of Hispanic voters in California. I guarantee there will more Hispanics voting Republican after I receive your nomination. How can I guarantee that?"

Don paused for a moment, and turned to Molly, sitting beside him, and said, "I would like to introduce Molly Dorman, my fiancée. I'm going to perform an experiment. Will those Hispanic Republicans stand up again, please?"

They stood up, and he whispered something to Molly. Molly fired off rapid chatter in Spanish, and one of the men replied, as his wife sat laughing beside him.

Don continued, "He's telling Molly that he heard that joke before, and his wife is laughing because she had never heard it. The point is that in California the Republican Party needs to attract the independent voters, because there are too many Democrats registered in the state to win without votes from independents. Attracting Hispanic voters is one thing we need to do, and Molly's and my fluency in Spanish gives us a tremendous advantage."

"Isn't that true?" he asked one of the men.

"Es verdad."

"Would you introduce yourselves?" Don asked, addressing the two Hispanic guests.

"George Ramirez," one of the men said.

"Fernando Martinez," the other replied.

Don replied, "And Mr. Ramirez and Mr. Martinez, if you'll contact my office and set up a meeting with some of your Hispanic citizens, I'll discuss my proposals for immigration reform with them when I'll be coming this way later in the campaign. Democrats or Republicans—it makes no difference. They are potential Republican votes."

Don continued, "Now to get down to business. I won't bore you with a long speech, but I'll answer all your questions. I took on this campaign because I know I can win this election and give the Republicans another seat in the Senate. First, a very brief personal history."

Don spoke about his parents and their struggles during the depression, and his own personal history, and how he worked to become a doctor.

In summary:

"1. I'm for a balanced budget amendment to the Constitution.

2. I'm for a strong military, as it lessens the chance of attack.

3. I particularly want to strengthen the CIA, the FBI, the Secret Service, and Immigration, putting someone in overall charge, forcing them to work together. They currently are jealous of one another and make too many mistakes.

4. I'm in favor of a beginning reform of the immigration policies, enabling long-time residents to apply for citizenship.

5. A great danger to our society are the Muslim extremists.

I'm not talking about average American citizens who happen to be Muslims. We must support Israel, and prevent damage to, or destruction of, Christian shrines. I'll do all I can to avoid foolish wars. All foreign wars are potentially foolish. Nobody wins wars anymore, which are fantastically expensive and cost American lives. This leads to cynicism among our troops and poor morale. Everyone remembers Vietnam and the disillusioned troops that returned from that conflict."

Looking around at the crowd, he continued, "Remember that President Reagan needs Republicans in the Senate and he knows that I stand the best chance of defeating Oates or any other Democrat. I'll again say that I have great respect for my opponents, who are good men. But California is full of Democrats and independents who tend to be moderate or liberal on social issues, and aren't likely to vote for Matthews or Sampson for that reason. We desperately need more Senate seats to ensure a balanced budget and financial stability."

Don added, "Oh, a final thought. Tough on budgeting, moderate on social issues. Who does that remind you of? Why, of course, our current senator, Peter Barton 'Pete' Wilson, the only kind of Republican who can be elected in California. I'm sure we'll work well together. Time for questions."

The chairman took over, but the questions were generally friendly except for the usual question on abortion.

Don said, "I'm not *for* abortion, but there are cases in which abortion is the lesser evil, as in rape, incest, and cases dealing with pregnancies of twelve and thirteen year olds. Americans generally favor Roe versus Wade, especially in a Democratic state like California. I respect the sentiments of people like Bob Matthews, who oppose any abortions, or George Sampson, who would permit very limited abortions, but I don't believe that either could succeed in the general election because of their stand on the abortion issue."

"My priest would kill me if he knew!" One man said, to the accompaniment of general laughter.

"Well, if you vote for me, I promise I'll never tell your priest," Don said, to more laughter. Don continued, "Remember, President Reagan knows the situation in California. He's a pragmatist and wants you to vote for me and win another Senate seat in California! Lose with Matthews in the general election, or win with Carter! Maybe your priest will give you a dispensation to vote for me. Your average priest is usually a good politician. And, as a bonus, you're likely to save money on your taxes when I get to Washington and balance the budget."

At the end, Chairman McCarthy thanked him and the group stood and applauded.

Members of the group followed Don back to the car, asking questions. He wrote down those questions that he could not answer, promising to respond by mail later, and Molly took down names and addresses.

Don asked Mike and Molly as they sped away, "Did I give away the barn? I feel burned out. I believe it will get better, less tense, as I make more presentations. I certainly hope so."

Molly laughed.

Mike said, "Great talk, Don. You added fifty believers and another fifty 'maybe's.'"

"Maybe so," Don said.

Maria, who had been a quiet observer during Don's talk, spoke up, saying, "You've got a terrific chance for Hispanic votes, with billboards in Spanish, maybe the 'He'll fight for you in Washington' bit, to capture the male 'macho' types, and emphasizing that both you and Molly speak Spanish."

She added, enthusiastically, "I'll talk to Joe about it when we get back. I know we'll get many more Latino votes this time."

"Good idea, Maria."

Don said, "Oh, since we'll be going to a different church

service almost every week, we'll probably start with a Catholic service this Sunday on the bus trip. Hopefully, it will be in a Hispanic church where they give the service in Spanish. And we'll publicize it!"

"Sounds like fun," Molly said.

"I agree," Maria said. "Great idea."

Don continued, "We'll attend Saturday Seventh-day Adventist Church services, Mormon services on the First Sunday of the month at the West Los Angeles Temple—that's when individuals speak out—Baptist services, Episcopal services, Muslim Mosques, and Jewish Synagogues, emphasizing that we're a nation of all faiths or no faith. And we'll continue the process after the election. Perhaps including more Spanish services to bring attention to my and Molly's language skills, emphasizing the importance of winning the Hispanic vote, which I feel is the key to winning the election. And Maria, if you want a job, either here in California, or Washington, making use of your language skills, that would be great! Just let me know, and talk to Joe."

That evening Don and Molly were tired, too tired to go out for dinner, and too tired to make dinner, so they ordered pizza and a salad, and when that arrived, they relaxed and talked.

Don said, "Guess what, Molly? Linda called and said they're all going to Italy for two weeks to see Benito and visit Vicenza. Robert has to get approval from Berkeley for the Palladian villa reconstruction and sign an agreement of some sort. And one of his instructors wants to go and look at the project. Benito agreed to pay the instructor's plane fare and expenses."

"That's wonderful!" Molly exclaimed.

Don said, "I decided to call Sam, your stepfather. I don't think you know, but he and I go back a long way, ever since I rescued your mother from being roughed up under the Steel Pier when you were only fifteen. We had not met yet. I never could figure out why this guy was dragging Hannah away. He was a big man, weighing at least two hundred pounds, an ex-fighter who had taken a few too many punches to the head. And the funny thing is that they knew him, and Sam said he worked for him. He seemed to be afraid of the guy who was with Sam—'Izzy' Singer. He was strong as hell, and if my partner hadn't arrived, I couldn't have held on. Max gave me twenty dollars, and my partner ten dollars, which was a hell of a lot of money in those days, and he asked us to keep quiet, which we did."

Molly spoke up. "That was 'Sal.' I never knew his last name, or what happened to him. He was supposed to protect my mother and me, but he was too erratic and quite scary. I never heard about that incident under the pier before, but he disappeared that summer when I was fifteen. Oh, it's not what you think! Sam was quite attached to Sal and would never hurt him, but Sal was quite confused and had to be put somewhere. But Izzy was another story—a psychopath if there ever was one. Sam got rid of him, paid him off with a big cash settlement, as Sam was rehabilitating his image in Vegas. Izzy died, eventually, in Lewisburg Prison from a brain tumor."

Don said, "Well, you solved one mystery for me—two, actually—and it also explains why Sal was so frightened of Izzy Singer. But you see why I needed to talk to Sam. When I spoke to Sam, he said he was pleased that I called, and he was going to call me, and claimed he was quite relieved to have the whole Arthur-Peggy business out in the open. I think he said, 'Now, maybe, I can get some work done around here.' Apparently, Arthur's trips were interfering with some of Sam's projects."

Don paused, and continued, "I thought I would have a little fun with Sam, so I said, 'I heard you have to be Jewish if you want to marry your stepdaughter.' And he said, 'Well, you can't have everything.' And I said, 'Would it help if I told you my mother was Jewish?' and he asked, 'Really?' And I said, 'Really.'

I could almost see him smiling over the telephone, and he laughed, and said, 'Pretty ridiculous, isn't it?' Oh, I saved the best for last. I asked Sam how Arthur and Peggy were getting on, and, of course, Sam realized that we knew about Peggy. Sam laughed, and said that now Peggy is after Arthur to get married, and Arthur keeps thinking up excuses, and that makes Peggy mad."

Molly asked, "Does this mean you'll be okay with a Jewish ceremony?"

"Yes, if you and your parents want it. I'll join a long list of Jewish atheists. But only if we continue our practice of visiting different church services. I want to keep them guessing."

Molly leaned across the table and kissed him, and said, "Listening to your talks, I came to realize the problems of organized religion, including Judaism. I'm not an atheist yet, but I'm heading in that direction."

Molly came across to the other side of the table and sat on Don's lap. "Let's go to bed. I want to thank you for being so nice."

The bus left at nine thirty on Monday morning, January 13, and Don, after talking it over with Joe, had decided to follow the English meeting occasionally with a Spanish meeting, sometimes reversing the order, as an experiment, consulting with local Republicans ahead of time to round up the groups.

Things started slowly driving up I-5 to Bakersfield. There was a moderate group for the English talk, but only six Hispanics, but things picked up in Fresno with curious crowds and many questions. By the time they reached San Jose late in the afternoon, they were attracting significant crowds, both English-speaking and Spanish-speaking. Most of the Spanish-speaking were Democrats or not registered to vote, but Don was receiving positive write-ups in the newspapers, focusing on immigration issues.

More importantly, some Republicans were coming over to Don and thanking him for urging Hispanic voters to vote Republican, and for taking a more positive attitude to immigration.

In San Jose, Don was greeting people just before the Spanish language talk when Maria recognized Fernando Garcia, the Democratic assemblyman from Fresno, in the audience, and she introduced Don to the assemblyman. They shook hands, and Fernando introduced his wife Anita, and Don called Molly over and introduced her.

"You're stealing my constituents away, so I wanted to see how you do it," Fernando joked.

Don laughed, and said, "No danger of that happening. I'm just borrowing them for my Senate race. I'll return them undamaged after they vote for me for the Senate."

Molly explained, "I'll vouch for that. Don always puts things back where he found them."

Fernando said, "The real reason I'm present today is that I plan to run for the House next year. I heard you were running a smart campaign, and likely to win a Senate seat in June.

"My problem is the reverse of yours," Fernando continued. "The seat I'll be running for is fifty percent Caucasian."

Mike Kelly had been watching the crowd, and he came over to Don and Molly, saying, "They're waiting for you."

Don hesitated, wondering about helping an opposing candidate, and said, "Sorry, we must go. My advice is to get a good campaign manager, consider separate meetings for Hispanics and Caucasians, involve your wife as much as possible without alienating male Hispanic voters, who think women should stay home with the kids, and raise lots of money."

He added, "Consider taking coaching lessons. I had someone critique my answer to political questions, questions you'll be asked in debates. Be sure you give the same answer to questions every time you're asked."

Don purposely gave generic advice—things that political candidates would read in most books on winning elections. He supposed there were such books. He had avoided mentioning Tom Brady's name, the man who had coached him and prepared him for debating. After all, there would be a Republican running against Fernando Garcia in the election.

Molly and Don left, greeting a group crowded into the small auditorium.

January 28, 1986

By the time of the debate in San Francisco, Don had passed George Sampson in the polls, but he was stuck two points below Bob Matthews and not making much progress.

Because of this, Joe Abrams decided to de-emphasize the Hispanic vote until the general election. There was only a small number of Hispanic Republicans. The emphasis now was going to be on the mantra of Matthews being unelectable because of conservative views in a liberal state like California—"Lose with Matthews or win with Carter."

Don had developed a smooth debating style, but was running into a roadblock with his permissive stand on abortion and, to a lesser extent, his ideas on homosexuality—that homosexuals would not automatically go to hell. Matthews was an experienced debater and hammered away on the abortion issue, while George Sampson believed that there were certain emergency situations where abortions were permissible.

After the debate, George Sampson approached Don and said he wanted to talk to him privately, and they met in the bar. Don had informed Joe where he was, and asked Joe to tell Molly they were not to be disturbed.

George was a courtly, older gentleman, with an unusually full head of hair for his age. Don judged him to be well over seventy. George got right to the point.

"Don, I don't agree with all your talking points, but I can't stand Bob Matthews for personal reasons, and I want to have him defeated. I have health problems and my wife wants me to give up politics. Plus, my campaign is underfunded. You have a great future in politics, and you have a strong campaign. You'll win the Senate seat if you can get past this primary, and I aim to give you this chance by halting my campaign and throwing my support to you."

Don started to express his thanks, but George held up his hand.

"My supporters are loyal, but in the past, we have had no one else recently in the primaries except a bunch of Bob Matthews's types. I feel comfortable that you and I share many similar views. Will you accept my support?"

"With pleasure," Don said. "I'm accepting with great pleasure!"

March 11, 1986

They were crowded around the large television screen in Joe's office after the polls closed. Early results were starting to trickle in. There was a feeling of anxiety pervading the room, in spite of Don's lead in recent polls. For many in the room, their jobs depended on the outcome of this primary, and the final results would not be known for hours.

Roberta watched the screen and remarked, "Don was leading the last poll by a significant margin, and the exit polls confirm that. It was close until Sampson threw his votes to Don, and now Don looks to be a shoe-in."

Joe walked over to get a drink of water, saying, "I've seen turnarounds. This is politics. You never know."

He turned and asked, "What about Don and Molly?"

Roberta said, "They're going directly to the Century Plaza Ballroom around nine. They said to tell you they'd be at the gym earlier, and they will be getting ready. Mike and Celia, too."

"Good," Joe said. "They shouldn't go anywhere unescorted from now on."

Checking the screen, he said, "This might be an early evening."

The crowds started gathering around 8:00 p.m. when the polls closed. Don and Molly stayed in their suite until around 10:00 p.m., when they began mixing with the crowd in the ballroom. Those in the ballroom cheered, as each count was read, groaning occasionally.

The reporters and TV cameras arrived early, as the voting clearly showed Don building up a substantial lead, and they were ready when Matthews conceded at 10:40 p.m. Loud cheers broke out and Don waved to Linda, his daughter, who was just arriving. The band played "Happy Days Are Here Again."

He and Molly stood at the elevated podium, as the noise swirled around them. The noise and the horns quieted down, as he held out his hands, and Don called Linda up to the podium and introduced her to the crowd.

The reporters asked for statements, and he made a short speech, complimenting Bob Mathews and George Sampson on a "clean campaign" and stressing the importance of a united approach to the final election campaign. He thanked George Sampson, who was present, for sending his votes to Don, and invited George to stand and receive a round of applause.

Don started speaking, at first thanking all the people who had helped him receive the nomination as the Republican candidate for the Senate. He recognized one after another, finally stopping with George Ramirez and Fernando Martinez from Orange County.

Don said, "There are more, but folks may be getting hungry. I'll be hanging around, and I would like to thank you all personally. But remember, we have a big campaign ahead, beating Dennis Oates, the Democratic candidate!"

The crowd cheered as he said this, and Don closed his

speech. He turned around, trying to locate Molly, and saw that she and Linda were deep in conversation at the back of the podium. Don's initial response was anxiety, but he saw the two of them laughing.

Mike, who had been shadowing Don at Joe's request, had looked over from below the podium and had seen them. He called up, saying, "Relax. They're getting along fine."

"Easy for you to say, now. You're going to have the same worries with your kids. And more anxiety if you marry Celia," Don replied.

"Well, we're talking about getting married—just talking, mind you."

"Yeah, right," Don replied, and greeted Tim McCarthy from Orange County.

Reporters had scattered to meet deadlines, but one, who was doing a feature article, followed Don around, asking questions, particularly about Benito. The reporter gave his name as Ray Cordero, and said he was writing about "some background material."

Don said, "Sorry, I keep telling you that Benito was my wife's uncle, not my uncle, and he never talked to me about his history. If you'll excuse me, I need to talk to my daughter!"

Don knew that the storm was about to break about Benito and the Mafia.

As he turned to where Molly and Linda were talking, Ray Cordero shouted after him, "Didn't your daughter just come back from visiting Benito in Italy?"

Don did not reply and continued walking. It was better for his campaign to have it brought up now, at the beginning of the general election campaign, rather than at the end. This way, Don would have time to respond. All the same, he felt a nervous excitement, a feeling of a challenge that he would have to take on.

He hugged Linda, kissed Molly, and asked Linda, "How was your trip? How is Benito feeling?"

Don had a chance to observe the two, side by side, both attractive, but both very different. They were about the same height, tall, but Molly was blond, with a robust, open, and vigorous personality. She had aged gracefully and her athleticism was obvious in her movements, and, as he was finding out, in her sexual performance.

His daughter, on the other hand, tended to be deliberative and thoughtful, even in her movements, yet she had been an excellent tennis player, and he had observed her occasional ferocious volleys and serves, playing on the Palisades High School tennis team, which took her opponents and her parents by surprise.

She had her mother's dark, Italian hair, and the two of them, the blond Molly and dark-haired Linda, appeared so different, yet it was clear that they had taken an instant liking toward one another.

"Oh, Daddy, Uncle Benito was wonderful to us. Even Robert was charmed by him. And the instructor from Berkley was very nice. He speaks Italian with a Scottish accent! But he does speak fair Italian and he's going to work with Robert on the project. He's coming back in the summer to work, and during the school year from time to time and over Christmas. It will give him a chance to visit with his parents in Scotland."

Don said, "I presume he's single."

"Yes, but how did . . ."

Don didn't remember ever seeing his daughter blush before.

She said, "Andrew is really nice."

"Yes," Don said, and he laughed. "He must think he landed in 'hog heaven' with re-building a Palladian villa, expense-paid trips in business class, and a beautiful girlfriend."

Linda said, "It *is* a bit much. Andrew is an expert on Palladio and is very excited about the Palladio villa project. He's thirty years old, never been married, and born is Scotland."

Joe rushed up, saying, "I've been looking for you. You're needed for a TV interview. And Molly, too."

"Good-bye, Linda," exclaimed Don, climbing down. "Call me about how Robert and Andrew get along, about Gina, and about Benito's health."

Molly and Linda followed, and Linda received a hug from Don and Molly, and Molly, Don, and Joe left to go to the other side of the ballroom for their interview. Joe hurried them along, frequently explaining they had a television interview to do, as Don and Molly paused to greet well-wishers.

Thoughts about Benito and the Mafia reappeared briefly, and disappeared.

Chapter Eight

March 12, 1986
12:20 a.m.

THE PHONE WAS RINGING, as he and Molly walked into the apartment, and Don hurried to pick it up before it switched to the answering machine.

"Yes? Who's calling?"

"This is Joe, damn it, and why didn't you tell me about your uncle and the Mafia? Why did I have to hear about it from a *Times-Tribune* reporter? And it will be all over the news tonight and in the papers tomorrow morning and . . ."

Don interrupted, "Don't get your bowels in an uproar, Joseph. I was waiting for those charges to come out. The truth of the matter is that both of us were working for the CIA. And the CIA will deny that they know me, and I'll say the magic words, they will confer, and they will say that someone with a similar name once worked for them. And, I'll say that isn't good enough, and . . ."

"Stop playing around," Joe said, almost shouting into the receiver. "What the hell is going on?"

"Sorry, Joe. The CIA is a secret organization and sometimes

they go overboard. Just play it up in all the papers, that Don Carter, the duly selected Republican candidate for the United States Senate, is going to Washington to force the CIA to admit that he and his dying uncle were working for the CIA. I'll leave for Washington tomorrow. And Joe, cancel the Reagan campaign appearance—he won't want to show, anyhow, with all this Mafia business going on."

Joe was silent for a moment, and said, "You've got 'balls,' Don. You've got the balls to be a great senator!"

"Thanks, Joe. I'll have to think about whether that's a compliment or not. We'll have a send-off with all the bells and whistles—meeting with reporters at the airport, pressure by you on Pete Wilson's office to arrange for my interview at the CIA, tearful leave-taking by fiancée of candidate. Cancel that last item, I'm just kidding. But I'm serious about the pressure by you, on Pete Wilson's office, to force the CIA to give me an interview. And I'll have Benito phone to Wilson's office through his Washington contact. You have time to make the morning papers."

"Okay," Joe said. "I'll arrange for the publicity and put pressure on Wilson and the White House. I'll have my fingers crossed. And you realize how important this is to the campaign. It's crucial, absolutely crucial!"

"Joe, I'm sorry to put you through this, but it was necessary. The timing is ideal. What if this had come out the day before elections, without time to refute this action? Believe me, we have the weapons to force the CIA to acknowledge our involvement with that organization, weapons which we can't reveal, obviously."

Joe said, "Okay, but I won't be sleeping until this mess is straightened out." He thought for a moment, and said, "Maybe the president can put pressure on the CIA."

After Joe had hung up, Don made his flight reservation to Washington for Thursday morning, and Don called Benito. It was early in the morning in Sicily, and Benito, through his connections, had uncovered more information about CIA activities in Nicaragua. He spoke with quiet assurance.

Benito said, "I am now sure that there is funny business going on with Nicaragua, and it is connected to the American hostage situation in Iran. President Reagan does not want to know about what is going on, in case something goes wrong, but trusts the CIA and Poindexter to get the hostages back. That is his mistake. Iran is buying missiles from the U.S. through Israel for their war with Iraq, and the money is being used to supply arms to the Contras, all of which are illegal and against U.S. laws. The Contras are making more money by flooding the market in the United States with crack cocaine, with help from the CIA."

Don interrupted, saying, "I still don't understand why my stargazer was killed."

Benito continued, "Your stargazer must have gotten in the way, maybe proclaimed that he would not agree because his income would be reduced, or he would no longer be in charge, so he was killed. You do not screw around with the CIA. Remember how the CIA pressured the treasury boys to ignore my foreign investments in return for knowledge of the cocaine trade in Colombia? What is another death in the Colombian jungles?"

Benito thought, and explained, "It is a spy caper that is bound to come apart because it involves too many people—Iranians, Israelis, CIA, and Contras. How many people can keep a secret? That is why the CIA has not protected you. They realize that it is all unraveling and are beginning to panic. Mark my word. It will all come crashing down within a year, maybe sooner."

Don mused, "Besides, if they kill someone, the records are classified, or maybe there are no records, or perhaps they contract someone else to do the killing."

Benito said, "You are catching on, Don. Remember, Don, be sure that the person you are speaking to has been cleared regarding 'Iran-Contra' because that is the way the CIA operates. Just ask if he has been cleared for 'Iran-Contra,' even if you are pretty sure that he has. It gets their attention, impresses them, and makes them understand that you can keep a secret."

Don thought about it, and said, "You aren't saying that you, yourself are cleared, but implying you know about it and may spill the beans unless they acknowledge that we're operatives."

"Precisely," Benito said. "You have just successfully passed the course in CIA-speak."

"Thanks. I certainly hope José Ramirez is around," Don said. "He's been involved since the beginning."

Benito replied, "He is around and available. It is just after midnight your time. I will be calling Pete Wilson's office, through my intermediary, to set up the interview with José. Also, President Reagan should be contacted. After all, he needs another Republican in the Senate. I am sure your situation will be picked by the European newspapers. They are always ready to sniff out CIA screw ups. You used good judgment to publicize it as much as possible, and it should be decisive in your Senate campaign."

"Thanks for the compliment. I learned from the master."

"Cut out the bullshit. You may be a model student, but this incident is not over, and you need to be very careful in what you say. Enough to show that you know, but they have to be sure that their secrets are safe with us. You are to say 'Iran-Contra' as a sort of mantra, and not much else. Period!"

"Got you, boss."

Benito laughed. "And go easy on the 'boss' business."

Benito said, "There is always a possibility that this call may be monitored, but I do not think so. There may have been some changes in the local Mafia, so we should keep that in mind. If the situation changes, I will contact you at the airport."

Don said, "I did get a congratulatory phone call from Wilson last night. He stayed up to call. Sounds like a nice guy."

Benito said, "Well, he may sound like a nice guy, but he will keep his distance from you now that this Mafia business has surfaced. But when he finds out we were working for the CIA, Wilson will be happy. Say hello to Molly for me. She is a wonderful girl and quite loyal, but intelligent and not afraid to question your decisions in private, to prevent you from doing something stupid."

Don said, "I know, and I love her dearly, but why not tell her yourself? She's right here. Just hold a few seconds." Don got Molly from the living room.

While Benito and Molly talked, Don stepped out of the room. He agreed with Benito and Joe that this could be the key to the whole campaign. It was make or break time, but he was confident, and also emboldened by Benito's confidence. He had to learn whatever he could from Benito, and, at the same time, prepare himself for life without Benito.

Later, when he and Molly were in bed, they held each other, and Molly said, "I know you're worried about tomorrow, but I know you'll do all right."

He kissed her. But he was not worried, really—more excited than worried. It was hard to describe how he felt, and he remembered feeling this way when he was in kenpo karate competitions, just before the match started.

Don and Molly turned off the phone and slept in on Wednesday. He read the *Times-Tribune* when they got up at 10:00 a.m. It was all over the headlines. And it reported that Don would be flying to Washington to force the CIA to reveal that he and Benito were working for them, which was what Don was looking for.

He kept a low profile on Wednesday afternoon, avoiding reporters and phoning Joe occasionally. Don talked again to Benito, who confirmed that he had reached his contacts in Washington.

On Thursday, March 13, Mike drove Don to the airport for

the 8:00 a.m. flight, and he and Mike went to the United Airlines First Class counter. The reporters were expecting him, and he waited for them to quiet down.

He said, "I have a statement to make. Since it involves certain government secrets, I can't be completely open. I'm going to the CIA headquarters to ask them to reveal the fact that I was working for them and Benito Desimone was working for them."

Don went on, "Naturally, we wrestled with this decision for some time, attempting to decide when we should clarify our relationship with the CIA, and went back and forth on this issue. I feel relieved that we have been forced into a decision, and Benito is also relieved. As you probably know, he's been diagnosed with invasive prostate cancer and only has twelve to fifteen months to live. He's now with his family in Sicily, but will return, somehow, someway for my inauguration as United States Senator from the State of California."

"What, exactly, did you do for the CIA?" one reporter wanted to know.

Don said, "One more question."

There were several competing voices, and a loud voice rang out, "How are you going to get them to admit that you worked for them? They're pretty secretive."

Don recognized the voice, and said, "Ramsey, we'll find a way, I'm sure," as he turned and walked away.

Their flight took off on schedule, with first class about three-quarters full. Mike talked about his life growing up in California, and they watched a movie for a few minutes. Don turned the movie off, while Mike continued watching. Several people on the plane recognized him from the picture in the *Times-Tribune*, which featured a headline saying, "CARTER IN TROUBLE. Heading for Washington and the CIA." They gave him a thumbs-up.

He showed Mike the paper. Mike read it and looked worried. Don reached over and patted his shoulder.

"Not to worry, Mike," Don said. "You'll look back on this someday as the defining point of your life—whatever the hell that means."

Don dozed, and when he looked over, Mike's eyes were closed. He remembered again how he felt when he was lying in bed with Molly, like he was waiting for his kenpo karate match to start, and he settled into a half-awake state, almost hypnogogic, dreaming about kenpo, meeting Elvis at the kenpo studio in West Los Angeles. Now he was more awake, but still thinking of Elvis and his three loaded guns he carried under his jacket, and what a nice guy he was, and how thin he was.

Mike was now awake, and he said, "You were smiling in your sleep."

Don responded, "I wasn't quite asleep, just daydreaming, like I frequently do to distract myself with happy thoughts when I feel pressured. It takes my mind off of stressful situations. I've had this dream before, about the time Elvis Presley came into the kenpo karate studio looking for Ed Parker, his longtime instructor. But Ed generally did his instructing in his Pasadena Studio, not West LA. This actually happened, by the way."

He thought a moment and said, "There were just three of us in the studio, and it was about seven or eight in the evening. Anyhow, this was about 1970, and I was commenting to my friend about how good Elvis looked, and how thin he was, and my friend said, 'Look at his pupils. They're pin-point!' His pupils were small, and he was thin, and I knew he had a big-time weight problem, and I knew he supposedly used speed, but he was a really nice guy. He showed us his three guns, which he carried in pouches inside his jacket, and he showed us his license for the guns."

Still remembering, he said, "He had a seventh or eighth

degree black belt in kenpo and was pretty serious about his karate for a while. Elvis stayed about forty or forty-five minutes while his manager tried to reach Ed Parker. I don't know if he found Ed. They were traveling in two cars, the three of them. One guy looked like a bodyguard, and the other guy may have been his manager. I was one-on-one with him for maybe ten or fifteen minutes, just talking, mostly about karate. I told him I had studied hapkido. I didn't tell him I preferred hapkido, which I do. My instructor in hapkido was Bong Soo Han, and he had reached only seventh degree at the time, and I think he was at the highest level in the country, so you see, there were differences in the way degrees were awarded in different styles of karate."

Don continued, "I also didn't tell Elvis I was about to quit kenpo. The reason I was quitting? They were always pushing competition, and I was the oldest in the group. I started competing, but developed a fear of being injured. It wasn't so much the pro's I was afraid of, but at my level, there were a lot of the young competitors, with their wild kicks. Bong Soo Han, my hapkido instructor, left suddenly to work on the Billy Jack movies, and he worked on other movies—*Force Five*, *Kentucky Fried Movie*, and *Cleopatra Jones*."

He finished his reminiscing with, "See, Mike, it works. Talking about Elvis has taken my mind off current problems, and I'm relaxed. It works better when you have someone else along to talk to. Of course, it doesn't work if you're not completely prepared."

Their flight was late and it was almost seven in the evening when they arrived at Dulles. He was not surprised when they were greeted at the plane by someone named "Frank," and taken to a limousine parked on the tarmac, before the other passengers had been deplaned.

Frank was apologetic and gave his full name as "Frank

Humphries," indicating that they were to get in the limo, and told them that their luggage will be at their hotel.

Mike interjected, "Just a minute, do you work for a private firm or do you work for the CIA?"

Frank said, "I work for a private firm. Sometimes, we pick up people and take them to Langley, and usually we wait for them. In this case, I'll be waiting for you, probably in the reception area, because it will be getting dark. We get paid for the trip to Langley by the CIA, but there's a lot of searching of the car and the customers. It takes a lot of time."

"Okay," Don said, as he got into the limousine followed by Mike.

When they got to Langley, they were searched at the gate, and again as they entered the building. There was a guard on duty who guided Don into an office.

A few minutes later, José Ramirez entered the office and greeted Don. "Sorry to get you out so quickly, but we thought we should meet before you approach the press."

"I'll get right to the point," Don said. "As you know, I was just elected to serve as the Republican candidate for the U.S. Senate in California, and we were hit by charges about Benito's criminal background. You and I met three months ago when I brought up the subject of acknowledging the work we did for the CIA."

"I, also, will cut to the chase and say that I brought it up with my superiors yesterday and the decision is still pending," José replied.

Don expected that he would say that, and Don asked, "Are you cleared regarding Iran-Contra?"

José was obviously startled by this question and took his time in answering.

He finally said, "Yes," in a low voice.

"Good," Don said. "We can talk freely. I have a statement to make."

Don said, "You know, you guys could have avoided a lot of trouble if you had just thanked us for our work in locating cocaine shipments and indicated that we were not needed anymore. Instead, you started your own operation suddenly and left us in the dark and confused as to what was going on, why we were not hearing from Carlos anymore, and why the cocaine shipments stopped."

Don paused, and continued, "We learned that Jimmy Calver, a.k.a. Pedro Cuevas, a.k.a. the 'stargazer,' had been killed. I knew that he was causing a problem for your work because he was so intent on killing me that he didn't have any room in his crazy brain for any CIA business. We don't know who killed him, and we don't want to know. When I spoke to you on January 4th of this year, I told you that we had reason to believe that he had paid for a hit on me shortly before he was killed, and you said you might notify Los Angeles, presumably to provide some protection. Nobody contacted me. Was I being protected?"

José shook his head, and said, "I was in favor, but my supervisor killed it for two reasons. First, the idea seemed far-fetched, but more importantly, it might have compromised our plans. I can't say more."

Don replied, "I understand fully and anticipated your problem. Pedro Cuevas, shortly before he was killed, actually did hire a Cleveland hit man to kill me. The Cleveland hit man didn't know that Pedro was dead and attempted to carry out the assassination."

Don could see that he had the full attention of José Ramirez.

Don continued, "As I'm obviously alive, he wasn't successful. With the aid of my bodyguard, he was disarmed outside of my house in Pacific Palisades. And I succeeded in convincing him, through my knowledge of the Cleveland mob scene, that Pedro was, indeed, dead. As you might know, this was especially difficult because it's typical for the hit man to not know who hired him. They work through an intermediary. He told me he received thirty-five thousand to kill me, which seems high. My bodyguard disposed of the gun and silencer."

Don paused, and went on, "We didn't report this because the only charge that would stick was carrying a concealed weapon, and the story would open up a can of worms and jeopardize national security, or force us to commit perjury."

José nodded understandingly.

Don said, "I want a statement from the CIA that Benito and I were operatives who were recruited by the CIA, that we served with honor, and that we no longer have any association with the CIA because of my political career. And, of course, I swear that we'll never divulge any information that we have come across, accidentally or otherwise."

Trying to establish a bond between José and himself, Don said, "Incidentally, my mysterious behavior—delaying my return from Italy and Sicily for months because of fear of assassination, unable to tell my wife the reason—was one of the factors in my recent divorce. I imagine that the pressure of leading a double life must affect the marriages of many of the CIA operatives."

José said, "I was just divorced." He said, "Wait here. I have to make a phone call. It may take a while."

José was gone for some time. When he finally returned, he said, "We can do it. Frankly, it's quite unusual. But President Reagan called somebody a few minutes ago, and so forth, and someone high up decided it would look good if we did it for you, this being a Republican administration."

Don thought José was being surprisingly frank and open. He doubted that it was due to their recent mutual divorce bond. Don suspected it was, as least partly, that José had told his supervisor that the cat was coming out of the bag regarding Iran-Contra and they needed to do damage control.

He guessed that José might have pushed for Don's viewpoint, and a higher-up agreed with this point of view because it made political sense. Don was glad there was a Republican in the White House.

"What do I tell the media?" Don asked.

"Tell them it was settled to your satisfaction and a statement from the CIA will be forthcoming, probably by mid-morning."

"Sounds okay," Don said. "Thanks and good luck with your career."

They shook hands and Don started to walk toward the door.

Don turned, and said in a low voice, "I hope you're off the case we were talking about. It's likely to be a disaster!"

José looked up from his desk, slightly startled, and something in José's sorrowful look told Don that he already knew.

Mike and Frank were waiting, and Frank went to get the limousine from the parking area. Don gave Mike a thumbs-up as they waited. When the limo arrived, the two of them said little and didn't talk on the way to the hotel.

Don impetuously gave Frank a $20 tip when they got out of the car at the hotel, starting to realize the enormity of his success. Of course, the call from President Reagan had been important, but hadn't Don been the one who decided on the big publicity campaign?

He called Benito from the hotel room and told him what had happened at the meeting and why he had made his speech instead of being quiet. He mentioned President Reagan's intervention, and he could tell how happy Benito was about the outcome.

Remembering Benito's admonition about tapped phone lines, Don asked, before he spoke, whether the "neighbors" were concerned about his notoriety. Benito understood and said he had explained satisfactorily and there wasn't a problem. When news reporters call, his sister tells them he's "too sick" for interviews.

He called Joe Abrams, who had been unable to sleep. Joe was especially happy about Reagan's intervention and its potential benefit to the campaign. Finally, he called Molly, who was also unable to sleep, and told her the good news and said he loved her.

Molly said, "I was really scared. I knew how much this meant to you."

He and Mike headed to the restaurant, where they found two reporters who had stuck it out and were waiting. The reporters introduced themselves, and Don told them that "it was settled to our satisfaction and a statement from the CIA will be forthcoming, probably in mid-morning."

Repeated questioning followed, but Don refused further comment, saying only, and as gently as possible, that he could not say more. He told the reporters that the hotel restaurant had stayed open at his request, that he and Mike hadn't eaten since early afternoon, and that he had told the reporters all he could. The reporters left, unsatisfied, but understanding, because it was the CIA, and they had probably dealt with that agency before.

He and Mike celebrated with a glass of Champagne at dinner. They were alone in the restaurant, which was officially closed. Don felt drained, but happy.

When they arrived back in their room, he arranged for a return flight for the next day, close to noon. He wanted to talk to the press after the CIA official announcement. He went to bed and fell into a deep sleep. Mike woke him in the morning at 8:00 a.m., and they went down to breakfast.

No reporters had appeared at the hotel. Don and Mike left for Dulles Airport early and entered the United Airways lounge, ordered coffee, and settled down to wait.

What if the CIA had changed their mind?

They hadn't. At 10:14 a.m., the lounge news channel picked up the story: "The Central Intelligence Agency announced today that Senate candidate Donald Carter and Benito Desimone had been employed by the Central Intelligence Agency, and both had resigned their positions. They have served honorably, and were no longer involved with the CIA because Dr. Donald Carter is a candidate for the United States Senate and Benito Desimone is adviser to Dr. Carter. This would be a one-time exception to the policy of the CIA, which maintains the utmost secrecy for the protection of its operatives."

"Yes!" shouted Don, jumping up from his seat, and spilling his coffee as he thrust his fist into the air. In a matter of minutes, television cameras and reporters appeared, and a press conference was hastily arranged. People were pumping Don's hand, congratulating him.

When the group had quieted down, Don began speaking. "I'm grateful to the CIA for making an exception in my case and revealing my service to the government of the United States. It was touch and go, because I was asking the most secret branch of the United States government to reveal the name of two of its operatives."

Don explained, "Of course, I feel vindicated, both for myself and Benito Desimone in Sicily. I'm almost certain he's watching this on Italian television. As some of you know, he's a United States citizen who had returned to his Sicilian roots because he has terminal prostate cancer and wants to die in his home village. He has one final wish, to see his nephew elected to the U.S. Senate from California. As I said, it's very likely that he's watching Italian television as I'm speaking. Benito, we're catching up and I expect to pass my Democratic opponent in the near future."

Pausing for a moment, Don continued speaking to Benito, "Starting as a complete unknown, never having been elected to public office, I'm convincing the public that I'm the better candidate. Untarnished by election promises, I can vote freely on any issue. I promised you, Benito, that I'll become the next Senator from California, and I intend to keep that promise."

Addressing the reporters again, Don said, "Gentlemen, I have a plane to catch and sleep to catch up on. We have time for only a few questions."

Roy, one of the reporters asked, "How did you convince the CIA to change their policy and reveal your name, and your uncle's name?"

Don replied, "Roy, I'm not sure. I like to think that even the CIA is able to show compassion for my situation and Benito's situation, but what went into their deliberations is unknown to me."

Roy said, "I have one other question. How the hell did you remember my name? You just met me briefly yesterday."

There was general laughter.

"Roy, I'm new at this game. I thought that's what politicians did, remember names. Did I do something wrong? I remembered your last name, also. It's Andrews, Roy Andrews. But they're boarding my plane, and I'll leave you with one thought. I'm a very happy man today, a very happy man."

As Don and Mike walked toward the boarding area, he found himself thinking about Nucky Johnson, "The Crime Boss of Atlantic City." *Why am I thinking about Nucky, of all people?*

He remembered Roy's question, about how he was able to remember his name. That was Nucky's specialty, remembering faces and names.

"I guess we do have something in common. Eidetic memories."

Mike turned, and asked, "Did you say something, Don, or were you talking to yourself?"

Don said, "My mother used to say that when you talked to yourself, that meant you had money in the bank. Well, votes are like money to a candidate. And we're a lot richer leaving Washington than when we arrived—a lot richer!"

CHAPTER NINE

June 10, 1986

THE MAN WAS LYING IN BED, hands behind his head, as though he was deep in thought, which he was. He had the heavy frame of a former football player, which he had been. And with his full head of dark hair and still-faintly blue eyes he appeared young, which he wasn't. He was sixty-six years old.

Carl Bainbridge turned, nudged Delia, and said, "I'm endorsing your former husband."

Partially awake, Delia turned and asked, "What did you say, dear?"

"I said I'm about to endorse your former husband's Senate candidacy. The type is set for tomorrow, his picture is featured, and the phone lines will be crowded."

Now wide-awake, Delia sat up in bed.

She asked, "Why?"

"My newspaper is independent, sometimes Democratic and sometimes Republican. At first, I didn't think that Don had enough experience, but he's held up well and been consistent. He knows the Constitution, backwards and forwards. He's a very good speaker for a novice—has a sense of humor, too. Sort of reminds me of a smarter Reagan, but with less charm and less BS."

Carl continued, "Frankly, I thought his goose was cooked when the Oates Democratic campaign came out about your uncle Benito being connected to the Mafia, but it turned out that they were both working with the CIA, confirmed reluctantly by the CIA. Although he does have a suspicious past, Benito had never been arrested for anything and has settled his tax problems."

He turned to Delia, "Are you sure he never gave any hint about the CIA work?"

Delia shook her head negatively. "You asked me that before when we were discussing marriage. He was over in Europe, mostly in Italy and Sicily, for over three months, not discussing anything with me. He was meeting with Uncle Benito, though, almost every day, and he came back speaking perfect Italian. That's when he announced he was going to run for the Senate, and I thought he was going crazy. He wasn't the husband I had married. I had already decided on divorce and was seeing you."

Carl said, "Well, he sure knows how to keep a secret, a good quality in a senator. Lucky for us and our marriage that it came out that he was working for the CIA. As I told you, my board was opposed to my marrying a woman with any hint of the Mafia, but the CIA was okay, even an asset. It's funny because the CIA is somewhat like the Mafia, involved in all sorts of illegal activities, including some funny business down in Nicaragua, which our reporters are trying to figure out."

Carl said, "I've thought about this a lot, and I believe that Don was involved with the CIA for a relatively short period of time, but your uncle's involvement possibly went on for years."

Delia said, "Well, that makes sense."

She sighed, "At least Don doesn't go around quoting all the time. You know, Don has a frightening memory, and he used to annoy his friends by his quotations. I never knew whether he was showing off or just practicing. And he just stopped—boom—like that! After he returned from Italy, the quotes were gone, as if by magic."

"Did he quote just anyone, or did he have favorites?" Carl asked.

Delia thought a moment, and said, "Thomas Wolfe was a definite favorite. My mother lives in Craggy Mountain, North Carolina, which is just outside of Asheville, Wolfe's birthplace, and Don visited Wolfe's former home frequently. My mother, whom you'll meet at the wedding, likes Don, and the two of them stay in contact."

She continued, "Pirandello was another favorite—you know, 'What is truth? Truth does not exist: truth we have in ourselves, we are truth: truth is the representation that each of us makes of it.'"

Carl and Delia both burst out laughing, and Delia said, "See? Don's quotations are drummed into my brain! And Benito is also a lover of Pirandello!"

Carl asked, "Speaking of Benito, are you going to call him? You brought it up again yesterday, about feeling guilty over not calling your uncle."

"I finally did call. I cried. We made up. I blamed Benito for Don's abandoning me last summer, but now I realize that it was the best thing that ever happened, because it brought me to my senses and brought me to you."

Delia continued, "Benito told me he'll be leaving his Pirandello collection of almost five hundred books to UCLA, originally intended to go to an Italian university—he won't say which one—and will attend a ceremony at UCLA, date undecided. Benito will give a talk on Pirandello, his health permitting. He said the Italian university stated 'they will see if they have room' for the books, but UCLA was 'overjoyed' to receive them and appreciated their rarity."

"I may go to see this," Carl declared. "That will be a great news story—'Ex-CIA operatives, Benito Desimone and recently elected Senator Don Carter, to give Pirandello talk at UCLA as Desimone gives Pirandello collection to school.' And this was a man who never graduated high school and left regular school in the sixth grade! So much for higher education."

Carl continued thoughtfully, "And a good political move for Don if, as I suspect, Benito does have a criminal past. Writers at this very moment are interested, and when Don wins the election, there will be a flood of articles and, eventually, books about Benito and Don, and some truth and a lot of conjecture will come out. You may have to go into hiding, and I'm only half-kidding. Benito may become a folk-hero, except to Democrats. Then, the movies . . ."

Delia declared, "Stop! I hope not or I'll hide."

"Don't worry," Carl said. "My board is primarily interested in selling newspapers, and they know already that Benito has a past. They also know that articles about interesting people sell newspapers. And they believe that 'criminals' don't give Pirandello talks."

Neither spoke for few minutes, but Delia remembered something, and said, "Don didn't bat an eye when I told him I was going for a divorce. I don't think I mentioned to you that he had a choking fit when I told him that I was marrying you, and he was laughing while he was choking. Sort of scary. I was about to call 911, but he managed to get his breath."

Carl asked, curious, "Did he say anything while he was choking and laughing?"

"He said, 'You did it, Delia, you finally topped me!' All the while, he was laughing and choking. I didn't understand, but I've been thinking about it. Tell me, Carl, honey, why are men so fiercely competitive?"

Carl said, "Not only men. You should see women in my

newspaper office! After all, a newspaper is all about competition—competition in getting stories, getting 'scoops.' It's pretty healthy, usually. But it's tough on women trying to raise a family, especially when they're alone and raising children, and worried about their jobs. We're cutting back on staff all the time. Did Don say anything else? He's an interesting man."

Delia replied, "Well, he did say, after he was finished choking and laughing, something about how he would have to be 'vice president or president' someday, presumably to even things with me. At the time, I didn't know what he was talking about. It got me to thinking. The thing that bothers me about Don now is that he's lost his vulnerability. I mean, he no longer needs people to tell him he's great. He assumes it's true."

She paused in thought and continued, "I think it's the money. He was always moaning about flying on those cramped seats in tourist class. I don't know how much money Benito has, but it's a lot. And he's leaving it all to Don. He said he never has to work again, and he always flies first class. It's like I could see him changing before my eyes."

"My family has always had money," Carl said. "So I don't know how it's to be without, but I somehow know it would be awful, and I work to change things in the economy as best I can."

Delia said, "But I really don't like the new Don Carter, and I'm very happy to have found you, Carl. I love you very much. I could never talk to Don like this."

"And I love you very much," Carl said, and he kissed her, softly at first, then with more feeling, and finally they had an almost violent sexual encounter that left them both panting and exhausted. They lay there for several minutes in each other's arms.

Finally, Carl said, rolling over on his back, "It's always hard to think of an ex-anything in a positive manner. Don is running even in the polls in spite of California being so strongly

Democratic. They've spent a lot of money, much more than Oates, probably money from Benito. But, believe me, Delia, Don is the better man."

"By the way, I just got a call the other day from someone very prominent, asking whether I thought Don was 'presidential material.'"

Delia gave a gasp.

"Don't be so surprised, dear. Anybody who could beat the Democrats in California is considered 'presidential material.' If you just saw *Bedtime for Bonzo*, would you think Ronald Reagan was 'presidential material?' And Don's got an attractive fiancée who adores him, thinks he's the cat's meow—am I dating myself, dear?—speaks Spanish like a native, and has been waiting for him for forty years. She's vaguely reminiscent of Nancy Reagan in her fierce loyalty. A lot taller, though. Between the two of them, both speaking Spanish, they're pulling some of the Hispanic vote away from the Democrats."

Neither said anything, until Delia remembered the moment when Don told her he was engaged.

She said, "I was bowled over when he said he was engaged, literally speechless, if you can imagine me becoming speechless. But afterward, when I talked to my daughter, who went on and on about their beautiful love story, and his BS about how lucky he was to have married two wonderful women, I thought, who am I to argue with that? And, especially, when it relieves Robert and Linda from taking sides, and feeling guilty about it."

"And, most especially," Carl said. "When you are wonderful."

Carl bent over and kissed her.

"Speaking of Linda, how does she like campaigning? You told me she joined Don's campaign."

"I'm afraid she loves it. But she's traveling back to Vicenza and her Scottish boyfriend after our wedding, and she'll spend the year in Italy and France. Love has temporally triumphed over politics. I don't want another politician in the family," Delia said.

They were silent for a moment, and Carl said, "Getting back to Don, his opponent, Dennis Oates, the Democrat, is hard to pin down, and is unsure of himself on constitutional problems. I don't like the way he voted in the California Assembly, because it seems to me that he changed his vote under pressure from the teachers' union. Didn't you notice that, dear?"

Delia said, "I did notice. It's so hard to see Don as a United States Senator, but I have to admit that Oates is a slippery character, rather insincere, looking to see which way the wind is blowing and heading in that direction. I stayed out of politics this year because of you being editor of the *Times-Tribune*, and a candidate like Oates makes it easy. It's hard to get excited about Oates."

"I know how you love politics—well, how you used to love politics, before Oates," Carl kidded.

Delia said, "You know, I think I told you how I used to get furious because Don got all that Republican literature. I used to scurry around, hiding his mail when I held a Democratic fundraiser in my home. Someone told him you get two votes, one in the primary and one in the general election if you registered for the opposing party. That way, you could vote for the least offensive candidate in the primary. He might not have run if he were registered as a Democrat."

Carl thought about it, and said, "Except for the budget, he's pretty liberal, and he would be strong with the Latino population because of his language skills. It's a close call, running as a Democrat. Don was at Stanford for two years, according to his bio. I've been thinking hard about this and believe I may have met him in the weight room once. I remember talking to someone who was punching the heavy bag, and he went to the weights. Maybe I'm getting him mixed up with someone else, but I noticed him because he was quite strong—lifting very heavy weights for a person with a slender build. And he wrestled, as I recall."

Delia said, "No, you probably have the right person."

"I was a senior when he was a sophomore. I played football for Stanford in 1947, the year Stanford didn't win a single football game. We were 0-9 as I recall, and I snuck around the campus, hiding from the questions, so I wasn't paying much attention. Our coach was Marchmont Schwartz, who had been All-American at Notre Dame. We didn't even have a football team in '42 and '43, during the war, and that was one reason I signed up for the Navy."

He continued, "As you know, I spent World War II in the Navy, and had already completed my freshman year before I enlisted. I traveled for a few years before I settled down and went back to Stanford. Then I graduated and went into the family newspaper business. Anyway, I intend to do my best to get him elected, and I'm running a banner headline tomorrow supporting Carter, and giving my reasons for not supporting Oates. I think we can pull it off. Don't you agree, dear?"

He kissed her again, and Carl asked, "Are you happy, dear? Not mad because I'm going to elect Don?"

"No. I have to admit that Oates is an idiot, but must I address Don as 'Senator Carter?'" she asked.

"No, but, of course, there's the requisite bowing and scraping," he responded.

"When pigs fly," Delia said.

He kissed her and said, "Wedding in six weeks."

The following morning, Don was awakened at 5:45 a.m. by the phone ringing. He picked it up and asked, "Who is it?"

"It's Joe. The *Times-Tribune* has come out for us. Your wife's soon-to-be husband has come out for us. He came through! I told you he was a straight shooter."

Don sat bolt upright in bed. He shook Molly until she was

awake and said, "Joe called and he said the *Times-Tribune* will support us."

He picked up the phone again and asked Joe, "I can't believe it. What about Delia? I mean—you know what I mean."

Joe replied, "He made up his own mind and simply picked the better candidate. Delia must recognize that Oates is an asshole and she respects Bainbridge's logic, even if she doesn't like it. The *Times-Tribune* never commits until the final couple of weeks, and does it in a logical manner. Better come over as soon as you can, because the reporters will be calling."

He hung up the phone, Don looked at his watch and said, "I'm going to call Benito," but Benito wasn't available and he left a message, saying, "I have great news. The *Times-Tribune* came out for us. I'll call later."

Molly said she would be over as soon as she got dressed, and Don dressed quickly and left. When he reached the office, a small crowd of reporters was already waiting. Don noticed TV cameras, one reading, "CBS." The reporters peppered him with questions, and Don had to hold up both hands until the reporters had quieted down, and he spoke.

"I believe that the *Times-Tribune* has considered the issues carefully and reached a logical conclusion. I have consistently, over these past weeks, provided the same message to the people of California. I promised them that I would always evaluate the issues carefully, explain my position so that it's easily understood, and vote responsibly according to my conscience. The *Times-Tribune* has recognized my steadfastness under pressure, my refusal to insult the intelligence of the voters with easy answers, and my honesty during the debates. And above all, I want the *Times-Tribune* to feel that they made the right choice in honoring me in this manner."

Don said, "I know you have questions."

They did have questions and one in particular came up:

"What did you think about your ex-wife's relationship to Carl Bainbridge, the editor of the *Times-Tribune*, and did you think that influenced the recommendation of your candidacy by the newspaper today?"

Don briefly thought of a humorous answer, but he answered, "Absolutely not, Charley. You know that the *Times-Tribune* always makes its recommendations ten days to two weeks before the election, and I would never suggest that Mr. Bainbridge in any way would let a personal relationship influence a newspaper editorial decision that he makes, and I only hope that I have the '*coglioni*,' the character, to do the same when I become a United States Senator. Remember, the future Mrs. Bainbridge is a staunch Democrat, but Carl Bainbridge came out for my candidacy in spite of that. That's why I say that he has '*coglioni*' or 'strong character.'"

"What are '*coglioni*?'" someone asked.

Don asked, "Any Italians in the audience?"

Somebody said, "I'll tell him."

"All right, Phil, but whisper it," Don cautioned.

A few more questions and the reporters and TV cameras left to meet deadlines. He noticed some differently shaped cameras, and Joe introduced John Moyers and Bruce Avalon.

Joe apologized, saying that in the excitement of the *Times-Tribune* announcement he had forgotten that these two men would be videotaping their campaign. Joe announced that they would be making a documentary about "campaigning."

"So, be careful of what you say," Joe said.

Bruce Avalon, who was the spokesman for the two, said, "You'll get used to us quickly. I'll do occasional interviews, sort of a commentary on what happened that day. Most of our footage was taken in the 1984 elections, and we were making the final print selections when this special election came along, and, frankly, this was the most exciting of all."

Bruce continued, "It's a close contest, an underdog seeming to come out of nowhere, the CIA, the Mafia charges refuted, and we love it. We want to find out your secret in staying up with the Democrats in a state that mostly elects Democrats."

Bruce added, "And, if you ever want to have a private conversation, just let us know, and we'll withdraw and fade away."

Molly had arrived as the reporters were leaving, and she greeted reporters by name as they left. Don, Molly, Roberta, Linda, and Mike joined Joe in his office, along with Bruce, and John with his video camera.

Joe appeared energized and strode around the office as he spoke, "Okay, okay. We just got a nice note from Senator Laxalt of Nevada and an additional two hundred thousand from the Republican National Committee for our campaign. They got really excited when they heard about the *Times-Tribune* recommendation. Wants us to go all out. They need that extra seat in Washington. The contributions are really coming in from private donors.

"But almost all of them with an agenda," he said, as an afterthought.

Joe paused to introduce Molly and Linda to Bruce and John.

"We're going to San Diego, to LA, to San Jose, to San Francisco, to Del Norte and everything in between in ten days. You've been there before, but not as 'happy warriors.' Who said that? Al Smith?"

Don spoke, "Franklin Delano Roosevelt at the 1924 Democratic convention called Alfred Emanuel Smith, Jr, 'the Happy Warrior of the political battlefield.' But he didn't write the speech. Judge Joseph Proskauer did, and Roosevelt had to be forced to give it."

Joe nodded, saying, "See? We're just warming up our campaign, getting better all the time. They will see us in a different light this time. I realize that you can't be everywhere, but I'll schedule you where I think the votes are. You and Molly have been terrific."

Joe paused and continued, "But we need to be super-terrific! The *Times-Tribune* is sending a reporter for part of the trip, probably Phil Santoro, and a photographer. I'll make out a schedule and you'll get copies. Mike has already arranged for extra security. You'll go in the campaign bus, as 'Happy Warriors' and vote getters. I'd book a larger bus for this trip. Today you'll stick to our old schedule: shaking hands at the Santa Monica Mall until eleven thirty, lunch at the Jonathan Club, and off to Santa Maria for some walking around and hand shaking, and tri-tip barbecue at dinnertime."

He took a breath and went on, "South tomorrow on a new schedule targeting the coast towns, since we've covered the eastern cities pretty well. We'll end up in San Diego, and gradually move up the coast, stop in LA and Orange County, San Fernando Valley, city by city, and continue north of San Francisco. Okay, quick breakfasts, schedule, and you're off. And I'll schedule gym stops while Don gets his workouts. We sure as hell will get all the boxers and weightlifters voting Republican."

He added, "I'll fly down to the big cities—San Diego, San Francisco, Sacramento, maybe Fresno, San Jose, and Santa Rosa—to check how things are going. You'll hit Eureka, Crescent City, and Redding. Smaller towns have their own problems, which you've been briefed on, and on which I've prepared extensive notes. Read those notes," he added emphatically.

Joe caught his breath and went on, "Don, this is where you have a big advantage with your great memory. People in the smaller towns have a lot of local problems, and when you know about these problems, they will be impressed and feel that you care about local issues. These notes have information about sewer problems, agricultural issues, water problems, dams, drought, and the local economy. Okay, breakfast and you're off."

Don called Benito again in Sicily, and this time he answered the phone. Benito said there was a problem with the connection at the time Don left the message. Don repeated the news that the *Times-Tribune* had endorsed him, and he could tell that Benito was very pleased. He told Benito that Joe was feeling confident of victory, and that the National Republican Committee had sent an additional $200,000 for the Carter campaign.

"Joe is sending us on a victory march around the state to collect every possible vote," Don said. "He's hoping we could win by a big margin and avoid a recount."

He asked Benito about his health. Benito said, "I am having more pain in my back, but Dr. Romani changed my medication and the pain mostly stopped. And he says he is sure you are going to win the election. He sends his regards."

Benito told Don about Delia's phone call. "We had a good talk and I am very happy. We both apologized. The other news is that the woman I spoke to at the local university insulted me about leaving the Pirandello books to them in my will, and said they 'might have room.'"

At this point, Don asked the camera crew to leave, and Benito continued, "I decided, 'screw them,' and called UCLA and described the volumes, and they were exceedingly happy and want me to set a date soon for a short presentation on Pirandello. I told you, in Philadelphia, that I inherited the collection from Francisco Savio, with the understanding that they would go to the University of Palermo, but he would have been equally insulted by the response of that university and would approve of my decision."

Benito continued, "I am setting up a charity to support the collection, which will be known as the Savio-Desimone-Carter Collection, so-named to honor Francisco Savio, my good friend who willed me his collection; Benito Desimone because I expanded the collection with further purchases; and, yourself because you will support the charity financially to make future purchases, as well as sponsor Festschrifts, when appropriate. Also, when they learn the extent of my misdeeds in the past, this Pirandello gift will serve to mitigate their effect. Of course, you were unaware of any naughtiness in my earlier life."

Don thought about this proposal, and said, "I don't know, Benito. After all, Pirandello is a foreign author."

Benito replied, "Precisely. That is why you are going to support *The Thomas Wolfe Society* with an annual lecture, as well as establish the *Carter Foundation* and the *Carter Collection* of important editions of Wolfe literature and donate this to the University of North Carolina, which I understand Thomas Wolfe attended."

Don said, "Congratulations, Benito. One American author, Thomas Wolfe, to balance off an Italian playwright, Pirandello. Politically speaking, it will work."

"On another subject," Benito said, and his tone changed, "I might mention that Paolo, who represents the local Mafia, warned me that trouble is brewing. Men are asking questions about me, and Paolo says I should leave for a while. He acts very nervous and keeps looking around."

"He says you should leave?" Don asked. "This is directed at you, personally. I expected this to happen. It was only a matter of time. You're a very rich man in a very poor country, and I would be willing to bet that they found out about your money, perhaps by bribing someone in your Swiss bank. Remember when I almost delayed hiring a bodyguard and would have been killed? You need to hire protection right away or leave immediately, or both. You're especially vulnerable in Palermo when you go to see Dr. Romani, where you could easily be kidnapped."

Don asked, "When did you plan to leave?"

Benito replied, "I was planning to leave Saturday, the 14th

and go to Rome to take care of some will matters, including leaving the Pirandello collection to UCLA, and make an additional bequest to enable them to take care of the collection. But you are right. I will hire bodyguards, make an appointment to see Romani, but not keep it, and leave for Italy immediately. I was not thinking clearly."

"I was really worried," Don said. "You made the right decision."

Benito continued, "I can trust no one here, but I have good friends in Rome. I will stay in Rome to take care of legal business. I will travel to Philadelphia, unannounced, by way of Washington. My Pirandello collection is in my house in Philadelphia and has to be cataloged, insured, and carefully shipped to UCLA. There are lots of arrangements to be made. Technically, it will be on loan to UCLA until I die."

Pausing briefly, Benito went on, "From Philadelphia I will fly to California and go to the Sovereign Hotel in Beverly Hills that you recommended. You probably will not be back from your bus tour yet. I have Delia's number and Joe's office number. Dr. Romani gave me a good supply of pain pills."

Don said, "I'll call Delia. She'll expect you and take you to UCLA for a check-up. As you mentioned, Molly, Linda, and I start on an eight-day bus tour of California cities tomorrow morning, and we should be getting back a few days after you arrive. Of course, you'll stay with Molly and me as soon as we get back."

"How is Linda doing?" Benito asked.

"Great. She filled in for Molly the other day on the Spanish program when Molly had a little throat problem. She loved it and did a good job."

"I found her to be charming, smart, and loyal, when they visited me, with much more interest in the family than Robert," Benito said. "Robert was too tentative and seemed unsure of himself. You might keep that in mind when you decide about the fate of my estate after you die. Linda may have a future in politics, also, if she is interested."

"I agree completely with your feeling about Linda, and I'm going to talk to her after the election," Don responded. "Oh, I was thinking that if you decide to stay in the U.S., we could have your services here, and I can take your ashes back to Italy for a Church burial and funeral in Sicily, for the family's benefit. One good thing about leaving Sicily early is that you'll be here for the voting on the 24th of June. And, you might check with your local priest regarding his attitude toward cremation."

There was a pause, and Benito said, "I did not consider cremation and returning the ashes for burial, but that may be appropriate. That way, I never have to return to Sicily. The local parish is very poor, and, although the Church now permits cremation, they discourage it, so a cash gift might be necessary to arrange for it. I was going to leave the parish a significant gift in my will, anyhow."

Benito took a breath and said, "As you know, I rarely attend mass and do not go to confession, but I will get a priest in the United States to give me last rites. I have my family to think about. Please pay the fare for my sister, Talia, to attend my funeral, but not for my ungrateful nieces."

"One other thing, Benito," Don said. "Pain medication tends to cloud people's thinking, and I believe you should be careful in making decisions. The surgery should result in fewer pain pills being necessary, and thus you'll have clearer thinking and more energy. Remember, Dr. Romani and I told you that castration, either chemical or through surgery, won't alter the course of prostate cancer? Well, now recent studies show that, in some cases, patients live from a few months to a year longer. It's not clear how low the testosterone level has to be reduced chemically, but the goal is to get it down to the level achieved by surgery."

Benito replied, "Thank you, Don. That is good news. And I have been more forgetful and drowsy lately. I will have Delia make an appointment with UCLA when I get to Los Angeles."

Don told Benito he might not be able to call as frequently when he was on this busy campaign trek, but he would try, and Benito should let Joe's office know where he was staying in Rome.

Don rejoined Molly and Linda, but as they were about to get on the elevator, Joe called them back. "I changed my mind about distributing schedules. You'll get one copy and it stays in Don's pocket. I want to make it as tough as possible for any hired hecklers to know where we're going, especially in the small towns where the police are scarce or hostile."

Joe dismissed the cameras, and said, "The Oates people may have hecklers working because it scared them when the *Times-Tribune* came out for us. I'll call a day early to organize rallies, but the larger cities will have to be scheduled ahead of time. Remember, avoid confrontations, if possible."

Don asked, "Would you have hired hecklers if you were behind in the polls, Joe?"

"No, but not for the reason you think. Heckling often backfires on you. People know the opposing party sent them. But I've been known to sling mud!"

As they waited for their bus, Mike introduced Don to the special security force he had hired, all former National Football League players, and all towering above Don. There was Alan Cooper, who had last played for the San Francisco Giants, Sal Angelo from the San Diego Chargers, and Henry Walker from the Boston Patriots.

Mike had told Don that he had a tryout with a professional team, the New York Giants, after playing college ball, but he couldn't pass the physical because of an old knee injury. He had followed football avidly, however, and was able to recruit the former players.

The trip had started with a large and enthusiastic crowd in Long Beach. Huntington Beach had a smaller crowd, as expected, but also enthusiastic. Next came San Clemente and Oceanside on their "victory tour."

It was on the second day that they had trouble. They were on their way to a luncheon stop in San Diego, and Don's schedule was marked "La Jolla, if possible." As Don was preparing to speak in La Jolla, he sensed something was wrong.

A group of tough-looking men appeared and started booing and hurling epithets. Someone threw a bottle, hitting Mike on the forehead, and he fell to the ground. Phil Santoro was hit a glancing blow by someone's fist, throwing him off-balance.

The men recruited as a special security force, described by Mike as the "toughest of the tough," sprang into action and quickly corralled the troublemakers, who may have been so impressed by the size of the three security guards that they offered little resistance. Mike said he was okay, and he helped run down the last of the attackers.

A photographer from that *Times-Tribune* had joined the group prior to La Jolla, and he reported that he had gotten "some good pictures." Don's first thoughts were of Molly, Linda, and Roberta, but they all had maintained their composure and insisted that they were "fine."

The La Jolla police were on the scene quickly and took the attackers into custody, after getting a report from Mike. The hecklers were arrested on various charges, including assault and battery, and the police took pictures of Mike's forehead, but none of the attackers would admit throwing the bottle.

The video crew said they would have the relevant tape copied and sent to the police quickly. Bruce said he thought they had video of the bottle thrower, and he appeared very happy that the incident occurred.

The crowd had drifted back cautiously and applauded the

quick work of security. Most eventually returned, and Don began speaking quietly to the small group immediately, replying to the attacks.

Don spoke about violence in our society and the importance of maintaining law and order even if we become angry and frustrated, telling the group that people behave badly when they're desperate, or when they are hired by others.

Don said, "I have no reason to believe that my opponent in this election had any connection with this pathetic attack and will call him to say as much, and get on with the campaign. We have forged ahead in the polls since we received the support of the *Times-Tribune*, and I anticipate we'll pull ahead even more, as people get to know me and my platform."

Don continued, "But so long as we fail to deal with financial realities and financial limitations, so long as we get involved in foolish wars, we won't be able to pay more for education and for social programs, and these problems will continue to haunt us. Also, I believe a woman has the right to choose whether she should have an abortion or not, as affirmed by the United States Supreme Court in Roe versus Wade, and we should focus our attention on avoiding wars that never end, educating our children, and balancing the budget. The State of California has to balance its budget. Why doesn't the Federal Government do likewise?"

Don explained his views on religion, saying, "I hold the same religious views as our forefathers, who believed in a firm separation of church and state, the religion of George Washington, John Adams, Thomas Jefferson, James Madison, James Monroe, and John Quincy Adams. It's amazing how many people have been killed fighting over religious beliefs, which are basically unknowable. I respect all religious beliefs and believe in absolute freedom of religion."

Don paused, and went on, "In keeping with this approach,

Molly and I have attended services in different churches, temples, synagogues, and mosques each Sunday or Saturday throughout my campaign, and we'll continue this practice after the election. Have your priest, minister, or rabbi request attendance before the election, or when the Senate isn't in session, and we'll try to be there. I've learned a great deal, as I've attended different services, and I take careful notes on their problems and concerns."

Don concluded with, "I promise to do my best in the Senate to focus on the problems of our society and bring security, stability, and decent jobs to these United States. Thank you."

There was applause afterward, and questions, mostly about the "founding fathers" and their religions, and they left for San Diego and another speech.

Don ordered the bus to stop by a nearby motel in order to phone Joe, who had flown in to San Diego earlier, and Don reported on the attack in La Jolla. Joe said not to worry. The attack would help the campaign and show the desperation in the Oates's camp.

Joe's only question was, "Did they get it on tape?" And when Don said, "Yes," he was happy and said he would make sure that the tape would be released to the media. Don had talked to Bruce, who thought it would be good publicity for the documentary to release the segment showing the bottle throwing.

Bruce said "And besides, you'd probably throw us off the tour if we refused! That's dynamite campaign material!"

Phil Santoro phoned in his story, and he and the photographer went on ahead to San Diego. Don ordered Mike to go to the ER for an examination to determine if he had suffered a concussion. A large and bloody bruise had formed on his forehead.

He thanked the three security guards and Mike. Molly, Roberta, and Linda personally thanked them.

They proceeded into San Diego, picking up a police escort

along the way, and the police stayed with them until they reached the hotel, where reporters and Joe were waiting.

He told the reporters, and a crowd that had assembled, that he didn't know who had been behind the attack and that it was now a police matter. He introduced Mike and the three former professional football players who apprehended the hecklers, mentioning the pro teams they had played for. The crowd was amused at the idea of people attacking them.

The three players surprised Don by saying that they were all donating their salaries to charities and urged the crowd to vote for Don Carter for United States Senator, and the crowd cheered and applauded.

Finally, he introduced Molly, who told the reporters and the crowd that the same security group would be waiting for any future attacks. She noticed several Hispanics in the audience and gave the same report in Spanish.

Don excused himself and his group, and they proceeded into the hotel to get ready for dinner and the usual after dinner speech. He talked to Joe and discussed the attack, saying he felt he should call Oates and reassure him that he was sure that Oates had not been involved, and it was strictly a police matter as far as Don was concerned.

Joe was silent for a moment, and Joe said, "Yes, I see your point. We really don't know whether Oates is involved, and you'll need his help in your reelection campaign in four years, so go ahead. You have already made a statement to the press. I'll track Oates down and tell him. You can talk to him and confirm that you consider it a police matter."

Joe asked, "What will happen to those guys who were arrested?"

Don said, "We have video of one guy who threw the bottle, and he's being held without bail on assault charges, but the other three will be out on bail in a few days. They said they don't know who hired them, just told to 'cause trouble,' and they got carried away and started punching and throwing things."

Joe said, "Okay, your call, but I agree." Joe handed Don a slip of paper with the name of the hotel Benito was staying at in Rome, along with a message that he was okay, there was no need to call, and he intended to sleep late in the morning.

He talked to Mike, who confirmed that Joe had scheduled a workout for seven in the morning, which Mike, Molly, Linda, and the security team would join. The team would take turns watching the spectators, who already had been carefully screened, and the doors would be locked.

Don wanted to make better use of the former football stars, and spoke to this group about making short speeches on his behalf, taking turns. They were very comfortable on stage, with great stage presence, and enjoyed doing this. Don told them to mix with the crowd more, getting to know the audience, and identify any suspicious characters.

Like many former players, they had continued eating the same amount of food as when they were playing football, and, as a result, had gained a great deal of weight. So, they enjoyed the idea of regular workouts, especially the heavy bag work, which made them sweat and (hopefully) lose weight. And they were strong as hell, with all of them easily bench pressing over three hundred pounds.

The bus, itself, was huge and luxurious, with many seats, as large as legally possible, enabling the former football stars to stretch out in solitary splendor and even nap, but confining, nevertheless. It took its toll as the days passed. Ordinarily, they stopped in motels and hotels, but once the bus was delayed by a flat tire, and they slept on the bus to make their scheduled city stop. As a result, they all became more and more rest-deprived as the trip progressed.

And there was a new problem cropping up, hinting at things

to come. Now that people realized that Don might actually win the election, he was getting increasing requests for favors. His stock response was, "Talk to me after I'm elected," but he realized that this was only postponing the issue. He would have to talk to Joe about this.

One day followed another, until eventually the days blended together—speeches, dinners, lunches, and more speeches. There were speeches in Spanish to groups of farm workers, hoping that some were legal and able to vote. And there were speeches to friendly and not-so-friendly crowds, trying to turn the unfriendly groups into votes for Don Carter.

Molly and Linda took the lead when he was too tired to think in Spanish. They both seemed to be tireless. Molly seemed to enjoy supervising her protégée, and you could see Linda's improvement as the tour bus went from city to city.

Don realized how dependent he was on Molly, and how much he needed her. Benito's words came back to Don, telling him he always could depend on Molly—"You are her true love."

CHAPTER TEN

June 23, 1986

DELIA WAS SAYING, "It's funny how things seem to be turning out."

Carl paused from his work at his desk, looked up, and said, "I can't imagine what you're talking about."

"Be serious, Carl. It's as though I was never married to Don. I was listening to him talk on television the other night and, I swear, he even speaks somewhat differently. I listened very carefully and finally noticed what it was, at least it was one of the things he did differently."

Carl turned, interested. "What did you notice?"

He and Delia were in the bedroom in pajamas. Carl was typing at his desk, seeking creative ideas for an editorial on the elections but not having much success.

"Did you ever notice that he never says 'can't' or 'don't,' usually 'cannot' or 'do not?' He's restricted his contractions! It's kind of weird—oh, there I go, saying 'it's'!"

They both laughed.

"I realize that he's making a formal speech, but I'm not used to it. I almost don't recognize his voice," Delia explained. "Plus he has more self-confidence than I can remember. He seems like a different person."

203

"Even the 'Great Communicator,' our president, Ronald Reagan, hardly ever uses a contraction in a formal setting, except when quoting someone else," Carl said. "If you want colorful language with lots of contractions, read General George Patton's speech to his troops, getting them ready for D-Day, in 1944. But he's an exception."

Delia shook her head. "It's not just that. I think I was holding Don back and he was holding me back. I didn't say anything to you, but I've been able, for the first time, to start on my novel. I've got an outline plus a first chapter sketched out, and an idea for a children's book, all since I decided on a divorce."

Delia paused and continued, "Also, I resigned from all the committees I was on with the Democrats and will be devoting my time to writing during the day and going with you to some newspaper functions, most of which I enjoy. I often meet other writers there."

Carl said, "Frankly, I'm greatly relieved. I was feeling guilty about being too tied to my job, with the elections and all. I'm very happy that you're writing, and I promise not to pry, unless asked. So yes, I have to admit that you and Don are both doing splendidly, much better apart."

Carl thought a moment, and said, "Don is an effective speaker, clearly superior to his opponent, Oates. I'd say he has plenty of confidence. Carter won both debates, and the Oates camp cancelled the third one. Oates kept accusing him of 'inexperience,' but the public is looking for new faces. For a novice, he was very good, and going to get better as he becomes more experienced."

Delia said, "Pirandello said something very important, although I didn't pay attention at the time, because I was mad at Don, but he kept repeating it, as he so often did. Pirandello said, 'Each of us is lots and lots of people.' I think Don and I were poisoning each other, and we both blossomed when we became untethered from the other. Only then were we able to let the other person out."

Carl said, "You may have hit on something important. But many people can't act so quickly because of money problems or lack of talent or fears of the unknown. So, they spend their lives wishing they could break away."

Carl hesitated, and went on, "On a related subject, I've had some thought about Don's speech pattern and why he was able to become so effective a speaker so quickly. You introduced me to Benito briefly the other day, and he spoke in a sort of courtly manner, as though he were making a speech. Don was hanging out with Benito for three months. Don is a quick study and he likely absorbed Benito's speech patterns. He sure is good for a novice."

Delia, who was listening intently to Carl's words, said, "I think you're right. Benito has the same speech pattern, but he's *always* spoken that way. Don has changed, at least in his speeches, so I noticed it."

Carl said, "Speaking of Benito, he appeared very frail when I met him. Will he be able to do the UCLA Pirandello presentation on Thursday?"

"He's doing better and appears recovered from the surgery," declared Delia. "When the doctors disagreed over how much the testosterone level should be reduced by chemical means, he decided on surgery. Molly has been going over his notes with Benito, and she says he's ready and will charm his way through the program. The doctors are pleased and feel he's added four to sixth months to his life."

Still thinking about Benito, Delia continued, "The Italian faculty at UCLA is very impressed with his knowledge, and they say he's part of a group of Pirandello fanatics in Italy who meet regularly in discussion groups, and it's remarkable that he absorbed so much in four or five years of study, alone and in these groups. They feel he has a brilliant mind. I think Don attended two meetings of this group. And Benito, when he was living in Philadelphia, would go back to Italy just for the meetings."

Delia suddenly remembered and said, "Oh, the talk has been moved to Royce Hall and the Italian Department is going all out, putting on a sort of Italian festival, starting at six thirty, with my uncle at eight. I've ordered tickets for us, which have to be picked up at the box office because Royce Hall became available at the last minute."

Carl nodded.

"It's funny," Delia said tentatively. "Back to being introspective—I've been thinking about this a lot—Molly is happy to have found her 'true love,' and I'm happy to have gotten rid of the same individual. I really like Molly and I respect her thinking. I think Benito views her as a substitute daughter, just like Don is a substitute son. He has no children of his own.

"My conclusion?" Delia asked, in response to an unasked question. "My conclusion is that love and happiness are often matters of timing. I may explore this in my novel."

There was a silence, and Carl said, "I'm afraid to enter *that* discussion. By the way, what's happening with the children tomorrow? I mean, are they going to the Century Plaza to celebrate? It certainly looks like Don will pull it off, maybe by a good margin."

Delia responded, "Linda, of course, is going to the Century Plaza for the election results, bringing Benito. Linda has joined Don's campaign for the general election. She's a linguist and fits right in with her Spanish, and was all excited when they were attacked by hecklers in La Jolla."

Carl said, "A dumb move by the Oates camp, even if Dennis Oates was unaware of the planned attack. And a lot of positive publicity for Don, giving the ex-professional football pros a sort of hero-celebrity status for a day or two. That was the death knell for the Oates campaign."

"Robert, also, will be there, probably with Gina," Delia explained. "And Bernie, Molly's daughter, will make her first appearance. She's coming in from New York. Linda, Robert, and Gina will be leaving for Italy sometime in July, after our wedding on the 20th. I think Linda is anxious to see Andrew again, the man whom UC Berkley sent to monitor the Palladio project.

"And, speaking about children, how about Mary, your daughter?" Delia questioned.

"Things are finally looking up in that area," Carl said. "Her mother has been in AA for two years and sober now for almost a year, as I mentioned, and has a boyfriend, so that's a load off of Mary. I told you, Mary wouldn't talk to me for almost a year after the divorce from Amy, blaming me for not sticking by my wife, and for the last three years, she's been very cool."

Carl continued, "And I know what people are thinking, that Amy couldn't stand the pressure of being married to a man trying to run a big city newspaper. I always suspected that was true. I know she's definitely doing better since the divorce. Now, much to my surprise, Mary is coming to the wedding, as you know, so you'll meet her. I told you she's been working as Press Secretary to State Representative Cormack in Riverside. And, I hate to say this, but I'm suspicious that she wants something. She's attractive and can be quite seductive, when she wants to be."

Carl hesitated, and said, "Well—and this is the kicker—now she's interviewed with Joe Abrams, among others, for a job as Press Secretary to a senator or representative in Washington. Obviously, she's thinking about a job with your ex. So, what do you think?"

Delia was quiet and said, "Didn't you tell me that Mary and her mother took the mother's maiden name after the divorce?"

Carl replied, "I thought about that. Joe Abrams would have no way of knowing that Mary Royal was my daughter."

"We don't want people thinking that your newspaper was involved in getting Mary a job," Delia said.

"Mary is very savvy about politics," Carl said. "I know what you're thinking. Mary must be aware that this is a very tricky job move, to work for Don."

Delia said, "I'm going to call Don first thing in the morning and warn him. It will give me a chance to check on his contractions."

Carl laughed and said, "Good." Carl appeared pleased. "I will—notice the lack of contractions—be headed to the paper early. Oates orchestrated a late get-out-the-vote campaign, dragging all the union members out of their houses, so it might be closer than expected, but Don should win."

Carl gave up on finishing his typing. He crawled into bed, kissed Delia goodnight, and soon fell asleep.

At that moment, Joe Abrams was putting the final touches on his own get-out-the-vote campaign in West Los Angeles, working late at his Century City office. He was on the phone, urging the President of the Young Republicans to make a greater effort, and trying to avoid being distracted by John Moyers filming the election documentary.

Joe said, "Remember, Hal, you're the difference between victory and defeat. If we make inroads on the Hispanic voters we've got it made. But they will need rides, many of them."

He listened as Hal apparently reassured him, and said, "I know you planned this out weeks ago, but I was checking. Good. Have you got rides scheduled in all the rural areas?"

Joe listened some more, and nodded. "I know that Don and Molly did a great job with the Spanish speakers, but we've got to get them to the polls. Right. We're depending on you. I'll be in the office all night, so call if there's a problem. Right. Right.

Keep up the good work. Right. I know, you've got workers checking the houses all over the state. Good work. Thanks."

Joe hung up the phone and said, speaking to the camera, "I think we locked up the Hispanic vote! Of course, it helps if your candidate and his fiancée both speak Spanish. We've plastered the Hispanic community with posters in Spanish emphasizing that Don and Molly are both Spanish-speaking. Let Oates mobilize the unions—there are a lot more Hispanics in California than union workers!" Joe made a bed for himself on the office couch, lay down, and looked up at Bruce Avalon and John Moyers.

Bruce laughed when they had finished filming Joe's dramatic move to the couch, and said, "We'll be following Don all day tomorrow, election day. People are really interested in how candidates spend that day, how they deal with their anxieties, and even if they are ahead in the polls."

"I'll tell you how one candidate deals with his anxieties," said Joe, leaning on one elbow on the couch. "Don works out three days a week, regular as clockwork. He tries to not let anything interfere with his workout, and he doesn't think about anything else when he's working out."

"Yeah," Bruce said. "That's true about workouts clearing your mind, but it takes one and a half hours to do a complete workout, and it's hard to find the time. Don has given me some tips, and I'm starting to work with a heavy bag. But Don will have a hard time finding time in Washington for his workouts."

The next morning, Don was talking to Benito and Linda, explaining what was likely to happen that day. He was somewhat uncomfortable because of the presence of the camera and had warned Benito about it.

Don said, "If all goes well in today's voting, and Oates doesn't demand a recount, and when the state verifies that I've won, I'll be sworn in by Vice President Bush, who requested to swear me in personally. That will occur in two or three weeks. There's often a foul-up on the voting machines in a county or two, and the absentee ballots have to be counted."

Don continued, "The Senate goes into recess for two weeks on the 26th of June, and Molly and I'll be getting married on Sunday, the 13th of July in Las Vegas. Delia filed for divorce in California in December, but I didn't get the papers until January 6, and in California, there's a six-month and one day waiting period. So, that's the earliest Sunday the wedding can be held. Delia is getting married the following Sunday."

Benito said, "I will hold off the congratulations until all votes are in. I told you about having the surgery while you were on your bus tour. The doctors at UCLA advised it be done quickly. It was done under local anesthesia. So, now my *coglioni* are gone, and I am having less pain and need less pain medication. As you predicted, I feel less sleepy and more alert. There was a difference of opinion among the doctors about how far down the testosterone level should go, so I voted for bilateral orchiectomy, because that is the gold standard."

Don had sent Bruce and John and their camera out of the office, and had also asked Linda to leave while he spoke privately with Benito.

"This is actually the first time I've spoken to you alone. How are you feeling? I wondered if you had called Dr. Romani."

Don thought Benito had lost more weight. His skin was darker than when he first saw him in Philadelphia a year earlier, and he was more stooped. Benito had been a man of average height, as Don recalled, but now he appeared to be much shorter. His mind, however, was clear, and he seemed to have more energy, which Don attributed to a decrease in pain medication.

Benito said, "To answer your first question, I am getting some of my strength back. I felt weak and tired for a few days after my surgery. Now I feel better, and by Thursday I will be ready. To answer your second question, I called from Philadelphia to Dr. Romani in Palermo. He said he was worried about me, and had called the house, but a man's voice answered the phone, so he hung up. A few days later, he called again, and my sister answered. She said two men were hanging around the house for three days. She kept telling these men that I had gone to the States for treatment and would not be back for thirty days. Finally, they left."

"Close call," Don said.

Benito said, "Very close. Thanks to you, I got out in time. I had always prided myself on thinking ahead and seeing trouble coming—avoiding arrest, for example. But my thinking is not as sharp now, probably due to the medication. I had been living in a dream world, believing I could stay in Sicily."

Benito went on, dissecting his mistake, saying, "I had made my peace with the local boys, for the time being, and I was paying a modest amount, and they, in turn, saw that my phone was clear. I was nostalgic for my Sicily, a characteristic of Sicilians far from home, well-portrayed in Pirandello's *Limes from Sicily*, and thought I could return, but as your Thomas Wolfe says, you cannot go home again. There was the prospect, for a time, of a change in the Mafia hierarchy, but nothing came of it, and I thought that things were okay until I got Paolo's warning. But I did not act on his warning until you, Don, brought me to my senses."

Benito paused briefly, continued, "I believe you were correct. They planned to kidnap me and hold me for ransom. They were not local and were undoubtedly Corleonesi making a raid. Of course, the Corleonesi are ruthless and are likely to kill their victim after they receive the money, in order to prevent identification. But it would be foolish of me to go back to Sicily, in any case, now that I've been singled out as a millionaire. Even in southern Italy, there are criminal gangs—the Camorra Mafia in

Naples, the Calabrian Mafia in Calabria, and the 'Ndrangheta in Calabria and Lombardi—there are others."

"So, it is 'good-bye southern Italy and Sicily' except for short, unannounced visits," Benito said, and there was sadness in his voice. "Sicily reminds me of the American 'wild west,' that I used to see in the movies, except that there are no cowboys on white horses riding up to save the day."

Benito changed the subject abruptly, saying, "I flew to Philadelphia by way of Washington, deliberately avoiding announcement of my arrival. Charlie Marturano and Al are still living in my house in Philadelphia. Talia, my sister, is there most of the time and reported no problems. Charlie and Al send their regards, by the way, and wish you luck in your election fight."

Benito explained, "But I cannot return to Philadelphia for more than a week. Even then, I need to stay hidden in the house. The Mafia boss, 'Little Angie,' is a very violent man, and I am told that he is angry about my working for the CIA, so I left for LA in about three days. I was in Philadelphia just long enough to get my collection cataloged and shipped by a special flight to UCLA. I did not leave my house the whole time I was in Philadelphia. Angie will be in jail soon, but I am sure he will run his operation from whatever prison he is in."

Don was doubtful about Angie running his operation from prison, and declared as much to Benito, but Benito was certain he would be able to do it.

Benito explained, "Luciano continued as the head of the Commission—'boss of bosses'—while he was in prison in Dannemora, New York, sentenced to serve thirty to fifty years. He only served ten years and was deported to Italy because he supposedly helped the war effort during the American invasion of Sicily, which he later denied doing. Luciano could just order someone killed and it would happen, even while he was in prison. The same with Angie."

Don responded, "You have convinced me, Benito. Today they want film of me voting, and I'm expected to be modest about my election chances and congratulate Oates on a clean campaign. Joe is going to set up my office for me in Washington and Mike and Celia—she's the gal that runs Joe's office—are going to work in Washington for me. She and Mike are probably getting married, and I offered the two of them jobs."

His phone rang. It was Delia.

With no preamble, Delia said, "Don, did Joe Abrams tell you about a job applicant named Mary Royal?"

Don thought a moment, "Yes. He described her as a great prospect for Press Secretary. But I had someone else in mind, and I was going to talk to Joe. Why are you calling about Mary Royal?"

"She's Carl's daughter, that's why!" Delia declared. "We're afraid that people will say that you traded the job for a recommendation from the *Times-Tribune*."

"Wow! That's incredible!" Don exclaimed. "Is Royal her married name?"

"Single. Never married. After the divorce, she was so mad at Carl that she took her mother's maiden name."

"Thanks, Delia. I've got to run, but I'll call Joe right away."

Delia said, "Good luck in the voting today."

The phone rang immediately after Delia had hung up. It was Joe.

"Are you ready to leave for the polls? Has Mike arrived?" Joe asked.

"Wait a minute, Joe. I want to check the office door."

Don opened the door. Bruce and John were talking in the living room with Molly and Linda.

Benito had listened to his conversation with Delia. Don picked up the phone again and asked, "Do you know that Mary Royal is Carl Bainbridge's daughter?"

There was silence, and Joe said, "Well, I'll be a monkey's uncle. And I was about to hire her!"

"Well, don't. Anyone who takes her mother's maiden name has father problems, and her father happens to be the editor of the *Times-Tribune*. Some people will say that we traded a job for an endorsement."

"She sure is highly qualified," Joe said, wistfully.

Don asked, "She doesn't happen to be very, very attractive, in addition to being 'highly qualified,' does she, Joe?"

Joe was silent, and said, "She's quite attractive."

Don laughed and said, "Joe, I'm glad that you're still alive down below. I haven't been subject to Mary's charms, so I can speak dispassionately. I believe that she would be dangerous in an office. Have you approached Roberta about the Press Secretary job?"

"Well, no. I was thinking I would hire Mary. And Roberta has a husband and children, and I thought . . ."

"Never mind," Don interrupted. "I'll talk to Roberta. I had the same problem, once, with a woman back in Atlantic City, and Benito cured me." Don looked over at Benito and winked. "Even if Roberta can only stay long enough to get the position started and maybe train someone else for the job, that will be a help."

"I'm sorry, Don, my head must have been up my ass."

"Maybe not up your ass, but somewhere else where it shouldn't have been," Don declared. "And if you keep feeding me straight lines, we'll be here all day.

"I just saw Mike arrive. He's driving us to the polls, and I have to leave. Don't worry about Mary Royal. She'll survive. And enjoy our victory tonight!"

Don hung up the phone, and Benito said, "An occupational hazard for people in politics—attractive women. But Joe is a good man, and smart. You handled it well."

"Thanks, Benito."

Don said, "On another subject, I want to keep you under wraps, for the most part, until the Thursday presentation, both to preserve your strength and to heighten interest. We expect a large crowd on Thursday, trying to see the man who put Don Carter on the road to stardom, but, more importantly, the man who loves Pirandello and can describe what Pirandello is trying to say to his audience."

Don continued, "I told you it has been moved to Royce Hall because someone cancelled. Royce Hall is a beautiful old building with wonderful acoustics holding over eighteen hundred people, modeled after Milan's *Basilica of Sant'Ambrogio*."

Benito said, "I have been to that church years ago. The professors in the Italian department were quite excited when they found out Royce Hall was available."

Don nodded and said, "And we signed a contract with Bruce Avalon of *Avalon Productions* to film, edit, and produce your talk in its entirety, using two cameras. Bruce has permission to include approved highlights in his own documentary. It's your legacy to the world, on film. I'll interrupt occasionally when I see you getting fatigued, or when I have something to say about Pirandello's plays or his philosophy. Does that sound okay to you?"

Benito placed his arm around Don's shoulders and said, "Thank you, Don. That is a good plan." He declared, "Before I forget, there is good news from the financial front. As you know, my bank in Switzerland originally offered twenty-three million as compensation, to right their wrong regarding Herr Schultz's manipulations of my account."

Benito continued, "After I told them I was going to get another estimate of my losses from a different accountant, they said that they had made an 'error' in their calculations, and they are offering an additional three point seventy-five million. I out-bluffed them. Or rather, you out-bluffed them. I believe I will accept their offer. Also, I complained to my attorneys about their accountant's error, and they apologized and said they had fired the woman who made the mistake, and she had made other errors. Who knows?"

Don countered, "More likely your attorneys were afraid of offending the bank, but this time, the bank has sweetened the pot with a mildly generous offer, so take it and be done with it."

"Now I want to talk to Joe, alone," Benito said.

"We'll drop you off at Joe's office on our way to vote. Then, we'll return for Joe's regular meeting," Don said.

The two embraced, and Don called Joe and dropped Benito off at Joe's office. The four of them continued their drive to the polling place. Mike and Linda looked on as Don and Molly pushed though the crowd of waiting reporters. The police watched carefully to see that reporters stayed behind a rope barrier that the police had set up.

After voting, Don moved with the reporters onto the lawn of a neighboring property at the legal distance from the voting. Don said that he was "hoping to win" and how both sides ran a "clean campaign," and excused himself after answering a few brief questions, saying he was expecting a "close contest."

As Don was leaving, he spoke with Bruce, who had been supervising the filming of the voting, confirming that arrangements had been made for a second cameraman for Thursday, and discussed other details, emphasizing that this might be the last chance to film Benito because of his health problems.

Afterward, as they traveled back to Joe's office in Century City, Mike said that Celia had told him that Roberta was upset about not being considered for the Press Secretary job and was looking around for another position. So, Don corralled Roberta as soon as he arrived, closing the door behind him as he entered her office. He announced he was offering her the job.

Roberta looked startled and said, "Are you sure? I thought Joe had selected 'Royal Mary,' or whatever her name was."

Don laughed. "She may have the technical skills necessary, but I felt that she would be a problem in my office for a number of reasons, some of which you may guess, plus she's the daughter of Carl Bainbridge."

"You mean *the* Carl Bainbridge from the *Times-Tribune*?"

"Yes, I do mean *the* Carl Bainbridge from the *Times-Tribune*," Don replied. "And she did not tell Joe, who was so besotted by her charms that he was ready to hire her on the spot. She's never married, but took her mother's maiden name. I can only assume that she had her reasons for not disclosing her relationship to Carl. You were my choice from the beginning, and it was my fault for not letting you or Joe know."

Don asked, "By the way, Roberta, have you had any problems with Joe?"

She replied, "Not that I'm aware of. Of course, you know he's a womanizer, but once you tell him 'No' he's okay. Supposedly, the reason for his divorce was other women, and I can believe that!"

Don said, "Well, that explains the 'Royal Mary' effect."

Roberta replied, "Yes, she's quite a package."

Don asked, "Is it a done deal, about coming with us to Washington?"

Roberta nodded and said, "Yes, a done deal."

Don and Roberta shook hands, and Don said, "Let me know what job you believe you qualify for. I'm confused about the difference between Press Secretary and Communication Director, for example, but Communications Director is scheduled for a higher salary."

Don continued, "And let me know if others should be brought along. Rents are high in Washington, the pay is modest, and the work can be tough. Joe will be there to set up the office. Oh, and you'll receive round trips back to California."

Roberta replied, "I have a sister in Washington who's divorced and works for the Department of Interior, and she's always asking for me to stay with her," Roberta said. "And my husband is from the East and has relatives in Virginia and New Jersey, so we'll do fine. My children are away in college, or will be after my youngest, who just graduated from high school, leaves for Bryn Mawr this fall. Bryn Mawr is very close to Philadelphia, and not very far from Washington."

She added, "Besides, I enjoy working with you, and it will be exciting working in Washington in the political atmosphere, with senators and congressmen."

He concluded, "Great. We're all set. I appreciate your confidence. Now all we have to do is win this election."

Don and Roberta went into Joe's office, accompanied by Molly, Mike, and Linda. Benito was sitting in a chair, enjoying Joe's telephone performance, and Don introduced Roberta to Benito in a whispered voice.

John was filming, following Bruce's hand-signaled directions, and Joe was on the phone, hustling the Hispanic vote. They heard him asking, "Where are those rides in Fresno? What the hell's going on up there?"

Joe noticed them and waved and finished his telephone conversation, saying, "Okay, the rides are on the street. Sorry I gave you a hard time. Keep up the good work."

Joe continued, "It's early, only eleven thirty, but exit polls show Don leading fifty-two percent to forty-eight percent. It's quiet now, but as soon as it's clear that Don is the winner, the stuff will hit the fan and phones will be ringing continuously— congratulations, people asking for favors, some cursing you out, reporters looking for dirt, and television interviews."

Don said, "On another subject, I offered Roberta a job and she accepted, on a permanent basis. It turns out that she has a sister in Washington, so she's the only one who has a place to stay."

They applauded, and Don said, "Mike, get Celia to come in, and we'll have a group good-luck toast to a successful election—non-alcoholic, of course."

Joe said, "Donna Boyd, Senator Boyd's widow, called this morning and offered her home in Washington for you or Oates to use temporarily, rent-free for a month, and then she's going to sell or rent it. I've been in it and it's quite nice. Not too far from the Senate building with good security, fenced, four bedrooms, circular driveway, air-conditioning, on about a half acre—one of the nicer homes in a good neighborhood."

"Donna Boyd also said that most of Senator Boyd's staff would like to stay on, if that's possible," Joe declared. "They know that you and the late senator have similar views on most things. I told her that it's usual for most of the secretarial staff to stay. I'll be interviewing higher-up staff to find out if there are suitable positions for them."

"That's very kind of Donna Boyd," Molly said. "I'll call her today and thank her for her offer. That will be one less worry. We never did get around to finding a house here, and I've got a wedding to plan. To be honest, it's mostly my mother doing the planning—I just haven't had the time."

"Benito will have one of the rooms in the Boyd house, and Mike and Celia another, until they find a place of their own. And Joe already has a place," Don declared. "But first things first. Time for a 'good-luck' toast for a successful election. It has been great working with you, and I'll see you again in Washington." Don led the small group as they clinked glasses. They had to drink again as Maria arrived, closely followed by John Stewart. Don introduced Benito to John and Maria.

Don walked into the outer office and spoke to the thirty or so staff there, saying, "This will be the last few weeks for some of you. It has been a pleasure working with you. You have all worked hard, and you'll all receive a three thousand dollar bonus, regardless of the outcome of the election."

Don went on, "Talk to Celia if you want a job in my office. Washington is a high-rent town. If you have relatives living there whom you could stay with, or a burning desire to live there, talk to Celia. Salaries for government employees tend to be modest. Celia, Mike, and Roberta will be coming along. And there may be some jobs locally in field offices in different categories, so, again, talk to Celia and Joe."

Don explained, "Mr. Abrams has informed the field offices personnel, with the consent of Mr. Oates, that they will be employed at least until he or the Oates campaign manager has interviewed them after the election. It's lunchtime, and I've sent for food to be delivered, and you're welcome to come to the Century Plaza later for all the excitement."

The group applauded and broke up into smaller groups. Molly, Roberta, Mike, and Celia had been listening as Don spoke, and Joe was on the phone as the phone calls increased. People were sensing a winner. Roberta started to answer calls on another line as the volume picked up. Don had instructed Joe and Roberta to say that he would not take calls before the vote was decided.

Linda came over to take her Uncle Benito back to the apartment to rest and said she would return with her uncle after the polls closed.

Just then, Bernie Stoller, Molly's daughter, arrived, breathless, and apologetic, explaining that she had been working late on a film for television in New York and had to leave her boyfriend behind to finish up.

Don knew she was twenty-five years old. She was shorter than Molly, but quite attractive in her own way, vivacious, and energetic, and genuinely happy about her mother's upcoming marriage. Mother and daughter embraced, and Don received a hug.

Don and Molly left to go over to a suite at Century Plaza with Mike driving. Molly was quiet, and after they arrived and they were alone, Molly explained, saying that Bernie said she knew about the affair with Peggy, but Arthur kept saying he was going to terminate that affair and asked Bernie to not say anything.

Don switched on the television as they arrived. He switched it off when an advertisement came on, and lay down on the bed. He heard the faint voice of Molly on the phone in the other room, and the last thing he remembered was wondering whether she had turned off the phone by the bed. He fell asleep.

He awoke to find Molly shaking him gently.

"Wake up, sleepyhead. It's four o'clock. Time to take a shower and do your thing. Exit polls show you leading Oates fifty-three percent to forty-seven percent, and the early balloting shows about the same margin."

He was now wide-awake and hurried into the shower, and toweled himself off. Why am I rushing? He deliberately slowed down, shaving slowly and carefully, and put on fresh clothes and a tie. Don looked at himself in the mirror, adjusted his tie slightly, and was ready to face the world.

Molly was remaking the rumpled bed as Don exited the dressing room of the suite. He seized Molly from behind, declaring, "You gorgeous creature. Let me take you away from all this. You'll never have to make another bed!"

She giggled as she leaned back against Don.

Turning around, Molly said, "Joe called and said people were looking for you. The ballroom is about one-third full, gradually filling up, and it's only five thirty. He expects Oates won't concede early, and not until well after the polls close. Joe feels you should make a tour of the ballroom, with Mike and me along, and retire for something to eat, returning later after the polls close. There's a buffet, but nobody looks statesman-like when eating, according to Joe."

Molly said, "The press especially likes to get pictures of politicians eating hot dogs. Joe has been here since four o'clock, and Alan, Sal, and Henry—the football guys—have been screening people at the door since the doors to the ballroom opened."

Mike was waiting at the suite door, and three of them took the elevator down to the ballroom and walked onto the floor. The room was filling up rapidly now. Everyone seemed to be in a happy, holiday mood. Catching sight of Don, Molly, and Mike, the crowd converged toward them in a friendly wave, and they were soon engulfed.

Don was shaking hands with friends, acquaintances, and complete strangers, and exchanging hugs occasionally with close friends. He thought to himself that this was the perfect nirvana moment, the moment before he had to say "No" to someone and piss him off.

Medical colleagues were in the crowd, most saying that they were surprised that he had "really pulled this off." That was it. That was the look that he was trying to identify—"surprise." And many of the other guests had that same look of surprise on their faces, as though they never expected to actually be here.

Suddenly, Joe Abrams appeared, rescuing Don from the hand pumping and hugging, which he was actually enjoying, and dragging Don away, telling the crowd, "Don and Molly have to leave for a 'handshake break.'"

As they entered the elevator, Don noticed that his hand and arm were tingling.

Molly said, "I've been careful with my hands, just offering a few fingers, if possible."

"I've ordered a room service menu for the two of you," Joe said. "I recommend something light. I'll call your suite when it's time, probably an hour after the polls close at eight. Mike, why don't you send one of your boys up to stand guard, and you and

Celia eat at the buffet. Actually, the food is quite good."

Joe said, "I don't know when I've enjoyed a campaign more. Excitement, ups and downs, and then, we wupped the Democrats' butt! Lovely! We're going to get over fifty-three percent of the vote! The problem is, they will be expecting the same result next time, and it's not going to happen. The newspapers and magazines will be analyzing these results and re-analyzing them, trying to find the 'secret.'"

"And don't forget the CIA excitement," Don said.

"Yeah," Joe said. "I almost had a coronary that time. And you and Benito had it planned, all along. That's when I decided you would make a damned good politician!"

Molly smiled at Joe's statement, found her key, and she and Don entered the suite, while Joe took up temporary guard duty outside.

Don switched on the television, and found a local station in Los Angeles, which was interviewing somebody pontificating on the likely sweep that Carter was demonstrating over Oates, but warning that the rural vote could turn things around.

Yeah, right, Don thought.

He called out to Molly, "Here is a guy who says the rural vote might change things for Oates."

Molly, who was just entering the room, exclaimed, "After us visiting small towns all over the state? Whoever that is doesn't know what he's talking about."

She said, "I called Donna Boyd about her offer on the house in Washington, and she was pleased that we would accept her offer of free rent for a month, and also pleased that you would continue most of Senator Boyd's policies, if elected."

Molly added, "I called her in Sacramento, where she lives. The caretaker has a key to her house in Washington, and it's furnished."

"Fine," Don said, but he seemed distracted.

Don got up and decided to change his shirt and tie. When he

returned, room service arrived with their orders. He picked at his Cobb Salad, while Molly ate and watched television.

"It's staying the same, fifty-three percent to forty-seven percent, with forty percent of the ballots counted," Molly said.

But Don was really not listening, and he said, "It's funny. Somehow, I can't believe this is happening. It's like a dream. It hit me suddenly, but now I'm slowly coming out of it. I was thinking a lot about Rosie, my mother, how proud she would be if she were alive."

Molly got up and sat down on the edge of his chair, leaned over, and kissed him lightly on the forehead, but didn't say anything.

The phone rang, and Don got up and answered it, listened, nodded, and said, "Okay, we'll be coming down."

He reminded Molly that he would introduce her and she was to say a few words, not forgetting the Hispanic voters, and she nodded.

Don opened the door for Molly. He greeted Sal Angelo with a few words in Italian, and the three of them entered the elevator, descended, and exited toward the ballroom. The crowd, anticipating their arrival, let out a cheer when they came into sight, the band opened with a processional march, and he and Molly walked across the ballroom in the direction of the podium, as the cheering increased.

The television blaring in the background was announcing that the polls had closed almost an hour earlier and that "Donald Carter had a commanding lead" over Dennis Oates, but Oates "had not yet conceded."

It took him the better part of an hour to reach the podium platform and another half-hour to separate himself from the crowd around the podium stairs. But he was not in any hurry.

Before the television had been turned down and moved, the voice of someone was talking about a "new force in national politics" who was "coming out of nowhere" for a "resounding victory."

Molly, Linda, Robert, and Bernie followed him up the short set of stairs. He introduced them to the crowd, gave their occupations, and he acknowledged Linda's great help in the campaign with Hispanic voters, and released all except Molly to return to the ballroom floor.

Don said, "Now I want to introduce a man who made all of this possible, the Century City miracle worker, my campaign manager, Joe Abrams!"

He had Joe come up on the stage, and Don noted, "We would not be standing here tonight if it were not for Joe."

There was loud applause, and Joe waited for the applause to die down and said, "Don might not have received quite as many votes without my work, I don't know. But he did everything I asked, and then some. I can't remember having as much fun in an election battle and being so close to a heart attack, when the going got rough, as it occasionally did."

Some in the audience laughed, remembering the CIA crisis.

"I tell you one thing. He's the candidate I learned the most from in all my years of running political campaigns. He's honest, a straight shooter, had a quick and bright mind, a fantastic memory, a good right hook, and even has a good sense of humor. Ask him any question about the U. S. Constitution and you'll get a quick and accurate answer. Also, he has a good stage presence and is a skilled debater."

Joe continued, "One final thing. As you may know, Don is fluent in Italian and has advanced my own knowledge of Italian—now I know what *'coglioni'* are. And he's got them!"

The audience in the ballroom burst into thunderous applause as Joe finished, and Don embraced him. The applause continued as Joe stepped down from the platform.

As the applause died down, Don said, "Most of you have met

my fiancée, Molly Dorman, whom I dated only once, forty years ago when I was a lifeguard in Atlantic City. She had just turned seventeen and was leaving with her family, the next day, for Las Vegas."

Don said, "Because of a mix-up in communications, I never saw her again until January of this year, when I went to Las Vegas on business, and we fell in love all over again. She was on the campaign with me almost from the beginning, and has worked alongside of me to bring the Hispanic vote back to the Republican Party, with her warm personality and a complete fluency in the Spanish language. We'll be married on Sunday, July 13, in Las Vegas, where her family lives. May I present Molly Dorman, my first and only love."

There was spirited applause. Molly spoke briefly about some amusing experience as the fiancée of the candidate, and of the many new friends she had made, thanking her friends for helping her make the transition from painter to political spouse.

Molly said, "Don and I wish to say something to the Hispanic community. It's this. You have a friend in Washington. We're grateful for your help in electing Don Carter to the Senate, and we aren't to going to let you down. We'll continue fighting for immigration reform."

The crowd applauded Molly, and Don gave special credit to Roberta and others who had helped make his campaign so successful, mentioning each by name.

Don said, "And I wish to give special mention to Alan Cooper from the San Francisco Giants, Sal Angelo from the San Diego Chargers, and Henry Walker of the Boston Patriots. They provided security tonight, and on our campaign trips, and I want to invite them up on the stage. They will be making an announcement."

They came up to the platform, each announcing a particular charity that he was donating his wages to, and thanking Don for the opportunity of working in his campaign. Sal Angelo added the comment that the group had lost a total of forty-six pounds as a result of Don's workouts, and they were going to continue working out. Their wives and girlfriends wanted to thank Don for making life less dangerous for them.

Don said he was pleased that he had been able to help out, and he announced that Oates had not conceded yet, that it was ten forty-five with eighty-three percent of the votes counted, and the ratio was now fifty-three point four percent to Carter and forty-six point six percent to Oates.

"The margin keeps growing!" Don announced.

Don continued, "This ends the formal part of this evening, and while we're waiting for the final election results, I have one announcement and one story to tell.

"The announcement is about the talk to be given by Benito Desimone, at UCLA Royce Hall the day after tomorrow, Thursday, the 26th of June. Admission is a modest ten dollars, five dollars for students. All ticket receipts will go to the Savio-Desimone-Carter Foundation for the Advancement of Pirandello Studies at UCLA. The event has just been moved to Royce Hall because of the demand for seats, and all Royce Hall program expenses have been underwritten by the Foundation. Fortunately, Royce Hall became available when another event was cancelled."

Don explained, "It has turned into an Italian festival and starts with a mixture of Italian opera and Italian romantic songs at six thirty, and includes an excerpt from Pirandello's *Six Characters in Search of an Author* in English at seven thirty, performing from a script. The UCLA Italian Department is handling this. The tickets will have to be picked up at the box office, and this will enable you to attend events early to avoid the rush, or arrive later and still see the main Pirandello program. You also can pick up the tickets at the box office starting tomorrow at eight in the morning and avoid any lines."

Don continued his announcement, "Benito Desimone is a remarkable speaker who is able to turn the plays and stories of Pirandello into vibrant English, which has meaning for life in today's world. I'll occasionally insert comments, and there will be time for questions.

"We will be celebrating a gift to UCLA of 483 volumes of the plays and short stories of Sicilian author Luigi Pirandello. Many of the volumes are quite rare and one-of-a-kind, collected over the years by Francisco Savio, and, after Mr. Savio's death, by Benito Desimone. They were close friends."

Don paused for a moment, and said, "This gives the community a unique opportunity to hear a non-academic speaker who's a true expert on Pirandello. The talk will be in English and may not be repeated, due to Mr. Desimone's health problems. However, it is being filmed and will be available later."

He continued, "Be sure to look around you after finding your seat on Thursday. Royce Hall is modeled after Milan's *Basilica of Sant'Ambrogio* and has seating for 1,833 persons. Built in 1929, it's a fitting setting for an Italian festival, has remarkable acoustics, and no bad seats."

Don paused and said, "Now I want to tell you a short story about my mother, Rosie. You have never heard this story before. I've been saving it for a special occasion, and I believe this is it."

There were scattered laughs from the ballroom audience.

He again paused and went on, "Rosie left school in the fifth grade to work in a cigar factory to help support her immigrant parents' large and growing family, and she married my father at age fifteen."

Don continued, "In 1927, she had had three living children and several miscarriages by the time she was sent by her Atlantic City doctors, at age forty-two, up to Philadelphia for surgery to be performed by an eminent University of Pennsylvania

Professor of Surgery, for a mass in her abdomen. Her youngest child, at the time, was thirteen years old. Rabbit test for pregnancy was negative. Any graduates of Penn Medical School in the crowd?"

Two hands went up.

"Well, I won't mention this surgeon's name, but a set of surgical retractors are named after him."

A voice from the rear of the crowd in the ballroom shouted, "Deaver!"

There were laughs from the audience, and Don said, "Precisely."

He continued, "In defense of the surgeon, I might mention that my mother was quite stout and had been heavy all her life, and the rabbit test, the only screening for pregnancy available in those days, was notoriously inaccurate or misread. Anyhow, to shorten the story, she claimed she felt 'pregnant' and the eminent surgeon said, 'You older women always think you're pregnant,' and he opened her up, expecting to find an abdominal mass, but, of course, she was pregnant, so he closed her up again and sent her home to Atlantic City."

Don said, "That isn't quite the end of the story. The end was, as I was growing up, my mother would occasionally, in front of her friends, introduce me proudly as her 'little tumor' and I would usually leave the room, embarrassed when that happened, but as I grew older, it didn't bother me, and I laughed along with the visitors. And after the surgeon died, a few years after my birth, she would claim credit for his death, saying he had never gotten over being ashamed of his mistake. And she would smile triumphantly."

Don paused and said, "My mother died six years ago, and I dedicate this apparent victory to her memory. I only wish she were here to join in the celebration. Old-timers would stop me on the street when I would return to Atlantic City, and ask about her, referring to her as 'the best hotel lady in Atlantic City.' And so, I dedicate this victory to the memory of my mother, Rosie Carter."

He put his fist in the air—"'the best hotel lady in Atlantic City.'"

As a cheer went up from the crowd packing the ballroom, a voice from the side where the television had been moved tried to shout above the cheers for Rosie—"Oates concedes. Oates concedes." Then, the public address system blared out, in defining fashion, "Oates concedes, Oates concedes."

The crowd, packed into the ballroom, primed by Don Carter's emotional tribute to the memory of his mother, let out a roar that shook the ballroom and reverberated out into the street through the ballroom doors left open to relieve the over-burdened air-conditioning on this warm June night.

Feeling the crowd roar, Joe Abrams looked up to the podium and saw tears streaming down the cheeks of Donald Carter, and a tearful Molly, now holding onto his arm.

Joe Abrams, thinking about future campaigns, turned to make sure the television cameras were catching it all.

Linda Carter, who had been supporting her great-uncle Benito as the audience exploded, her arm entwined in his, looked at Benito closely and noticed a single tear coursing slow-ly down his cheek. But his gaze was locked on Don and Molly on the podium, and he was smiling.